Praise for the Transplant Tetralogy series

"His wit and style are as compelling as his tightly wound thriller plots, and his thoughts on the world we live in are fascinating and, often, spot on… An awe-inspiring feat." *Washington Post*

"Fitzhugh's stuff is unique. It's also alarmingly accurate. That's what makes it so good." *Clarion-Ledger*

"Bill Fitzhugh just gets better and better." *Christopher Moore*

"A thrilling tale of science run amok… laugh-out-loud send-ups of the madness of modern life." *Booklist*

"Fast, funny, deft action… You have to experience it, hanging on tight and keeping those pages turning." *New Orleans Times-Picayune*

"Where Bill Fitzhugh earned his Ph.D. in street smarts is a mystery. The wicked sense of humor he must have been born with." *Dallas Morning News*

"Genuinely funny… his satiric eye spares no one." *Publishers Weekly*

Human
RESOURCES

THE TRANSPLANT TETRALOGY, BOOK 2

BILL FITZHUGH

This edition published in 2021 by Farrago,
an imprint of Duckworth Books Ltd
1 Golden Court, Richmond, TW9 1EU, United Kingdom

www.farragobooks.com

First published in 2017

Print ISBN: 9781788423281
Ebook ISBN: 9781788423274

Cover design and illustration: Christopher Sergio

For Kendall, always and forever.

Special thanks to Dr. Chris Glick who had the answers to all my questions.

This is a True Story

In July of 2007, a police task force in Houston was tracking a ring of cargo thieves. Acting on a tip, they followed two suspects in a tractor truck as they targeted a semi-trailer parked in a drop yard a few miles from Houston Hobby Airport. The logo on the trailer indicated a brand of high-end electronics. The thieves cut the gate chain, backed their truck up to the trailer, hitched it, and drove away.

Hoping the thieves would lead them to a warehouse of stolen property, the cops followed at a distance. Half a mile later the back door to the semi-trailer opened and a man looked out with a panicked expression.

Fearing the thieves had stumbled across a trailer filled with illegal immigrants whose lives were now endangered, the officers decided to effect a traffic stop. This led to a high-speed chase that ended when the driver tried to take an exit at sixty miles an hour. The trailer flipped several times then wrapped itself around a bridge abutment.

When the cops opened the trailer, hospital equipment spilled out the back door: a vital-sign monitor, an infusion pump, a scrub sink, and an articulated surgical light, still warm.

Scattered among the debris were nine bodies.

Eight of the bodies were dressed in full surgical scrubs. The ninth body, that of a seventy-two-year-old man, was naked, save for a blue shower cap. According to one cop, the man's sternum was split wide open and there was no heart in his chest cavity.

Investigators concluded the thieves had unwittingly stolen a mobile, state-of-the-art operating room while an illegal heart transplant was being performed inside. Based on evidence collected at the scene, they also concluded this was not the first such transplant.

Two months later, after consulting with the Department of Justice and the FBI, the U.S. Department of Health and Human Services instructed the Deputy Inspector General to create a new office tasked with finding and stopping illegal organ transplant organizations. It was called the Office of Assistant Inspector General for Investigations, Division Four.

The following story is based on one of their case files.

1

Room 465 at St. Luke's Hospital held two beds and two comatose patients, John Doe and Yuri Petrov, each on a ventilator, oxygen saturation meters clipped to fingers, EKG leads on their chests. The only sounds in the room came from the machines, beeping heart monitors and whooshing air forced into lungs, keeping things viable.

No one at the nurses' station even glanced up when the man wearing blue scrubs and a surgical mask walked into the room. He drew the privacy curtain around the first bed, blocking the view into the room.

The man placed a small box on John Doe's table then went to Yuri Petrov's bedside. He looked at Petrov's face, nodded, then patted his cheek. Using his foot, he released the brakes on the bed's wheels and rolled the two patients closer together. He removed Yuri's oxygen saturation meter and placed it on John Doe's finger. Working quickly, he did the same with the eight EKG leads.

Then he paused to listen.

At the nurses' station, a brief glitch flashed on Petrov's monitor. A nurse looked up from her paperwork just as the monitor returned to normal. She didn't give it a second thought.

The man unplugged Petrov's ventilator then reached into the box and removed a jar half-filled with a pale pink liquid. He set this on Petrov's bedside table. He did the same with a snare wire loop and a pair of curved enucleation scissors.

Behind him, Petrov's body jerked suddenly as he lurched into agonal breathing, a horrible gurgling from deep within.

The death rattle.

The man in scrubs spun around, unnerved by the unexpected movement and the ghastly sound. He pinched Yuri's nostrils closed and clamped a hand hard over his mouth. It looked like some ghastly human rodeo with the man holding on as Petrov's body bucked and struggled against the pressure. The man jerked the pillow from under Petrov's head, pressed it hard against Petrov's face, putting all his weight behind it. The man glanced around the curtain, but no one seemed to notice. He held the pillow until Petrov surrendered and all movement ceased. Once again the only noise in the room came from the machines.

The man took a deep breath and glanced around the curtain again. Nothing to worry about, so he resumed his work. He unscrewed the lid on the jar and set it aside. He took the snare wire loop and the curved enucleation scissors and leaned over Yuri's head.

A moment later, an eyeball splashed into the pale pink liquid.

The other eye soon followed.

***

Jake Trapper was walking down a hall in the north wing of Ascendant Medical, on his phone. "I know Pete put it in the system that way, that's why I'm calling. He's got it backwards. How do I know? I looked at it. Have you ever tried to breathe through a liver? No, that's right, so you see my point. That's why we need to fix this, send the… no, we *don't* need to go through channels. What we need to do is send the *lung* to San Francisco and the liver to San Jose. And if they ever figure out how to transplant a brain, send one to Pete."

Jake ended the call when he reached the hemodialysis unit. He walked in, passing the nurse on the desk with a wave, heading for the row of dialysis recliners. Eighteen of them were currently occupied with patients hooked to dialyzers. They were young and old, brown, black, and white. Some were talking to visitors, some had nodded off, some were staring despondently into space. No amount of cheerful wallpaper could brighten this grisly process.

When they saw Jake, the patients looked to him with hopeful eyes. Jake was a transplant coordinator.

He moved down the line acknowledging the patients with a nod here, a smile there, a thumbs-up, offers of hope. He stopped at the bed of a black man in his sixties. Jay Carlton was not at death's door but he could see it from where he was.

Jake fixed Mr. Carlton with a rueful expression. "Mr. Carlton, how long have we known each other?"

"Too damn long."

"And have I ever brought you good news?"

"Not a bit of it."

Jake nodded with regret. "Yeah, well, things change."

"Yeah, they get worse," Mr. Carlton said.

"Sometimes," Jake agreed. "But not today, Mr. Carlton. Today I've got a six-point match for you."

The news was transformative. Mr. Carlton tried to say something but he choked up, couldn't get it out.

Jake put a hand on Mr. Carlton's shoulder and they shared a smile. Jake dug into his pocket and pulled out an airline bottle of vodka and a cigarette.

Mr. Carlton took the gift with surprise. "What's this?"

"Celebrate a little," Jake said. "It ain't gonna kill ya. But you might want to wait till after the surgery. And if your wife catches you, leave my name out of it."

3

Jake continued down the row, approaching a sixteen-year-old girl named Angel, a poster-child for teen rebellion. Angel presented a punk-goth hybrid of dark makeup, tattoos, and piercings calculated to shock. She was inspecting some recent ink on her arm, wondering if it was infected.

"Hey, Angel, how's it going?"

"Just peachy," she said, glancing around. "Really lookin' forward to spending the rest of my short life with this cheery group of dick blisters."

Jake was used to it. It wasn't her fault, really. Teenage girl from a broken family dropped into the middle of a medical nightmare. He smiled. "Yeah, well, it's only temporary. We'll know more when we get the test results."

"Yeah, right. Temporary." Angel had her arms tight by her sides, fists balled in knots.

"Cold?"

"A little."

Jake grabbed a blanket from the shelf and noticed the man visiting a patient a few recliners away. Jake had seen him visiting others previously. He was in his fifties, wearing a sport coat over a mock neck sweater. The patient was Scott Daniels, late forties, a real prick in Jake's experience.

Jake covered Angel with the blanket and received a grudging smile of thanks. She closed her eyes, exhausted from the process. Jake stayed while she rested, keeping an eye on Scott Daniels and his visitor. After some whispered conversation, the visitor glanced around the room and scooted his chair back. He reached under his sport coat, slyly lifting his shirt tail to reveal a surgical scar on his flank.

Jake would bet the man was a kidney broker.

Angel bolted upright and shouted, "Oww! Jesus, fuckin' leg cramp!"

Jake took her foot and stretched her calf as Angel continued yelling. "Ow, ow, ow!"

"Sorry," Jake said. "The fluid loss causes that. It'll get better."

"Stop lying. This sucks ass."

"I know but you're almost done for the day, so…" Jake's phone chimed a text alert. He glanced at the screen, looked closer, then mumbled, "That can't be right."

***

At two-thirty on that clear December afternoon in Los Angeles, Tom Breland took five thousand dollars in cash from a man who rode away on what had been Tom's Harley-Davidson Sportster. It was the latest in a series of desperate transactions intended to help Tom keep his house. At least that's how it started. Now, it was simply a matter of getting rid of his stuff. There wouldn't be any room for it where he was going. Barring some sort of miracle Tom Breland would soon be renting a six hundred square foot apartment in Van Nuys.

A late model Mercedes pulled to the curb. A man got out, dressed business casual. When Tom looked over at him, the man waved at him. "Mr. Breland?"

Tom slipped the five grand into his back pocket. "You with the bank?"

"No," the man said with a pleasant smile. "I'm one of the good guys."

"What's that supposed to mean?"

"I'm here to help."

Tom had his doubts, suspecting the man was there to pitch a loan modification scam. "Whatever you're selling, I'm not interested."

"Not here to sell anything," the man replied. "I'm here to buy."

"Oh." Tom gestured at his driveway. "You're here about the 'Vette?"

"No, and I don't want your eighty-inch flat screen, your jet ski, or your pool table either," the man said. "In fact I'd like to help you keep all your stuff *and* the house."

Tom looked him over, wondering how the guy knew about the pool table and the flat screen. "Who the hell *are* you?"

"Mr. Kaye." The man extended his hand, an expensive watch peeking out from under the cuff. "Pleasure to meet you."

Tom reluctantly shook the man's hand. "Mr. Kaye, I know enough that when something sounds too good to be true, it is." He thought of that teaser rate he'd gotten on his first mortgage.

"Perfectly understandable," Mr. Kaye said agreeably. "The thing is, I've got friends in the real estate business. We share information, and sometimes I find I'm able to help people like you, in your circumstances."

"What do you think you know about my circumstances?"

"Everything."

"You think you know what I owe the bank?"

"I wouldn't be here otherwise." He pulled a slip of paper from his pocket and handed it to Tom. It had a dollar amount printed on it. Exactly what he owed.

"How can you know that?"

"The same way I know you came home three weeks ago and found that notice of foreclosure taped to your front door," Mr. Kaye said. "You're not the only one, Mr. Breland. A lot of people got caught up in it and if you ask me, it's not your fault."

"I agree," Tom said. "Thank you. They never should have approved me for the loan in the first place, but they did and the housing prices kept going up so, hell, I kept taking money out, having some fun until that adjustable rate kicked in, nearly tripled my monthly payment." He held his hands out in a plea. "I tried to keep up but there was nothing I could do."

Mr. Kaye offered a sympathetic nod. "The good news is it's not too late. I can help you with your problem and you can help me with mine. You want to talk about options?"

Tom was trying to make sense of it. A stranger shows up in a fancy car, seems to know everything there is to know about his situation and offers to give him enough money to keep his house. And it was a *lot* of money. What could he possibly expect in return? Tom thought whatever it was, it couldn't be legal. Only half joking he said, "Okay, who do I have to kill?"

Mr. Kaye chuckled politely and pointed at Tom. "You're not the first one to say that, Mr. Breland, but no."

"So what exactly *do* you want?"

"One of your kidneys."

***

The Los Angeles Medical Complex was a vast sprawl of buildings in a range of styles, each reflecting the decade in which it was built. Anchored by two hospitals, like bookends to the complex, it covered nearly a square mile in the middle of the city. At one end was Ascendant Medical, a gleaming ten-story model of modern corporate medicine-for-profit. At the other, St. Luke's, the original hospital from the 1960s, running on outdated technology and plagued by inadequate retrofitting. It was as good a metaphor for the nation's crumbling health care system as you'd find.

Between and around the hospitals were a dozen other buildings housing a variety of institutes and facilities funded by a sea of public and private money. Specialists and opportunists; geniuses and quacks; biotech firms and medical tourism outfits; doctors-for-hire conducting FDA experiments on paid volunteers at the behest of Big Pharma. It was a small city, humming with hope and despair, crisis and calm, the living, the dying, and the dead.

In short, the medical-industrial complex.

Jake had been called regarding a potential organ donor. It took him fifteen minutes to get from Ascendant Medical to St. Luke's. He rounded a corner on the fourth floor and saw a crowd gathered outside Room 465, nurses and orderlies rubbernecking to get a glimpse. An LAPD uniform was keeping them back.

Jake pushed through the crowd. The cop stopped him at the door. "Can't let you in."

"Got to," Jake said.

The cop chested up to Jake, trying to intimidate. "Yeah? And why's that?"

Nose to nose with him, Jake said, "Because I'm the organ grinder. Wanna see my monkey?" He thumped his clip-on ID.

After reading it, the cop leaned into the room. "Hey, Detective? Guy out here from So-Cal Organ Procurement agitating to get in."

"All right. Let him."

Jake stepped into the room and came to an abrupt halt. Leaning over Yuri Petrov's bed was a striking woman in her thirties wearing bright red lipstick and a dark skirt tight on generous hips. In Jake's mind, she looked like a cross between Mamie Van Doren and Courtney Love. Although Jake ran into cops now and then on the job, this one stood out.

When the jolt of her appearance passed, he took in the rest of the scene: the beds side-by-side, the unplugged ventilator, the heart monitor turned off.

Jake felt cheated, like someone had stolen some merchandise from his warehouse. "What the hell happened?"

"That's what I'd like to know," the detective said without looking up. She carefully tweezed some evidence into a bag, sealed it, and then caught Jake in the act of admiring her from behind. She smiled. "Detective Densmore. LAPD Homicide."

"He's dead?" Jake stepped toward the bed, reaching for Petrov's hand.

"Hey! No touchy! Crime scene. Jesus, don't you watch television?"

"How long ago?"

"My guess? About an hour."

Jake was incredulous. "What? They just paged me. Why would anybody… I mean, shit, why didn't the goddamn nurses notice?"

Detective Densmore showed him how the two oxygen meters and the EKG leads were attached to John Doe, giving the appearance of life for both men. "Let me ask you…" She glanced at his ID, "… Jake. You turn off a man's ventilator, won't he just… die?"

"Not necessarily."

"Huh. Learn something every day."

"Why do you ask?"

"I'm pretty sure this man was suffocated."

Jake glanced at the ceiling in frustration. "Jesus H. Jones." He stood, staring down at Petrov. "What a waste."

Detective Densmore thought about that a moment then said, "Oh, his organs."

"Eight lives, down the drain."

"Well, nine if you want to count Mr. Petrov here." She arched an eyebrow. "Or had you already counted him out?"

Jake ignored the comment. "You know who did it? Or why?"

"Give a girl a minute, would you? I just got here for chrissakes." Detective Densmore motioned to Jake, almost mischievously. "Come here. Look at this." She lifted Petrov's eyelids, revealing the two gaping sockets.

Jake stared at it for a moment. "Jesus."

"So that's unusual, right?"

2

Alex Carr was a slim, attractive fellow who, for most of his adult life, had made ends meet by burglarizing homes. He hadn't gotten rich but he hadn't gone hungry either. He'd done two stints in prison, both times after making the mistake of taking on a partner. Both times they'd been caught, and both times his partner had rolled over on him. Alex didn't mind the jail time so much as the awkward and painful prison romances he was forced to endure as a result of being such a slim and attractive fellow. So after his latest release Alex decided it was time to go straight. Finally do something to make his mother proud of him.

He planned to start a mobile pet grooming service. He'd done his research and crunched the numbers. The biggest upfront cost would be the customized van with the plumbing and the industrial strength hair dryer. And for that he needed some cash.

To that end Alex had been doing day labor, most recently on a landscape crew working at an estate in Beverly Hills. They were laying a paver stone pathway one afternoon when the estate's owner appeared on the elevated terrace overlooking the vast property. Alex recognized him as Mitchell Wick, the creator, producer, and host of the reality television show *One Hit Wonder* which featured

Buddy, a black-handed spider monkey, who acted as the head judge on a panel of C-list celebrities. The show was number one in its time slot.

Mr. Wick stood at the edge of the terrace surveying the crew's progress. A minute later, Buddy wandered out of the house, loping along lazily like he'd had a few drinks. He went over to Mr. Wick and climbed up into his arms.

That's when Alex had what seemed to be the best idea of his life. Sure, he'd have to put his dream of going straight on hold for a little while, just long enough to do one last job. Then he'd have enough money to get the pet grooming van of his dreams.

All he had to do was kidnap that monkey.

***

Jake was crossing the Medical Center grounds when his phone chirped. One of the lists was being updated. A man named Leonard Prentice had died after a year waiting for a heart. Now someone else was moving up a notch, a man by the name of Toby Castro. After saving the update, he heard a familiar voice from behind him.

"Hey, aren't you the guy from that press conference?" It was Dr. Mark Simmons, a cardiologist pal.

"It wasn't a press conference," Jake said. "A reporter asked me a question and, off-the-record, I gave an honest answer."

"Boy, no kidding," Simmons said. "I'm guessing the folks upstairs are beside themselves, what with you being so honest and all."

"That's my guess," Jake said. "I've got a face-the-music meeting this afternoon."

"Well, it's been nice working with you."

"I'm not done yet," Jake said. He wiggled his phone at Mark. "One of yours just got to the top, guy named Toby Castro." Jake cocked his head. "Why is that name familiar?"

"He's the death row inmate who sued for the right to get the transplant. I can't believe that landed on my plate."

"Yeah, well, we don't want 'em to die before we get a chance to kill 'em, do we?" As they continued toward Ascendant Medical, Jake entertained his friend with a recount of events at St. Luke's.

"When was this?"

"An hour ago," Jake said. "Took the poor bastard's eyes too."

They entered the hospital and hustled to the elevator bank, catching one about to go up.

"And you should have seen this detective."

"Hot?"

"More like dangerous."

"Single?"

"Didn't see a ring."

"Get her number?"

"No. Oddly I was distracted by the murder victim with the empty eye sockets."

The elevator doors opened.

"You do like girls, right?"

Jake batted his eyelashes. "Why do you ask?"

"Yeah, that's what I thought." Mark stepped out. "I'll see you this afternoon."

Jake caught the closing doors at the last second. "For what?"

"The Fontaines?"

"Oh, right," Jake said. "The man with the unrealistic expectations."

"That's him. Three o'clock."

***

The next afternoon as the landscaping crew was leaving the estate, Alex Carr slipped into the privet hedge that lined the east side of the property. He waited there until Mitchell Wick got into his Range Rover and drove off.

Alex watched the tail lights wind down the driveway to Coldwater Canyon and turn toward Beverly Hills. When the gate closed Alex emerged from the privet and brushed himself off. He circled the mansion to check for a security system or a lingering housekeeper who might call the cops. Satisfied he was alone, he walked up the stairs to the big terrace. He was pulling his bump gun and lock pick set from his bag when he saw that Mr. Wick left his house wide open when he went out.

Alex didn't see any motion detectors or infrared sensors so he walked into the vast room off the terrace, all white marble floors and silk upholstered furniture. In the corner was a large walk-in cage, almost an aviary, fitted out with all manner of children's playground equipment.

Alex stopped at the cage door and looked in. Buddy was nowhere in sight but Alex suspected he was in the large nesting box up in the corner. To one side of the cage was a table stocked with diapers, diet supplements, and prescription bottles. Alex looked to see if there was anything worth stealing. He didn't recognize any of the drug names, which was too bad because if he'd known Telazol was an animal tranquilizer, and if he'd had the wherewithal to put two-and-two together, things might have gone better.

Alex slowly opened the door. "Hey, Buddy, you in here?" he said quietly. "Uncle Alex brought you something." He pulled a banana from his bag.

Buddy peeked out from the nesting box curiously.

Alex held the banana up to him.

Oh, I like those, Buddy thought.

"It's okay, go on," Alex cooed.

Buddy snatched the fruit from Alex and tore into it. As he ate the banana, he noticed the cage door was ajar. *Finally,* Buddy thought, *freedom.*

Alex slowly reached up for Buddy. "I got a lot more where that came from."

His cheeks bulging with mush, Buddy gave Alex his best good-natured-monkey look while he calculated distances weighed against what he knew of human speed and reaction time. When he was satisfied with his plan, Buddy threw the peel out the cage door, pounced onto Alex's head, wrapped his prehensile tail around his throat, and started screeching.

"What the hell?" Alex wailed. "Get off my goddamn head!" Alex bucked and twisted around the cage, but Buddy held on like a rabid bronc rider.

When Alex reached up to grab him, Buddy bit his index finger clean off. Alex screamed like a howler monkey while Buddy scampered out of the cage.

Hunched over his pulsing wound, Alex tried to give chase but Buddy was too fast. He disappeared through the terrace doors.

Blood spurting from his hand like a lawn sprinkler, Alex grabbed a diaper from the table. He bound the wound as best he could. Now what? The kidnapping plan was clearly off the table, so Alex resolved to find his finger and get to a hospital ASAP. After all his trouble, he couldn't bring himself to leave empty-handed, so while he searched for his missing digit, he kept an eye out for something small and valuable to steal.

In his first (and only) bit of luck for the night, Alex found his index finger straightaway, on the floor by a Wellington chest where, one would guess, Buddy had spit it on his way out. Alex pocketed the finger and quickly frisked the Wellington. In the third drawer down, he found a Colt .38, customized with ivory and gold inlay, worth a few hundred at least. Maybe enough for an industrial strength hair dryer.

He tucked that in his waistband and headed for the door, which was when he saw all the flashing blue lights. He would later discover he had failed to consider the possibility of pressure-sensitive tiles in the marble floor connected to a silent alarm.

A voice from the next room, "Police! Hands up!"

Alex quickly reviewed his options. A shootout with the Beverly Hills Police Department seemed like a bad idea and suicide was off the table for philosophical reasons.

"I'm coming in!"

If Alex was going to get his life together and start his pet grooming business, he knew surrender was his best choice. He pulled the .38 from his waistband to hand it over.

The cop rounded the corner and saw it. "Gun!" He ducked back to the other room. "Drop the weapon!"

"Okay, okay." Alex set the gun down. "It's on the floor."

"Kick it over this way." The cop heard the gun slide across the marble. "Now, hands up!" The cop came in with his Glock leveled on Alex. "Okay, good choice," he said. "Now, turn around, face away, and lace your fingers behind your head."

Alex did as he was told.

"Walk backwards toward the sound of my voice."

Alex did so.

"Nice and easy," the cop said. "Nobody gets hurt."

Which was true until Alex slipped on the banana peel, flipping ass-over-tea-kettle, the back of his head hitting the marble floor hard enough to crack his skull.

3

The CCTV system at St. Luke's consisted of more than sixty cameras covering the grounds, loading docks, hallways, supply rooms, and the two dozen entrances of the hospital. Everything was archived on hard drives in bite-sized files.

Detective Densmore was in the security office watching video from that morning. The guard on duty set her up in front of the off-line monitors, while the live feed continued on the screens behind her. Since she didn't know who she was looking for, or which entrance or exit might have been used, Densmore had to work backwards, starting with footage that covered the hallway and nurse's station on the wing of the fourth floor where Mr. Petrov was killed.

Twenty minutes in, she saw what she assumed to be the killer. It was a man, certainly. Caucasian, apparently. Muscular, around six feet tall. Densmore guessed he was in his thirties, in his physical prime. He was wearing full surgical scrubs, mask, cap, and sensible footwear popular among hospital workers. He was carrying a doctor's satchel that looked like black leather with nickel-silver hardware.

According to the time code, the man emerged from Petrov's room ten minutes after entering. He walked casually past the nurses' station, down the hall, past the elevator bank to the stairwell. He took the stairs down to the first floor, into the lobby, and walked out the front door. No one gave him a second look. By all appearances, he was just another doctor.

Switching to footage from the exterior cameras, Densmore watched the man walk away from the parking garage and off the hospital grounds. When he was nearly out of range of the last camera, the man removed the mask and cap, slipped them into the satchel, then walked off the edge of the screen. If Densmore was lucky, or if the man wasn't as smart as he seemed, she would be able to find footage from ATMs and other CCTV in the surrounding neighborhoods that might help identify him. But since she had no idea which way he went after he fell off their radar, that could take a while.

Detective Densmore backed up to retrace the man's route into the hospital. Behind her, on the screen showing the live feed from the camera on the front entrance, a black SUV pulled into the No Parking Zone. A security guard approached, pointing at the parking garage. The driver, a spidery-looking fellow around forty, wearing a dark suit and dark glasses, got out of the sedan, looking serious. The security guard tried to block the entrance but the man in the suit held up his hand, showing credentials, and blew right past him without slowing down.

Densmore used the time codes to see how long it took the killer to get from Petrov's room to the edge of surveillance. She added the ten minutes he was in the room to get an approximation of when he might have entered.

What she found was the man came in the same way he went out. It took Densmore a while to figure that out because the man was dressed differently when he came in, wearing slacks, a shirt, and leather shoes. But he had the surgical mask on from the moment he was under surveillance. Still, no one paid him any attention. Why would they? He wasn't the only one in civvies wearing a mask. There were half a dozen others; people with compromised immune systems and run-of-the-mill germophobes wore them all the time on hospital grounds.

The man walked in the front door, satchel in hand. He went to the elevator bank but didn't get on the first one going up. There were others getting on. He waited until he could be alone. He took the next elevator. He got out on the fourth floor and went into a restroom. Five minutes later he came out wearing the scrubs and still carrying the satchel. From there he walked straight to Petrov's room.

Now Densmore had the whole picture.

She was making notes when the door behind her opened. Densmore kept writing and didn't look up.

A voice behind her said, "You Densmore?"

"Who's asking?"

"Special Agent Fuller." It was the spidery man in the dark suit.

Densmore swiveled in her chair, surprised. "FBI?"

The man held up his ID, the same he'd shown the guard downstairs. "OIG, Division Four."

This made Densmore smile. "The hell is OIG?"

"Office of Inspector General."

She leaned back in her chair. "Doesn't quite have the ring of FBI, does it?"

"No, but it sounds better than DHHS."

After a moment's thought she said, "I give up."

"Department of Health and Human Services."

"I see your point."

"Thought you might."

"So what's OIG?"

"Criminal investigators for DHHS," he said. "Same training and authority as ATF, DEA and FBI. They even gave me a gun and permission to use it."

"So you got everything but the good initials."

"We all have our cross to bear." Fuller gave Densmore the onceover, taking in the tight dress and the lipstick. "You're a detective?"

"Why do you say it like that?"

"Would have thought LAPD had a stricter dress code."

"Well, I hook on the side," Densmore said.

"Ah. That explains it."

"Yeah, so what exactly do you and your unimpressive initials want?"

"I'm looking into the Petrov case."

"Is that right?" Now she was intrigued. "And why would the Feds be interested in a murder in my jurisdiction?"

He leaned over and said, "The murder's not what we're interested in."

4

Detective Densmore and Agent Fuller walked down a corridor in the hospital's basement, Fuller examining Petrov's driver's license. He said, "Looks legit."

"Yeah, I'm pretty sure it's DMV-issued," Densmore said. "But the organ-procurement guy couldn't find any next-of-kin for that name so I thought, what the heck, let's check his prints." They turned, following signs to the morgue. "So why are you on this instead of going after Medicare fraud and that sort of thing?"

"That's for the older divisions," Fuller said. "I'm with Division Four. Illegal transplants is our whole mission."

"You catching a lot of bad guys?"

"Chasing a lot more than catching," he said. "We got started after this deal in Houston. Cops there stumbled on a mobile surgical center doing illegal transplants. Not long after that we fielded a complaint from some guy who had a liver transplant off-the-books. It didn't take," Agent Fuller said. "When the man failed to get any satisfaction from the man who arranged the surgery, he contacted us, wanted us to prosecute. He knew his days were numbered, decided theirs should be too."

"What happened?"

"Before we could open a file, the man turned up about as dead as you can get. And no eyes to boot. That sorta got our attention," Agent Fuller said. "But you wouldn't believe some of the stuff we find. Remind me to tell you about the fat lab in Alabama."

At the morgue they asked an intern which drawer for Petrov. The intern walked them through the autopsy suite to the cooler room, opened Petrov's drawer, and left them alone.

Fuller and Densmore pulled their phones out and tapped at the screens. Fuller glanced at Densmore's phone. "You using the FAFA app?"

"You kidding? That piece of crap?"

"Works fine for me," Fuller said. He tapped at his screen, waited, tapped some more. "Usually."

Densmore took Petrov's hand and, starting with his thumb, pressed his fingers to the screen. "Here's my question," she said. "Who designed the interface on that, a mole-rat?"

"What do you use?"

"An open-source app," Densmore said as she worked her way to Petrov's ring finger. "Tight as can be and ties in with all the print databases." She took the last print and hit 'send.'

Fuller continued waving his phone around trying to find a signal. "DOJ makes us use this," he said, looking around the room. "What are we, in a damn Faraday cage down here?"

Densmore shoved the drawer closed. "By the way, if you haven't downloaded the SOC patch, don't. I made that mistake and ended up getting a hit on Jimmy Hoffa last year."

Fuller's phone chimed. "Ha!" he said. "Got it." Just in time to see Densmore walking out the door.

***

Jake was at the SCOPE office downtown, sitting across from his boss, Amanda Rodriguez. She offered a sincere and sympathetic look as she said, "If it were up to me, Jake, we wouldn't be having this conversation."

"No?"

"No. We'd both be doing something more productive, like our real jobs."

"Yet here we are," Jake said, never looking up as he worked the SCOPE/UNOS app on his smartphone.

"Jake, could you put that down for a minute?"

"Hang on, trying to get a heart-lung from San Bernardino. You know, lives at stake and all that."

Amanda motioned her surrender while Jake did his work. A moment later, he put the phone on the desk and looked up. "You were saying?"

"The question the board would like an answer to is, why did you tell a reporter for the *Los Angeles Times* that one of your co-workers had killed a ten-year-old girl?"

"I never said that."

Amanda picked up the copy of the *L.A. Times* and showed him the headline that read: *Is Organ Distribution System Fair?* "It's right here in black and white. Little quotation marks around the words and everything."

"I was misquoted. I said he *might as well* have killed her. That's completely different."

"Not to the public, Jake. We need people to trust us or we're never going to get the donor numbers to improve."

"You want to talk about trust? I told the reporter I would only answer her questions off-the-record. Whatever happened to journalistic integrity?"

"Missing the point here, Jake." Amanda thumped the newspaper. "This is what the folks in public relations call a bit of a stinker. Not only did Pete not kill a ten-year-old girl, he arranged, according to our organization's policies and procedures, for a forty-two-year-old father of three to get a life-saving organ."

"According to our mission statement, the girl should have been at the top of the list."

"According to our policies, she was too young."

"By two weeks! Two damn weeks!"

Amanda nodded once, acknowledging his point. "I didn't make the policy, Jake. Besides, what was Pete supposed to do, lie about it? Don't you think that might surface eventually?"

"What if it did? Just say it was a typo and that you saved a little girl's life. That's what the folks in public relations would call a winner. But no, Pete's not going to take that chance, is he? No way he's going to risk hitting a speed bump in his career path."

"Is Pete a boot-licking careerist? Perhaps, but he's good at his job."

"Good at his job? Pete couldn't find a liver in the meat department."

"Jake, you might want to keep in mind that when it comes time for the vulgar stuff like promotions and raises, it's things like following the rules and not talking to the press without permission that gives you a leg up."

"That's your speech? A guide to career advancement?"

"Jesus, Jake, you're not the only one who cares, but if that's how you want to play it…"

"First, that's bullshit and what's worse is you know it," Jake said. "Second, instead of calling me on the carpet for being misquoted when I was speaking off-the-record in the first place, why don't we seize the moment and use the child's unnecessary death to institute some policy changes?"

Amanda sighed. "Because we don't live in Candyland, Jake. Oh, and by the way, what's this I hear about you handing out liquor and cigarettes in the Ascendant dialysis unit?"

Jake had the decency to look slightly chagrined. "Oh, come on, that's not what's going to kill anybody in that room and you know it. Let the man celebrate a little. God, what must your childhood have been like?"

Amanda stared at him for a moment, knowing there was no explanation that would satisfy. "Jake, you've maxed out on your vacation days." She paused to get his attention. "Since *policy* doesn't allow you to cash them out, you're going to have to use them, starting now."

"Are you kidding?"

"What do you think?"

"I thought you were worried about the donor numbers. Mine are three times what Pete's are."

"Yes, it will be a miracle if anyone survives while you're gone," Amanda said. "Three weeks, paid. Get some rest, have some fun, and keep your mouth shut."

***

When Detective Densmore walked into the hemodialysis unit, the nurse on the door did a double-take, as did several of the men undergoing treatment. And a couple of the women. It was the reaction she was going for. She looked like she'd stepped off the cover of some lurid pulp fiction paperback original. It was calculated to disarm and put her in charge and it worked more often than not.

Densmore approached the nurse, flashed a smile, followed by her badge. "I'm looking for Jake Trapper," she said. "I was told he might be here."

"You're a cop?"

"Yep."

"You don't look like a cop."

"Yeah, I get that a lot. I'm a detective. Get to wear what I want."

"You investigating that murder over at St. Luke's?"

"That's right." Densmore glanced around the room. "Now, Mr. Trapper?"

"He was here earlier." The nurse glanced at the wall clock. "He's either on a call or taking lunch." The nurse had a second thought. "No, wait, he had a meeting downtown, at the SCOPE office."

Densmore nodded. "Lemme ask. You know him at all?"

She shrugged. "A little, I guess."

"What can you tell me about him?"

"Like what?"

"Whatever comes to mind."

"He's not a suspect, is he?"

Densmore smiled enigmatically. "Whatever you can tell me."

The nurse thought about it briefly. "He was an army medic in Iraq or Afghanistan, I forget which."

"MD?"

"No, I think he's an RN though."

"He's a nurse?"

"Lotta men are nurses."

"I didn't mean anything by it."

"It's part of his training for what he does."

"He married?"

"Why do you ask that?"

"I'm a detective. It's what I do."

"I think so," she said.

"Is he good at his job?"

The nurse pulled a look and said, "You have no idea."

"Oh?"

"Trust me, that man can talk a mama out of her baby's eyes."

***

Jake had known Mark Simmons for ten years. They met as volunteers at the Southern California Transplant Games when they ended up as refs for the basketball championship. Things were going fine until halfway through the first quarter when Mark made a three-second call.

"What?" Jake couldn't believe it.

"Three seconds," Mark said. "He's in the lane too long."

"I know what three seconds is, dude."

"Okay then." Mark blew his whistle. "Blue team's ball."

"Whoa! Hang on. Jesus." Jake pulled Mark aside for a conference. "The man had a heart-lung transplant, what, a year ago?"

"I know. I did it. But the rules of the game are still in effect."

"The rules?"

"Yes, the things that keep civilization from devolving into chaos." Mark blew his whistle again. "Blue's ball, here we go."

Jake snatched the ball from Mark. "Dude, this isn't the NBA."

Mark snatched the ball back. "Look, dude, last I checked, the man's ejection fraction was nearly fifty-five. He's fine. And he can't just plant himself in the paint. Those are the rules."

"You're serious? The rules?" Jake snatched the ball back, blew his whistle, and pointed the other direction. "Red ball!"

"What's your problem? You can't overrule me." Mark tried to take the ball back and inadvertently caught Jake's chin with an elbow.

So Jake punched him.

Naturally, a fight ensued, one that was finally broken up when another player wedged himself between the two while shouting, "Don't hit my liver!"

And in the peculiar way that men sometimes form bonds with one another, Jake and Mark became friends. They were both jocks. Mark was the better tennis player while Jake won most of their one-on-one basketball games during which Jake made an inordinate number of three-second calls.

A decade later, they were sitting in Mark's office on the sixth floor of one of the buildings in the L.A. Medical Complex waiting for Mr. and Mrs. Henry Fontaine.

Mark said, "Three weeks paid? That's nuts. I would have fired you."

"I would have punched you again."

"So, you got plans?"

"How can I have plans? I didn't know I was going on vacation until an hour ago."

"You should go straight to Vegas."

"I'd rather be horsewhipped."

"You can do both. I know this girl there, very reasonable... oh, wait, you can't go, we're running that 5K."

"I knew you'd get there eventually."

Mark's intercom buzzed. "Your three o'clock is here," his secretary announced.

The Fontaines were old money for California: oil, real estate, and connections. Mrs. Fontaine had a steady gait for seventy-nine. She wore a salmon colored knee-length skirt with matching jacket, white blouse, pearl earrings, and a hat like Queen Elizabeth. She sat ramrod straight with the air of certainty that privilege brings. Mr. Fontaine was less stable, though no less assured. Dressed for a stockholders' meeting in a navy suit, white shirt, and red tie, he was slightly stooped and used an ivory-handled cane for support.

Jake sat off to the side, waiting to repeat what he'd already said. Mark spoke loudly as Mrs. Fontaine preferred to save the batteries in her hearing aide. She and Mr. Fontaine listened while Mark went through the preliminaries, then brought the bad news in for a landing. "I'm sorry, but your husband doesn't qualify for—"

"Dr. Simmons, that is simply unacceptable! We are—"

"Mrs. Fontaine, the issue—"

"Don't interrupt me, young man," she said. "You told us yourself—"

Mr. Fontaine stamped his cane and cut her off. "Let the man finish for god's sake!"

Mrs. Fontaine continued without missing a beat. "Dr. Simmons, you said yourself, Henry is going to die if he doesn't get a new heart."

"And, as Mr. Trapper here explained, there is an established set of criteria and—"

She waved him off like his words were nonsense. "I am not going to let my husband die because of the arbitrary rules of some government bureaucracy."

"Jesus, woman, let the man talk! I want to know my options."

"What do you think I'm trying to do, Henry? He's saying your only option is to give up and die. Is that what you want?"

A faraway look crossed Mr. Fontaine's face, just a brief look in his eyes as he entertained the thought of being removed from her constant badgering.

Mrs. Fontaine took in a long breath through her nose, a defiant, haughty sniff. She said, "We'll sue to get him on the list."

Jake said, "Mrs. Fontaine, trust me, our hands are tied. UNOS in general and the people at SCOPE in particular are sticklers for the rules. I know this first-hand. Even if Mr. Fontaine didn't have such extreme hypertension, he'd be excluded due to age limitations."

Now Henry took offense. "What! The law says I have to die simply because I'm old?"

Dr. Simmons and Jake exchanged a look.

"It's those death panels, isn't it? Well, our attorneys will—"

"Mrs. Fontaine, as a representative of the Organ Procurement Network, I assure you there's nothing your attorney can do. I'm sorry but—"

"Mr. Trapper, do you think it's a coincidence that the cardiac wing of St. Luke's bears our family's name?"

"Your philanthropy's not in question, Mrs. Fontaine."

Mrs. Fontaine touched her husband's arm. "Call Senator Leeson," she said. "He'll take care of it." She stood to leave.

Mr. Fontaine remained seated, his face growing red. "Screw the Senator and the attorneys! I have money, Mr. Trapper. Therefore I have alternatives. And I want to know what mine are."

5

Jake lived in a 950 square foot bungalow in Mar Vista, a half-hour drive from the Medical Complex, depending on traffic. Tucked away on a side street, a mile from the beach, it was cool and quiet. Overgrown pink bougainvillea crowded the cracked driveway and drew the eye away from the drought-brown lawn. Jake's landlord wasn't big on landscaping but lately he was selling it like he was all about water conservation.

Jake came here for lunch whenever he could. He liked the solitude. The calm was a good counterbalance to the stress and emotional complication of befriending anguished strangers and asking for their loved one's organs.

That kind of thing took its toll.

One of Jake's problems was his inability to recognize when he was overdoing it, probably left over from his time as a medic. His commanders had pulled him from action a few times when they discovered he'd been working for three days straight with no sleep. No surprise, they also found he had a pocket full of Provigil.

Working for SCOPE wasn't the same as being a medic in-country but the effect was the similar. With the clock ticking and lives at stake, once you got going, you fed on the critical nature of things and it was hard to stop. It was probably a good thing he'd been forced to take the vacation time.

Jake had the curtains pulled and the lights off, like his therapist said. He'd been resting on his sofa for a few minutes when he heard a car pull up. He peered out the window, saw a black sedan blocking the driveway. There was too much tint on the glass to see who it was. But when the driver got out, he knew. That lipstick was unmistakable, though he'd seen it only once. He got to the door just as she knocked.

Jake opened the door, squinting, as his eyes adjusted to the afternoon sun.

"Hello again," she said. "Detective Densmore."

"Sure, you're somewhat memorable," Jake said. "Can I help you?"

"I hope so. I've got some questions, thought you'd be the one with the answers."

"How'd you find me?"

"Not for nothing, do they call me 'detective,'" she said, smiling. "Got a minute?"

"I guess." Jake stepped back. "C'mon in."

Densmore trailed him into the room. Not much by way of interior decorating. There was a sofa and a table on one side, some framed photos on the wall. She didn't see any that looked like a wife. The other side of the room was a home office with a desk piled with paperwork and organ-related tchotchkes like the heart-shaped paperweight perched on top of some files. There were two monitors, one filled with current case information, updates blinking in every now and then. The other was linked to the Organ Procurement and Transplantation Network. Over the desk hung a wall map of Southern California with red push pins indicating hospital locations, yellow for transplant centers. Next to the map was posted a list of phone numbers for things like Air Ambulance Services and Human Organ and Tissue Couriers.

Jake gestured at the sofa but Densmore waved him off and said, "Tell me about the eyes."

Densmore had big green eyes that Jake was staring into when she batted her eyelashes and it dawned on him. "Oh, Mr. Petrov's?"

"Yeah," Densmore said. "At first I was thinking it might be some sort of revenge thing. You know, killer sending a message, something like that. Now I'm curious. Would they be worth something, like for transplant?"

"Just the corneas."

"The way they were taken? Corneas would be viable?"

"According to my eye consultant, yeah."

"You checked?"

Jake shrugged. "Color me curious."

Densmore wrote something on a note pad. "Yeah, well, the whole thing got me thinking about a possible black market connection. I was wondering what you could tell me about that."

"Well, the official line is that there is no black market in the U.S."

"And yet…"

"Where there's demand, supply tends to follow," Jake said. "Ask your buddies in vice."

"So you're saying there is a black market?"

"Well, if there's not," Jake said, "it's just a matter of time. We've got a hundred thousand people on our lists and seven thousand of them die each year waiting."

"And it stands to reason some percentage of them has the means to buy what they need."

"Transplant tourism's a growth industry," Jake said. "Sooner or later somebody's going to realize you might as well save the airfare and do it here. There's already a healthy gray market in the states for kidneys. Matter of fact, I saw a broker at a hospital this morning, acted like he worked there."

Densmore registered some surprise. "Did you call him on it?"

"Why would I?" Jake asked. "We're both after the same thing, and since he's drawing from a different pool of donors, that just keeps my lists from getting even longer."

Densmore stepped over to look at one of the framed photos on the wall. It was a group of soldiers and medics in a desert. She studied it for a moment then pointed at it. "That you?"

Jake confirmed that she wasn't wearing a ring on her left hand. "Yeah."

"Where was this?"

"Just outside Diyala Province."

"When was this?"

Jake looked away. "A while back."

"Well, thanks for your service," she said. "I was an MP but never deployed."

Jake responded with a nod giving the distinct impression he didn't want to talk about it.

She looked at the picture again. He had nice eyes, she thought, with a hint of forgiveness in the corners. "So, anyway, back to the black market."

"Yeah, the thing that doesn't make sense is the corneas," Jake said. "I might understand killing for a heart, but corneas?" He shook his head. "The wait list isn't that long and sight's not life and death. And even if you're willing to kill for them, why sneak in and out of a hospital to do it? That's just dumb, isn't it?"

"Yeah," Densmore said. "The murder was probably the thing and the eyes were secondary. An afterthought."

"Or maybe you're looking for a psychopath and trying to make sense of all this is a big waste of time."

"Possible," Densmore said. "Or maybe Mr. Petrov knew something he shouldn't have. Posed a threat to somebody."

Jake looked skeptical. "The man was deep in a coma. Not much of a threat as a witness."

"How deep? Like a three, four on the GSC?"

"You're familiar with the Glasgow scale?"

"I've picked up a few things along the way," she said. "Maybe the killer didn't want to take the chance Mr. Petrov would come out of it." She nodded at her reasoning. "And then the eyes... I like somebody sending a message for that. Feels right to me."

"Well, if that's the case, it makes you wonder what Mr. Petrov might have seen with those eyes of his."

Jake's smartphone chimed in the kitchen. He excused himself and went to take the call.

With Jake out of the room, Densmore stepped over to the desk and looked around. A past due cable bill, the current issue of the *Journal of Organ Procurement,* a dog-eared pamphlet on post-traumatic stress disorder, and a prescription bottle for some medical marijuana.

With the phone cradled on his shoulder, Jake came back and went to his computer where he dumped some information into the system, and ended the call. "Sorry," he said. "Potential donor."

"I thought you were on vacation."

He paused a second. "How did you know that?"

"You do know what 'detective' means, right?"

"Yeah, well, it appears you're one of the first to hear about my little holiday."

"I'm on your side, by the way," Densmore said. "In my experience, you can't trust a reporter any farther than you can comfortably spit a rat."

"So I discovered."

Densmore folded her notebook and headed for the door. "Listen, thanks for your time." She stepped outside and handed her card to Jake, saying, "If you think of anything, give me a call."

"Anything?" He looked her up and down like a cartoon wolf.

She smiled and left it at that.

"Okay then." Jake watched Densmore walk away. "I'll be thinking," he said.

***

Jake pinned his runner's bib to his shirt. "So he slips on the banana peel and cracks his head open on the marble floor."

"Poor bastard." Mark shook his head in wonder. "They ever find the monkey?"

"Don't know, but they found the guy's finger," Jake said. "In his pocket, collecting lint."

It was Saturday morning and they were at the 5K Renal Run. It started at the Santa Monica Pier and ended at Muscle Beach. The pier was crowded with a thousand or so runners and supporters. An event organizer was addressing the crowd.

"Every dollar we raise goes to support the Kidney Education Outreach Program and SoCal Pediatric Nephrology," she said. "Our mission is to reduce the presence and burden of chronic kidney disease and with your help, we will do just that!" After the applause, she continued, "And now, it's my pleasure to introduce the man who helps make all this possible, the president of The Medicus Group, Dr. Steven Brewer."

Dr. Brewer stepped forward and gave a modest wave to acknowledge the applause. He was a tall, dark-haired man in his mid-fifties with a paunch that said he'd never run a 5K and wasn't about to start now. "Thank you very much," he said. "The Medicus Group is proud to be a sponsor of today's run and I want to thank all of you for coming out to support this great event." He paused for another round of applause. "I'll be the first to admit that what I do is the easy part. All I have to do is write a check. The hard part is done by you and your families, everyone who is on dialysis, the great volunteers at Pediatric Nephrology, those waiting for a transplant, and the hard-working coordinators at SCOPE and UNOS."

Jake leaned toward Mark. "I read somewhere that Brewer's net worth is somewhere in the neighborhood of five hundred million dollars."

"Yeah," Mark said. "He's one of my heroes. Had the good sense to get out of medicine while the getting was good."

Jake gave him a look. "The way I heard it, he didn't 'get out of medicine' so much as the California Medical Board showed him the door owing to some Olympic-level misdiagnoses."

"So mistakes were made," Mark said. "Shit happens. Now he's one of the most successful entrepreneurs in the country. And God bless him, he donates a boatload to charity."

Dr. Brewer continued, "Now I want to announce that, in addition to the new dialysis equipment we are donating, The Medicus Group is also picking up the tab for one thousand kidney screenings throughout greater Los Angeles!"

"Wow," Jake said.

"Yeah, that's impressive all right," Mark said, applauding with the rest of the crowd.

"Not that." Jake nudged Mark, nodding toward a man in a sport coat who was lifting his shirt to show a scar on his flank to one of the runners. *"That's* impressive."

Mark looked. "I give up."

"That's the kidney broker I told you about."

Dr. Brewer held the starter's pistol over his head. "Runners take your mark…"

"Smart move," Mark said. "Came to the right place."

"…get set…"

"I mean if you can't sell a kidney to somebody in this crowd you need to…"

"…go!"

***

Detective Densmore and Special Agent Fuller retraced the killer's route to the point he disappeared from the hospital's CCTV coverage. They ended at the eastern edge of the Medical Center. To the right it was all retail: restaurants, banks, florists. To the left, across a broad avenue, a residential neighborhood.

"He went left," Fuller said.

Densmore nodded. "Probably. Avoids cameras. Unless the residents are paranoid."

They crossed the street, heading toward the houses.

Agent Fuller gestured broadly at the neighborhood. "You'd think people with the money to live here would have some stricter CCRs." He pointed at a house. "I mean look at that, you got a Tudor next to a modern next to, what is that, a miniature Taj Mahal?" He shook his head. "What is wrong with people?"

"It's a mystery to me."

Ahead, a woman was tending flower beds in front of a two-story colonial with a security company sign posted in the yard. They asked the woman if her security system had cameras. The woman said it didn't but she thought a neighbor up the street had them. They canvassed the neighborhood but didn't come up with anything useful.

On the walk back to the Medical Center, Densmore said, "Let me ask you a philosophical question. Earlier, I was talking to this organ-procurement guy. He said Mr. Petrov was what they call a 'beating heart cadaver,' essentially dead but on a vent to keep the organs viable until they're harvested for transplant."

"Right," Fuller said, "except now they call it 'recover' instead of 'harvest.' Something to do with marketing."

"Huh. Well, anyway, I'm here investigating a murder, right?"

"Yeah, so?"

"So here's my question: how do you kill a cadaver?"

6

Mr. Chad Huntington Yardsworth made a note on his legal pad, nodding sagely while expressing heartfelt sympathy and understanding as Mrs. Fontaine recounted the meeting with Jake and Dr. Simmons.

Mr. Yardsworth was a senior partner at the firm that had been handling the Fontaines' legal matters for three decades. Trusts, wills, contracts, real estate deals, the odd criminal matter made to disappear. The Fontaines were the sort of clients for whom the firm moved heaven and earth whenever necessary.

"Dr. Simmons' position is completely unacceptable," Mrs. Fontaine said. "And I fully expect something to be done about it."

"I understand, Mrs. Fontaine," Mr. Yardsworth said. "However, it is true that Mr. Fontaine does not meet the established legal requirements to be put on the list for a heart transplant."

Mrs. Fontaine drew an indignant breath, ready to voice further displeasure.

Mr. Fontaine put a firm hand on her arm. "Let the man finish."

Mr. Yardsworth nodded courteously to Mr. Fontaine. "You see, the UNOS system was established by Congress in 1984 in order to manage the Organ Procurement and Transplantation Network."

Mrs. Fontaine said, "Mr. Yardsworth, that system is for others."

"Yes, of course," he said. "That's exactly why I had one of my partners review your insurance policies, and we found what we believe is not only a viable solution, but one that's quite reasonable from a financial standpoint." The Fontaines' stony expressions led Mr. Yardsworth to say, "Not that you're concerned with such things, of course." He smiled at his gaffe, then continued. "Are you, by chance, familiar with Aadil Hospital?"

Mr. and Mrs. Fontaine exchanged a glance, then shook their heads. "Here, in Los Angeles?" Mrs. Fontaine asked.

"No, no," Mr. Yardsworth said. "No. Pakistan, in fact. Lahore, sometimes called the City of Gardens. A beautiful old place. I trekked through there during my senior year. Wonderful architecture, museums and, as it happens, world-class hospitals."

Mrs. Fontaine was genuinely confused. "Why on earth are you talking about Pakistan?"

"Well, because your insurance company has a relationship with Aadil Hospital."

The Fontaines stared at Mr. Yardsworth, waiting for some words that made sense to them.

"For transplants," Mr. Yardsworth added.

The Fontaines' looks of confusion evolved into sheer disbelief, prompting Mr. Yardsworth to shore up his proposal by saying, "Of course I did some checking with cardiologists I know – I wouldn't have brought this up had I not – and they speak very highly of the work done there."

"In Pakistan."

"Not just Pakistan, actually. Your insurance company has relationships with hospitals in India and Egypt as well. 'Transplant tourism' is the common phrase," Yardsworth explained. "It's good business actually. A heart transplant here in the States, including follow-up care and so forth, will run the insurance company upwards of a million dollars. In Pakistan, it might cost them one-fifth of that, so…"

Mrs. Fontaine looked at her husband as if Mr. Yardsworth had just proposed a ménage à trois right there in the office. Mr. Fontaine looked as surprised as she did.

"You must be out of your mind! Those people are filthy. Have you been to that part of the world? They defecate in the streets!"

"Well, no, I don't think that's quite—"

"You can't be serious," Mrs. Fontaine continued. "Not only is it unsanitary, it's halfway around the world." She paused as if consulting a map in her head. "I suppose we might consider something like Canada. At least they're white. But Pakistan?"

Mr. Yardsworth steepled his fingers and peered over the top. "Well, not to put too fine a point on it, Mrs. Fontaine, but what's key here is that in Pakistan or Egypt, we can arrange for the transplant to be, uh, to be done at your convenience."

"I understand what you are saying, Mr. Yardsworth, but it's completely out of the question." Mrs. Fontaine sniffed and said, "Now, I would expect that a firm such as this one, experienced as it is in providing all necessary services for clients such as ourselves, would be able to solve a problem such as this."

Mr. Fontaine aimed his cane at Mr. Yardsworth. "And I know for a fact that when Edward Winslow needed a liver, by god he got one. And we are both aware that he did not stand in line waiting for it, nor did he travel to the Third World."

Mr. Yardsworth nodded. "You understand I'm not at liberty to discuss the particulars of the Senator's situation owing to attorney-client privilege."

"Of course," Mr. Fontaine said, sensing some progress. "Just as everything that transpires between us is completely confidential."

"Exactly." Mr. Yardsworth tapped his Waterman pen on the pad a few times thoughtfully then said, "It isn't cheap."

Mr. Fontaine leaned forward. "We pay you, what, a thousand dollars an hour? What makes you think we are interested in cheap?"

***

Eight o'clock the next morning, Detective Densmore and Special Agent Fuller were driving to the California Highway Patrol's Southern Division tow yard. Stuck in traffic and fresh out of small talk, Agent Fuller was talking about his job with OIG.

"So TSA stops this guy while he's trying to board a flight to Paris."

"Out of New Orleans?"

"Right," Fuller said. "They ask him to explain this big jar of goo they found in his carry-on. He's evasive at first, then after a while he says it's human fat, not an explosive, not dangerous at all unless it's on your hips. Naturally they ask what he's going to do with it. He says he's selling it, what do you think? Says it goes for fifteen thousand bucks a liter."

"No shit? Who was he selling to?"

"Cosmetic labs in Europe," Fuller said. "They put it in their top-of-the-line cosmetics. They usually use animal fat but human fat's the gold standard. So naturally the TSA folks ask where the man acquired the fat. He says he bought it from a plastic surgeon who does liposuction. When pressed for the name of said plastic surgeon, the guy started to squirm and ask for legal representation. One thing leads to another and he makes an incriminating statement or two and his attorney suggests his client make a deal. That's what led us to the woods outside of Eutaw, Alabama."

"Never heard of it."

"Not surprised," Fuller said. "West-central part of the state, near the Mississippi line, middle of nowhere. We found an old airplane hangar out there, for crop dusters, I guess. We get our search warrants and we bust into the thing and you won't believe it. This little gang of hillbillies was kidnapping and killing people. But not just anybody, only folks who were clinically obese, mostly over three hundred pounds."

"Well, the Mississippi-Alabama state line is the place to do that, I guess. Those two always seem to make the top ten list for that sort of thing."

"They'd kill the victims and cut 'em up, hanging the torsos upside down on these big S-hooks. They had some space-heaters warming the room to help render the fat that seeped out of the thorax and collected in these big glass jars underneath."

"That's… wow," Densmore said. "Why don't cosmetics manufacturers simply get the fat from plastic surgeons?"

"They do, but there was something about the way these good old boys were refining it or filtering it or something that saved the cosmetics companies a lot of time and money. The man told us they were selling it as 'artisanally produced.'"

"Surprised they didn't say it was also gluten-free."

"No kidding. Come to find out they'd killed a few dozen people over the past year or two and made a ton of money."

Densmore shook her head. "I'd say you're making that up, but I don't think you could."

"Don't need to, truth being stranger than fiction and all." Agent Fuller took a right into the tow yard. Ahead they saw Sergeant Brian Miller waiting in his Crown Vic Police Interceptor. He was the first responder to Yuri Petrov's accident.

Sergeant Miller led them past the impound lot to the fenced area where the evidence vehicles were kept. They stopped in front of a badly damaged black Escalade. "It was on its roof when I got there," Sergeant Miller said. "Wheels were still spinning. Accident reconstruction team said it left the road doing near seventy, rolled five or six times. Would've done more except for the palm tree."

He pointed at the curved indentation, running from the roof to the running boards on the passenger side.

Densmore said, "Was Petrov conscious when you arrived?"

"No," Sergeant Miller replied. "Still breathing but non-responsive. EMT arrived ten minutes later, cut him out, transported him to St. Luke's."

"So what, he lost control of the vehicle?"

"Yes and no. According to witnesses, he had some help."

"What sort of help?"

"That's where there's disagreement," Sergeant Miller said. "One witness said it looked like two vehicles racing. Another one said he thought it was a road-rage thing, one cut the other off, hand gestures were exchanged, the usual. Couple others said it looked like one was chasing and one was trying to get away."

"Any agreement on the other vehicle?"

"Unanimous," Sergeant Miller said. "Also a black Escalade." He held up a hand to forestall the next question. "No plates. Tinted windows. No descriptions of passengers."

"And this one?"

"Plates were snatched in Sacramento earlier this year. The VIN matches an Escalade stolen in Phoenix two months ago."

"What's your take?"

"I like the chase scenario and I'll show you why." Sergeant Miller led them over to the other side of the Escalade and showed them the five bullet holes.

***

Jake was scheduled to meet Angel's mom at the nephrologist's office but she was no-show, so Jake met with the doctor by himself. The news was bad. It involved words like *inflammatory cell proliferation* and *reduced glomerular blood flow* but the key words were *renal cortical necrosis* and *transplant*. It was not a false positive, the files weren't mixed up, everything had been double-checked. Angel needed a kidney or she would die. Dialysis would only take her so far.

After the consult, Jake was waiting for an elevator down to the dialysis unit. The doors opened and there she was, Angel's mom, Nikki. She was only seventeen years older than her daughter, a little wobbly on cheap spiked heels, wearing an abbreviated skirt, and rubbing at her nose like she'd just snorted something.

"Oh, hey, there you are," she said. "We still good to see that doctor? I'm kind of in a hurry."

"You're late," Jake said. "The meeting was twenty minutes ago."

Nikki looked up and down the hall. "Really? Well, my bad, but traffic blows. I swear to God, they really need to do something about that, know what I'm sayin'?" She checked her phone for new texts or something. "So how'd it go?"

"It's not good, Nikki. Angel needs a transplant."

"Ohhh, man." Like this was going to be *so* inconvenient for her. She started to pick at the skin on her arm. "How come, I mean, what causes that kind of shit?"

"No way to know," Jake said. "Could have been drug use, could be viral or an autoimmune thing, but that's not really what matters right now, is it? We've got to get her on the list for a transplant."

"Why you keep saying that? She might get better."

"Meanwhile she'll be on dialysis three days a week and that's rough. She's going to need some support, like yours."

"How long's it take to get a kidney?"

"Varies," Jake said. "Could be three months, more likely five years." He refrained from telling her that Angel likely didn't have one year without a transplant.

"Damn, five years? Doing that dialysis? What's that gonna cost? I mean, this stuff's covered by, like, Medicare or Medical or medi-something, right? 'Cause I'm tapped out. Jesus, I can't believe this shit is happening to me right now, this is a bad time, you have no idea." She picked at her skin some more. "Is there a restroom on this floor? No, never mind."

Jake stared her. "Yeah, some of this is hard to believe, all right. And here's some more news for you, Nikki, I checked your records and you're not a match."

"What kinda match?"

"For Angel. You can't donate one of your kidneys."

"One of *mine?*" She looked insulted. "Who said I would anyway? Jesus, what a dick. I can't have a big nasty-ass scar across my stomach or whatever. I dance for a living for Chrissakes. How'm I gonna take care of her if I can't work?"

"Well I guess that's good news for you. What about her father?"

"What about him?"

"He should get tested."

"Oh, he's been tested," Nikki said. "Positive for HIV was last thing I heard, plus Hep C or some shit. I wouldn't know how to find him anyway. He's like that, makes it hard to track him down for the child support, right? He's way behind on that, which is another reason I can't afford this."

"You need to tell her," Jake said.

"Me?"

"Yeah, what with you being her mother and all."

Nikki glanced at her phone then hit the call button for the elevator. "I would but I don't have time right now. I'm gonna to be late for work as it is. I gotta drive halfway to San Bernardino, doing a private party. Besides, isn't that your job?"

"I'm on vacation."

The elevator doors opened and she hopped on. "Well get whoever's fillin' in for you, they can do it, that'd be cool, but listen, I gotta go, traffic's gonna be a bitch this time of day."

Nikki was still picking at the skin on her arm as the elevator doors closed and Jake briefly wondered if Nikki would live long enough to hit rock bottom, get straight, and assume her responsibilities as a parent. Then he wondered if Angel would live that long.

He got on the next elevator going down and headed for the dialysis unit. He couldn't leave Angel hanging, waiting to find out the results of her tests. He was from the school of thought that knowing was better than not knowing and being left to imagine the worst.

Angel was near the end of her session. She looked drained and fragile, a look intensified by her Goth makeup. Jake approached with a smile. He sat and made small talk until Angel asked about the test results.

"Well, Dr. Patak wasn't sure," Jake said. "She wants to run some more tests, so…" Jake tried to brush the hair from Angel's face, but she pulled away.

"So… what? I have to keep doing this shit?" Angel's hard shell started to crack under the pressure.

"Well, for now, yeah, you have to hang in there. But it's not forever. We'll just take it one day at a time."

Angel was fighting back tears. "Easy for you to say. You don't have to lie here and—" She looked at the tube running to her arm.

Jake said, "I know." He reached over to brush the hair again, and this time she let him.

"It's not fair! It's not fucking fair!" Angel started to cry without reservation. Her body trembling, tears rained down her face.

"No, it's not," Jake said, thinking of the hand Angel had been dealt. "It's not fair at all."

The unit nurse arrived with a cheerful tone. "Okay, Angel, you're all done. Let me get this for you." She took the needle from Angel's arm, disconnecting her from the machine.

While she did, Jake told Angel that he'd seen Nikki, that she was pretty upset about the whole thing, and she would have come down to see Angel but she was going to be late for work.

"She wanted me to tell you that she loves you and she'll see you soon."

Angel just stared at him. Jake wondered if she was expressing disappointment that her mother was so lame, or disbelief that she would actually say she loved her. Or maybe she was amazed that Jake was such a pathetic liar.

7

Jake was at home, looking at a map of state parks, thinking he might use some of his vacation to go camping. He couldn't decide between the coastal redwoods or the Sierras. He wasn't exactly focused. He couldn't stop thinking about Angel. Somebody needed to be there for her and he knew Nikki wasn't going to play the part. He decided to see Angel tomorrow, break the news, and make arrangements with a social worker to help with counseling and all the paperwork, maybe do a little hand-holding. If he could get her on the list, maybe he could stop worrying.

As he was folding the map his phone rang. The caller ID indicated it was his boss, Amanda Rodriguez.

"Hi, Jake, how's your vacation going?"

"Well, I can't decide whether I should go camping or head to Las Vegas for a little B&D."

"A little what?"

"Bondage and domination," he said. "Got a great price on a little flogging. Mark Simmons hooked me up, says this gal is terrific. Wanna join?"

An awkward moment passed. "I'm pretty sure I need to take a rain check on whatever that is," Amanda said. "But thanks."

"Up to you," Jake said.

"Jake, I, uh, as much as I hate to do it…" She hesitated.

Jake didn't like the tone of her voice. He sensed bad news. "Wait, you're firing me?"

"Worse," she said. "I have to ask you a favor."

Jake laughed. "That's pretty rich."

"It gets richer," she said. "I need you to go back to work, sort of."

"How do I *sort of* go back to work?"

"You heard of Toby Castro?"

"Yeah. Death row inmate sued for a heart?"

"Right. And we have one for him but we can't get the next-of-kin to budge."

"We?"

"Okay, Pete can't get her to budge. Says he's done all he can."

"This is the same Pete you were telling me was so good at his job?"

"I know…"

Jake let her twist in the wind for a second. Then he said, "You'll owe me."

"Don't I know it."

Jake walked over to his computer. "Okay, give me the particulars."

"Donor is Alex Carr."

"The failed monkey kidnapper?"

"That's him. He's at Valley Memorial. Next-of-kin is Keri Carr, his mother."

"I'll see what I can do."

"Thanks, Jake."

"Yeah." He ended the call and tossed the map into a drawer. When his phone rang a second later Jake assumed Amanda had forgotten to tell him something. He answered with, "Changed your mind? Realize you deserve a little spanking for being such a bad girl?"

After a short pause the caller said, "Well, if you must know, I prefer to be the spank-*er*, not the spank-*ee*"

"Oh, god. Who is this?"

"Detective Densmore," she said. "You like handcuffs?"

Jake let out a little groan. "Oh, god."

"Coulda been worse, right? Coulda been your mom or your favorite aunt."

"Listen," Jake said, "it's not what—"

"No explanation necessary," she said. "I'm all in favor of consenting adult activities, and we can get into specifics later if you'd like, but that's not why I called."

Jake's doorbell rang. "Uh, hang on a second, somebody's at my door."

"I'll call you back," she said, and hung up.

Jake crossed the room, opened the door, and found Detective Densmore standing there, playfully spinning her handcuffs on her index finger. "Surprise!"

He looked at his phone, then at Densmore. "What're you doing here?"

"I was over at Pacific Division. I got a hit on Mr. Petrov's fingerprints, thought you'd want to know who he really is… or was."

"You could have just called."

"I did call."

Jake laughed. "You want to come in?"

"I got a better idea," Densmore said. "Why don't we go out? You hungry? I'm hungry."

***

They went to a seafood joint in Venice, ordered fish tacos and beer.

Detective Densmore said, "It turns out Mr. Petrov's real name is Alphonzo Blount. "And he's in the system not once, but twice. Once for employment purposes, the other for an arrest."

"What for?"

"Possession of stolen goods."

"Okay…"

"And what kind of goods do you think Mr. Blount was in possession of?"

"I dunno, TVs and computers?"

Densmore looked disappointed in the level of Jake's imagination. "I wouldn't tell you the story if it was stolen electronics."

"Okay, jewelry and priceless art?"

Densmore noticed the only jewelry Jake wore was a gold band on his left ring finger. She smiled. "Tendons and ligaments."

"You don't say."

"Yeah. Remember the willed-body scandal over at the U a while back?"

"Sure, they made a fortune selling parts."

"Yeah, so our Commercial Crimes Division decided to run a sting to see who else might be engaged in like activities. They advertised as a medical research lab looking for connective tissue. Our Mr. Blount took the bait, showed up with an ice cooler full of patellar tendons and some other gristly bits and soon found himself under arrest. In his defense Mr. Blount said he worked at a mortuary and had all the paperwork to show chain of title, though he was unable to provide it upon request. Next day he made bail and was tooling up the 405 when someone started shooting at him for reasons unknown. A high-speed chase ensued, ending when Mr. Blount lost control of his vehicle and rolled it into a palm tree, resulting in a coma and a free ride to St. Luke's."

"Interesting."

"Right? You wanna know about the employment fingerprint?"

"Apparently so."

"It seems that Mr. Blount worked in hospital administration."

Jake was skeptical. "You don't get printed for that, do you?"

Densmore grinned slyly. "You do if the hospital is in a state prison."

"Okay, and do you have some unifying theory to connect all these intriguing facts?"

"Nope," Densmore said. "It could all be coincidental. Could be that the ligaments were his to sell. It's entirely possible somebody shot at him on the freeway because he was driving slow in the fast lane. I've had that urge myself," Densmore said. "However, it's hard to imagine there's no connection between a man trying to sell body parts, who gets shot at and later killed, and then has his eyes removed, right?"

"A fair conclusion," Jake said. "So now what?"

"Heading up to Carrizo State Prison tomorrow to see what else I can find out about our Mr. Blount." Densmore finished her beer and waved for the check. "Want to tag along?"

"Tempting," Jake said. "But I've got to work."

"Wow, worst vacation ever."

"Yeah, but next time you're going to a penitentiary or a leper colony or whatever and you want a date, I hope you'll give me a call."

***

The next morning Jake started the paperwork to get Angel on the kidney list. After he met with a social worker about the interviews and made arrangements for counseling, he went to the dialysis unit to see Angel.

Halfway through her session, she was lying there staring at the ceiling, her pale arm stretched out with thick white tape obscuring her tattoos and holding the tubes and fistulas in place.

Jake tried some small talk but she wouldn't engage, and only halfway pretended to listen. He eventually told the truth about her test results and the fact that she was going to need a transplant.

Angel never stopped staring at the ceiling. "Well, maybe I'll get lucky and die of an infection or something."

"C'mon, Angel, don't talk like that."

"Why not?" She looked at him with bloodshot eyes. "You notice how my luck's run so far?"

Jake frowned a bit. "Are you high?"

"Hell yeah," she said. "You ever done this? Jesus." Like he was an idiot. "But don't worry, I got a prescription."

"Look, I know it's boring. You want me to get you a book or video game or something?"

"How 'bout a kidney? To go, if you don't mind."

Jake put a hand on her shoulder. "I'm going to do everything I can to make sure you get what you need, Angel. You just need to hang in there for me, okay?"

"Yeah, whatever."

***

Ten minutes later Jake was winding his way through Beverly Glen heading for Valley Memorial to see Alex Carr's mother. He was still thinking about Angel. She'd have to submit to hours of testing, counseling, and evaluations, and failure at any stage would be a death sentence. If it came to that, Jake wondered what she might do.

Then he wondered what *he* might do.

A few minutes later at Valley Memorial, he took the elevator to the third floor and headed for the North Wing nurses' station. Jake knew someone at every hospital in Los Angeles – doctors, administrators, and lots of nurses. There were four nurses at the station. Jake recognized three of them.

Maria Saldana was the first to notice Jake. She was forty, petite, wearing a sweater over her scrubs. "Hi, Jake. You here about Mr. Carr?"

"Yeah. What's neuro say?"

Maria handed him the chart. "Couple of days, maybe. GCS is five and dropping."

GCS was the Glasgow Coma Scale, a neurological measure of consciousness. The scale ran from fifteen, meaning fully conscious, to three, meaning deep coma, on the verge of death. Why it stopped at three remained a mystery to Jake. All he knew for sure was that a score below eight was considered severe.

Jake glanced at the chart. "Mom's name is Keri?"

"She's in there now."

"And?" He knew Maria would have a preliminary assessment.

"Pete says it's a waste of time."

"Pete's a douchenozzle." He handed the chart back to Maria. "Okay. Introduce me."

Maria led the way. She tapped on the door and took Jake into the room. Alex Carr was lying on the bed, not a man so much as a vessel, a container of goods Jake needed to acquire for the benefit of others.

Jake focused on the mother. He guessed she was around fifty. She was wearing an old pants suit, some shade of eggplant, with a gray striped shirt. Her brown hair was going a bit gray with bangs held back by a plastic barrette. She was sitting, reading a celebrity magazine.

Jake believed in first impressions and something here was a bit off. He usually got a sense of the stage of grief the family member was experiencing. Non-verbal cues, body language, he wasn't sure what it was, but more often than not he could tell who would agree quickly to consent, who would refuse, who needed to be talked into it. But not today. The only impression he got about Keri was 'cold-blooded.'

Maria spoke softly as she approached. "Keri? This is Jake Trapper. I mentioned him to you earlier?"

Keri looked up briefly with flinty eyes and a smirk. "Oh, right, the new guy from the parts department." She tossed her magazine on a table. "I hope you're the first string," she said. "That last one was useless."

Maria flashed Jake a sideways glance on her way out. In situations like this, the next-of-kin was usually sleep-deprived, fatigued, dehydrated. People tended to stop taking care of themselves, parents especially. Mothers had usually cried and wiped their eyes so much that there was either a raccoon effect or a complete absence of makeup. Keri didn't fit any of it.

Following protocol, Jake kept a respectful distance between them. He was a stranger, after all, here with an awful request. In his gentlest voice, Jake asked, "How's he doing?"

Keri looked up. "What would you say if I told you he's starting to respond a little?"

Jake gave an affirming nod, despite the impossibility of her claim. "I'd say that's good."

Keri heaved a sigh of disappointment. "Seriously? That's how the first guy played it," she said. "Like I'm in denial or whatever. For Christ's sake, I talked to the neurologist. I'm not an idiot. Alex is done. We can stick a fork in him." Keri opened a bedside drawer, pulled a hypodermic and jammed it into Alex's arm.

"Jesus!" Jake's head snapped back.

"See?" She left it sticking there like a dart in a board.

"What is wrong with you?"

"What're you, squeamish? Get over it," she said. "He doesn't care. Why should you?"

Jake removed the needle. "That's your son!"

"Not anymore," she said. "That's why you're here, right? Beating heart cadaver and all that? Point is, there's no need for all the pussyfooting. You're here for the parts, I'm the one who can give the permission. I don't need your metaphors about how the situation here is like when little Alex leaps off a diving board and the board keeps moving even after he's gone, okay? He's out of his misery, so we might as well talk turkey."

Jake never knew what he was going to get. Some people were receptive and grateful for the opportunity to donate. Others were all denial, hostility, or refusal. And every now and then he ran into someone who wanted to play *Let's Make a Deal* with their loved one.

Jake put the hypodermic into the sharps container on the wall. "When you say 'talk turkey' what exactly did you have in mind?"

"Nothing unreasonable." Keri gestured at Alex. "We've got, what, a million-five worth of goods here? Solid organs, corneas, veins, arteries, skin, marrow, and it's all good. He's a dream come true for you and all the recipients. I just want to make sure I don't walk away empty-handed."

"I see you didn't have any trouble decoupling."

"Decoupling," she repeated with disdain. "I love that. No, I managed to work through the grieving process pretty quick. I'll let you in on a little secret: just because someone's family doesn't mean you have to love 'em. Alex was a third-rate criminal and a fourth-rate son, never did a thing in his life to be proud of, all culminating in his kidnap-the-monkey get-rich-quick scheme. Christ. The saddest part is, that was one of his better ideas. At least now he can do some good for me and whoever gets his parts."

"That's very touching," Jake said. "You understand it's illegal for me to—"

"Here's the deal," Keri said. "I know how this works. Good friend of mine went through it with her daughter. One of you people got her to sign off on the donation. She went home, crazy with grief, and three days later she got a bill for seventy thousand dollars she didn't have. Hospital was demanding payment too. There was no more of that 'we understand what you must be going through' and no more diving board metaphors either. But you can't get blood from a turnip, so they handed the account over to a debt-collection agency, ruined her credit. She lost her house.

That's not going to happen here, okay? Not if you're serious about saving lives."

No wonder Pete bailed on this one, Jake thought. This was going to require some serious rule-bending. "I'll have to talk to some people," he said, pulling a consent form from his notebook.

Keri shook her head. "Not signing anything until we've reached some sort of agreement."

Once upon a time, Jake might have been appalled at the woman's callousness. However, after his years in the trenches and seeing how things worked, he couldn't help but admire the woman's chutzpa. She'd done her research, knew who stood to profit, and by how much. She wasn't going to be victimized. How could you not respect that? Jake put his form away. "I'll see what I can do."

8

Detective Densmore was heading north on Interstate 5 parallel with the towering Path 26 power lines. With an hour's drive ahead, she had called Special Agent Fuller to share her progress, see if he'd made any.

"B-l-u-n-t, like a dull blade?"

"No, b-l-O-u-n-t," Densmore said. "Alphonzo."

"Doesn't ring a bell," Fuller said. "I'll see if anything pops on the name at my end. You confirm his claim about the mortuary?"

"Not yet."

"You find anything at Carrizo?"

"On my way there now. What about you?"

"Got sidetracked," Fuller said. "Spent all of yesterday at the San Diego airport, following a lead that sounded like some major parts trafficking. Employee at Southwest Airlines had this big box with some discrepancies in the paperwork, so he opened it up, took one look at the contents, and passed out cold."

"What the hell was it?"

"Fifty human heads."

"Get out."

"Happens all the time," Fuller said. "Couple of years ago we got a call after a commuter jet went down in the middle of Ohio. Pilot did a pretty good job bringing it in, only a couple of serious injuries and one death. NTSB was on scene quick and called us, which we thought was weird until they explained they'd found eighteen heads scattered in the debris field. No bodies, just a bunch of heads scattered amongst the luggage and freight. They were being shipped to a research hospital in Cleveland."

"Research?"

"Yeah, training for ophthalmological, dental, and reconstructive surgeons. The San Diego heads were the same deal, whole thing was a paperwork snafu. Wasted my day."

"Sorry for your loss," Densmore said. "Do me a favor and check with CHP to see if they recovered any slugs from Blount's Escalade. I'll call you if I find anything at Carrizo."

Densmore ended the call as she was coming down the Tejon Pass into the San Joaquin Valley, the state's agricultural wonderland, producing vast quantities of grapes and cotton, citrus, almonds, and a dozen other crops, including a recent thriving addition.

California's prison population had grown nearly five hundred percent in the past two decades. Under contract with the state, private corporations had built twenty-five new prisons to deal with the state's 170,000 prisoners.

Convicts as a cash crop.

Just past Wheeler Ridge, Interstate 5 met California State Route 99, forming a huge Y. Half the traffic veered north on the 99 for Bakersfield and Fresno. The other half took I-5, heading for the Bay Area or points north.

Densmore and the eighteen-wheeler in front of her were the only ones not to take either of those. She was behind a Peterbilt Model 389, pulling a forty-five foot trailer marked with the logo of an American flag drawn as an eighteen-wheeler underscored with 'C.M.S. Enterprises, Los Angeles, CA.'

They took Route 166 west to Route 33. Fifteen miles later, past Taft and Ford City, they passed a sign for Carrizo State Prison.

The big-rig followed the sign for Deliveries. Densmore headed for Visitor Parking.

Set on three hundred acres of scrub, Carrizo State Prison was designed to house 2,200 medium-to-maximum security male inmates. Owing to a combination of factors, the current population was 4,195. Business was good.

A trustee escorted Densmore to the prison's hospital where she met with the Head of Medical Services, a woman named Kelly Bixby Mazzo, who said she'd be happy to answer any questions. Densmore had called ahead only to say she wanted to meet with Ms. Mazzo regarding a former employee, not wanting to name names on the off-chance that Ms. Mazzo had reason to hide anything.

They sat in Mazzo's office, which looked out onto the hospital ward.

"Ms. Mazzo, I'm investigating the murder of Alphonzo Blount," Densmore said. "He might be in your records using the name Petrov. Either name ring a bell?"

"Blount… Alphonzo Blount." Mazzo looked off to the middle distance and stuck out her lower lip in thought. "I vaguely remember him. Worked in records administration."

"You got a file on him?"

"Sure." Ms. Mazzo tapped on her keyboard to pull up the file. "What do you want to know?"

"Anything interesting."

Ms. Mazzo scrolled through the file. "Let's see, usual stuff, dates of employment, salary, emergency contact, performance reviews."

"Wait." Densmore stopped her. "Back up. What's the name and number for his emergency contact?"

"Uh, that was left blank. H.R.'s not real finicky about some of this stuff."

Densmore cracked a wry smile. "What did Blount do, exactly?"

"Data entry, more or less. Whenever an inmate is admitted for care, medical personnel gets a history and takes down the information on whatever medical situation they are presenting with, and that form has to get input and coded with whatever procedures are performed, along with results of blood and urine tests, X-rays, all that sort of thing."

Densmore gestured at the computer. "That indicate if Blount had any medical training?"

Ms. Mazzo scrolled through the file. "Doesn't look like it. He came here from C.M.S., where he worked in inventory control."

Densmore had just seen those initials on the Peterbilt. "What's C.M.S.?"

"Correctional Medical Supplies, the company that provides all the stuff we use," Mazzo said. "Syringes, thermometers, blood pressure cuffs, everything you need."

"How long did he work here?"

"Just short of a year."

"You know why he left?"

"No, but we get a lot of turnover out here. People come to the Valley thinking it's going to be quiet country living, clean air and all that, but they end up in an apartment complex outside of Bakersfield where it's dusty most of the time and the air either smells like pesticides, herbicides, or cow shit, depending on which way the wind's blowing."

"You have Blount's last home address, a forwarding address, anything?"

"I've got the old Bakersfield apartment number but I think he moved back to L.A. after he left here." Mazzo scrolled through the file a bit further then stopped to read for a moment. "Here's something," she said. "Blount was assaulted by an inmate here on the ward."

"Do tell."

"Man by the name of Thaddeus Dell, doing time for felony assault. Brought to hospital for a knife wound after a scuffle in the dining hall." Ms. Mazzo looked up from the computer.

"Apparently Mr. Dell didn't want to share his pudding. Got twelve stitches defending it. Chocolate, by the way."

"What was his beef with Blount?"

"According to Mr. Dell, Mr. Blount promised to sell him some painkillers. When Mr. Blount delivered two aspirin instead of something more substantial, he made the mistake of being close enough for Mr. Dell to grab him. Dell messed him up pretty good before the guards intervened. At the disciplinary hearing, Blount denied the drug accusation, said Dell simply attacked him for no reason."

"What do you think?"

"If his record's any indication, Blount's telling the truth. Mr. Dell's jacket is one aggravated assault after another, plus a rape."

"Can I speak with Dell?"

"If you can track him down, you can. He was released two months ago." Mazzo tapped a few keys and hit the 'print' button. "Here's his parole info."

***

Dr. Simmons arranged the four strips of bacon like a hash tag on top of the fried egg that was itself draped over a double cheeseburger. He buttered the toasted bun and pressed it on top, snugging it down like a warm hat on a child's head. Then he looked at Jake and said, "So what did you do?"

Jake shrugged. "Well, plausible deniability being what it is, I did the same as the other times. I had an extremely off-the-record conversation with a couple of unnamed members of unnamed departments of unnamed organizations all of whom are now speaking with in-house attorneys to cloak themselves in attorney-client privilege."

Dr. Simmons nodded like it was the most sensible thing to do. "Here's what I don't get," he said. "The donor's mom isn't on the hook for anything, right? Donor was an independent adult. She's not responsible for her son's hospital bill."

"No, but she can't just come out and say she's going to bury the organs if we don't give her fifteen grand. She knows I can't engage in a conversation like that. Woman did her research, knows our cost-benefit analysis says we're better off paying her than wasting the organs. She even low-balled it to make it easy."

"Smart cookie." Dr. Simmons took a sloppy bite from his burger. "So is there, like, a slush-fund for this?"

"I have no idea what you're talking about," Jake said. "And I was certainly never here having this conversation."

"I'll take that as a yes."

Jake snagged an onion ring from Dr. Simmons' plate. "What do you think about how we allocate organs? The system."

"I'd say it's a lot better than the way we're allocating onion rings here. At least the UNOS people won't take a man's kidney without his permission."

Jake took another onion ring. "Admit it. It's a complete disaster. We need an opt-out system if we're going to have half a chance. And for that matter, you ought to be able to sell a kidney if you want to, and without all the subterfuge of the directed-donation crap."

"That only benefits the wealthy."

"Everything benefits the wealthy," Jake said. "It's the money, I think. But, look, if people with means could buy a kidney, at least they'd be off the list, meaning less wait time for the rest of us."

Dr. Simmons set his burger onto the plate. "The rest of us? You need a kidney?"

"Not me."

"But somebody, right?" He stared at Jake. "It's that kid isn't it? The one with all the tats and meth-head mommy?"

Jake met his friend's eyes, but didn't answer.

62

"Jake, you can't let it get personal," Dr. Simmons said. "That will screw you up."

"Yeah, probably, but what're you gonna do?"

"Let me rephrase. I understand that we get to know these people and it's not always possible to be detached and impersonal. But don't get *involved.*"

Jake didn't seem to hear the advice. He was staring at the table, wondering if his HLA matched Angel's.

***

Detective Densmore was heading south on I-5 when Special Agent Fuller called. "You still up at Carrizo?"

"On my way back," Densmore said.

"How far out are you?"

"Just passed the L.A. County line. Why?"

"I'll tell you when I see you."

"Which is when?"

"Depends how fast you drive. Write this down…" Special Agent Fuller gave her an address in the north San Fernando Valley. "If you like fireworks, you won't want to miss this."

Detective Densmore wasn't sure what that meant but she liked the sound of it, plus she got a kick out of driving fast. She put the light on her dashboard and pushed her cruiser up to 115. Twenty minutes later she passed the gaudy stone entryway for Rancho Grandes, a new sprawl of McMansions looking south over the Valley.

Approaching the address, Densmore saw the first of the SWAT vehicles and the mobile command center. Fuller was out front talking to a guy strapping on the last of his Kevlar commando outfit.

The air was thick with testosterone as Densmore approached Fuller saying, "What in the world is all this for?"

"I promised you fireworks," Fuller said. "I hate to disappoint." He opened the door to the command center and ushered Densmore inside. "You get anything up at Carrizo?"

"Potential suspect," she said. "But he seems like a long shot." She gestured at one of the video screens showing a SWAT leader talking to his team. "I don't suppose this has anything to do with a man named Thaddeus Dell."

"Who?"

"Never mind," she said. "I'm just gonna guess, based on your assembled collection of big boy toys, that you found something?"

"Indeed we did. Couple of things actually." Fuller directed her attention to one of the monitors. "Watch this." He hit a button and a video began playing. It looked like it was taken with a cell phone camera from a speeding car that was changing freeway lanes without regard for any of the laws governing motor vehicles.

For example, the person taking the video was also narrating and driving. As the video would eventually show, he was a white, suburban teenager who was saying, "This shit is wild! Mu'fugga in the 'Sclade there been gettin' after dude in the 'Sclade in front of him for the last three miles. Man is pissed off over something! Whoa!"

The camera did a wild zip-pan when the kid was forced to grab the wheel and swerve to miss a car. When he recovered, the kid aimed the camera at himself and said, "Damn! That was almost some 9-1-1!" When he flipped the camera back to the chase, the man in the second Escalade stuck a Mac-11 out his window and started shooting.

"Holy shit!" The kid let out a giddy cackle, like he'd been transported into the video game of his dreams. "Yo, this is some wild ass Grand Theft Auto shit going down!" He put himself on camera again. "And I am all up *in* this shit, what?!" He flipped the camera back onto the gunman.

That's when the shooter noticed the kid taking the video. He aimed the Mac-11 straight at the camera.

"Whoa!"

The image then went black. Agent Fuller hit 'Stop,' then 'Rewind.' "Our young citizen then dropped his phone and, according to witnesses, made a remarkable exit from the freeway, crossing three lanes of traffic without hitting a thing." Agent Fuller paused the video where the gunman was looking straight at the camera. He tapped the screen. "So that's our man. Definitely the one shooting at Blount, and most likely the one who finished the job at the hospital and took the eyes."

"How did you get this?"

"The kid posted it on YouTube."

"Of course he did."

"Meanwhile the CHP recovered a slug from Mr. Blount's Escalade. They ran ballistics and got a hit on a Mac-11 as you might expect. They sent a couple of uniforms over to have a chat with the owner."

"Wait a sec," Densmore said. "The lands and grooves were in the database?"

"Yep."

"Meaning the gun had been used in the commission of a crime."

"Correct."

"And they gave it back to the owner?"

"Yes again."

"And he used it on Blount's Escalade?"

"No," Fuller said. "The *original* owner was one Shelton Birch who you may remember from the great recession."

"Not ringing a bell," Densmore said.

"Had a mortgage company that originated twenty billion dollars' worth of subprime loans, every one of them junk and he knew it. Bundled them into one big toxic asset, told investors it was good-as-gold, and walked off with four hundred million in his pocket. Unfortunately for Mr. Birch, when the wheels came off the economy's cart, you had to get in a long line if you wanted to investigate or sue the son of a bitch."

"Sure, I remember now," Densmore said. "Over-bleached teeth and complexion like smoked salmon?"

"That's him. Turns out Mr. Birch is a bit thin-skinned and as such took exception to something a newspaper reporter wrote about him, so he shot the man."

"As you do."

"Yeah, didn't kill him though," Fuller said. "Cut to some high-priced lawyering and the charges against Mr. Birch were dropped and he got his gun back. But the lands and grooves remained in the database."

"Only one problem." Detective Densmore pointed at the image of the shooter. "That's not Shelton Birch."

"No, it's definitely not. According to Mr. Birch, he was disappointed in the Mac-11, said he wanted something that would drop a newspaper reporter with one shot, so he sold the Mac to a gun dealer named Randell Harlow and bought himself a Desert Eagle, fifty caliber in the burnt bronze. CHP contacted Mr. Harlow, who said he'd sold the Mac-11 to a man named Bryce Weeks and provided an address right around the corner." Agent Fuller nodded toward a video monitor that showed the house in question.

"That's a big place," Densmore said. "What do you think, seven thousand square feet?"

"Something like that. Damn eyesore too, like the rest of this hideous development. What's the cladding on those dormers made of, for Christ's sake, vinyl?"

Densmore looked closer. "Can't help but notice all the windows are covered."

"Yeah, and all out of proportion too. The neighbors don't seem to mind though. Their only complaint is about the unusual late-night traffic. Large vehicles, they say, pulling around the back where you can't see what's going on."

"How large?"

"Large enough to bring people in on a gurney," Fuller said.

Densmore looked back at the house. "So you're thinking impromptu hospital and illegal transplants?"

"That big gaudy thing has all the space you need for an O.R., recovery, private rooms, the whole shootin' match."

The radio in the command center crackled and a man's voice said, *"SWAT Seven, going in!"*

Agent Fuller and Detective Densmore watched the action on the monitors. Black-clad men appeared on both sides of the house and fired flash-bang grenades into it. A moment later there were two furiously bright magnesium explosions, blowing out a couple of other windows. Simultaneously, two teams on the roof were rappelling down the sides of the house and flying in through the shattered windows as two other teams hit the front and back doors with battering rams. Fifteen heavily armed men poured into the house.

"I sure hope they weren't in the middle of an operation in there," Densmore said. "Hard to suture an artery with flash-bangs coming through the windows."

A looked crossed Fuller's face that said he'd never thought of that. Then he shrugged. "Screw 'em."

A moment later the radio crackled again. "All clear. House is secure."

Agent Fuller and Detective Densmore hustled down the street to the house. Even twenty yards away they could smell it, like skunk. Stepping inside they came to a quick stop.

"Wow!" Rows of grow lights suspended from the vaulted ceiling, a sophisticated irrigation system, and three hundred marijuana plants, each nearly eight feet tall.

Agent Fuller stared at it for a moment. "Huh. I'll be damned." He looked up to the ceiling. "I bet that crown molding is Styrofoam."

"In here!" It was the SWAT leader calling from the next room.

Detective Densmore followed Fuller into the kitchen of her dreams. An eight-burner gas range and indoor grill with a big stainless steel vent hood over it, marble countertops, three professional ovens, and a walk-in refrigerator. The refrigerator door was open. Inside was a man duct-taped to a chair, hands behind his back. Looked like he'd been shot several times in the chest.

Agent Fuller stepped inside and lifted the man's head. "I'd say that's our shooter."

"Yeah." Densmore came closer, leaned over, and opened his eyelids.

Two empty sockets.

"Whaddya know," Agent Fuller said. "They took his eyes."

"So you think this is Bryce Weeks?"

Agent Fuller shrugged and addressed the SWAT leader. "Get this man's prints, would you?"

The SWAT leader glanced behind the chair where the man's hands were taped. "No can do, sir. They took his fingers too."

9

Jake's HLA antigens and panel reactive antibodies were not a match for Angel. So he moved to plan B. He called the dialysis unit at Ascendant Medical, asked if Scott Daniels was still on the schedule. Jake wanted an introduction to the man he'd seen Scott talking to, the man Jake assumed was a kidney broker. The nurse said Daniels had stopped coming in. Jake asked if they had transferred his records to another unit. They had not. Jake assumed Daniels had opted for a gray-market transplant.

Jake found Daniels' home address and headed that way, to a sweet spot in the Hollywood Hills overlooking the L.A. basin. Scott was one of those types who had been born on third base but always acted like he'd hit a triple. As one of his best friends said, "Scott's problem isn't that he inherited a ton of money, that's not his fault. Scott's problem is that he's an asshole."

It was getting dark as Jake drove up the winding streets into the hills. On the way he called Mark Simmons.

"I need a favor," he said. "I need you to call me in five minutes and play along with whatever I'm saying."

"You're aware that I'm a heart surgeon, right? I've got important shit to do."

Jake said nothing.

Mark sighed. "Are we committing a crime of some sort?"

"Not that I know of."

"Okay, what're we trying to do?"

"I need some information from somebody."

"Did you consider simply asking?"

"I did. But answering would open a legal can of worms for him, so we're taking the indirect route." Jake pulled to the curb in front of Scott Daniels' house. "I need you to help me put the fear of God into this guy so he tells me what I need to know. Be ready to spout some medical gibberish that sounds scary as all hell."

Jake ended the call and opened his glove compartment. He rooted around until he found the stethoscope inadvertently left behind by a nurse he had fond memories of. He draped it around his neck and headed for the front door. He kept the phone to his ear and made pretend conversation in case Scott happened to see him coming. Jake rang the doorbell four or five times in rapid succession, then banged on the door with a fist. "Mr. Daniels! Are you home? Mr. Daniels! This is Jake Trapper! It's very important that I talk to you immediately!" He rang the doorbell three more times.

Presently, an irritated Scott Daniels jerked the door open. "Stop ringing my goddamn doorbell, asshole! Who the hell are you?" He was wearing a white terrycloth robe that sported his monogram and a bogus coat of arms.

Jake, still pretending to be on the phone, looked surprised and said, "No, he's here! I'm looking at him. He's not dead." Jake pushed past Scott and into the foyer. "I'll check. Call me back in a few and I'll tell you."

"Who do you think… why should I be dead?"

"Mr. Daniels, I'm Jake Trapper, Southern California Organ Procurement. When you stopped coming for dialysis we got worried. We checked around and found your records didn't get transferred. All we could figure was you had either died or gotten a gray-market transplant."

"None of which is your business," Scott said.

"Let me see your eyes." Jake moved toward Scott but he backed away.

"Get out or I'm calling the cops!"

"There's no time for that, Mr. Daniels. You're not in legal trouble, you're in serious medical danger."

"What trouble? I don't know what you're talking about, gray-market transplant. It was a directed donation, strictly on the up-and-up."

"I'm sure that's what they told you, Mr. Daniels, we don't care about that."

"Who is this 'we'?"

"Me, the CDC, the NIH, the AMA, you name it. Now let me see your eyes."

The fact that he recognized Jake from the hospital, combined with the medical authority the stethoscope conveyed, and the certainty with which Jake was presenting himself prompted Scott to take him seriously. He let Jake check his eyes.

"What's the Centers for Disease Control got to do with me?"

"A woman who went through the same people you did died yesterday. Autopsy showed they had done a xenograft on the woman, not an allograft." Jake took hold of Scott's arm, pushed up the sleeve, and pinched his skin as if doing some other test. Jake seemed disappointed at the results. "It held for a week," he said. "She seemed fine, then boom. Dead as the record business."

Scott was starting to look more than a little frightened. He put his hand over the stitches in his flank, his eyes growing wide. "What in god's name is a xenograft?"

"A cross-species organ transplant." Jake gestured at Scott's mouth. "Gums!"

"What?"

"Your gums. I need to check them!" Jake grabbed Scott's head, lifted his upper lip and pressed a finger to Scott's gums. "Shit."

"Shit what? Wait, what do you mean 'cross-species'?"

Jake put on the stethoscope and pressed it to Scott's chest. "Medical biotech companies are looking for ways to transplant animal organs into people. It'll mean huge profits. We think you got one of their transgenic baboon kidneys. You're a test subject."

"Jesus!" He looked terrified. "A test subject?"

Jake was trying to think of some other phony exam to perform when his phone rang, Dr. Simmons calling back.

"Yeah, it's me," he answered. "Doesn't look good. Pupils are asymmetrical, skin's in early stages of hipohydrosis, capillary reflex in gums shows abnormal perfusion." He waited a moment, then, "That's what I was afraid of. Here, you tell him." Jake held the phone aside, said, "This is Dr. Fowler at the CDC." Jake put his phone on speaker.

"What the hell is going on?" Scott said, panicked. "This man is saying I got a xenograft, something about other species?"

"It's possible, sir. Rogue surgeons working for the biotech industry. We've been trying to track them. You're our best lead. Please answer Mr. Trapper's questions."

"What questions?" Scott looked at Jake.

Jake said, "Who did the surgery and where?"

"I don't know," Scott said. "I was blindfolded when they took me there. My god, what's going to happen to me?"

"Depends on the type of xenograft."

"He told me it was some sort of baboon."

"Transgenic," Jake said.

"A transgenic baboon?" Scott said.

"Well, for your sake let's hope so," Dr. Simmons said. "They've been experimenting with goats too."

"Goats?! I might have a *goat* kidney?!"

"Afraid so. The immunosuppressants these days can allow you to function long enough for your check to clear even with goat parts. But who knows? Could just be baboon. Until we find these people, we won't know for sure."

"Holy shit," Scott said. "I just wanted off dialysis!"

"In the meanwhile," Dr. Simmons said, "it sounds like you're in the early stages of acute phagocytosis complicated by chronic secretory spondylitis. If we don't find these people we won't be able to treat you."

"What if I don't know *how* to find them? Which I don't!"

"You'll lapse into nephrotic folliculitis followed by a massive hemolytic ventricular bloat that will quickly rupture and you'll die. Christ, it's horrible. I suggest you do whatever Mr. Trapper says."

Jake said, "We really need to find these people."

"They told me not to say anything," Scott said. "They made it *clear* about the consequences if I told anybody anything."

"I understand," Dr. Simmons said. "But here's the problem. Based on what we know from the previous victim, the goat kidneys they work with aren't tested for eukaryotic parasites."

"Parasites?"

"Primarily the Guatemalan razor worm, but others too."

"Sweet Jesus."

"They multiply like crazy in the ureter and then start spreading, some move to the testicles, others move up the shaft, essentially chewing their way out. Jesus Christ, the pain these things cause is horrible. I mean, they didn't get the name razor worm for nothing."

Jake could see that he had put the fear of God into Scott, whose hand had moved from the surgical scar to his crotch. "How did you contact them?" Jake said. "Do you have a phone number, anything?"

"I've got his card!"

Jake followed Scott into the kitchen where he frantically rummaged through the drawers until he came up with a business card. He handed it to Jake with a trembling hand. It was white and contained only a phone number. "Got it," Jake said and headed for the door.

"Wait! What about me? What do I do?"

"Oh, right." Jake paused for a moment then spoke into the phone. "Something occurs to me. The, uh, pupil and capillary tests rule out the micturition test, right?"

"No," Dr. Simmons said. "Other way around."

"Oops."

Scott was sweating heavily now. "Oops? What oops? What does oops mean?"

"I hate it when I do that," Jake said.

"Don't beat yourself up," Dr. Simmons said. "I do that all the time. Mr. Daniels, let me ask, have you urinated today?"

"Yes, right before you got here."

"And?"

"And what?"

"On a scale of one to ten, how painful was it?"

"Zero. It was normal, felt great."

Dr. Simmons said, "Well, Jake, there you go."

"That's fantastic," Jake said. "I love a happy ending!"

"What does it mean?" Scott asked.

"Means you got a human kidney," Simmons said. "Take your meds, you'll be fine."

Scott staggered to a chair and collapsed into it. The last two minutes had left him too drained to speak. He could only stare, mouth agape, as Jake ended the call and headed for the front door.

"Sorry for the mix-up, Mr. Daniels. Have a nice day."

***

Cell reception was iffy coming down the canyon so Jake waited until he hit Sunset to make the call. It rang through to voice mail that was the service provider's standard outgoing message in a generic female voice.

At the beep, Jake simply said, "Please call to discuss a potential client." He left his number and disconnected. He had no idea if or when he could expect someone to call back.

He cruised down Sunset toward La Cienega past the clubs where kids were lining up for the night's fun. For a moment he thought he saw Angel standing outside the Whiskey. He slowed for a closer look, then realized it wasn't her, just a clot of kids in Goth regalia. It dawned on Jake that he'd gotten too old and too straight, that all he could see was the makeup, not the person underneath.

A mile down the strip, his phone rang. The area code was Cleveland or Cincinnati, somewhere back there, and Jake didn't recognize the number.

"Hello?"

After a pause, a man, speaking through a digital voice-altering filter, said, "Who is this?"

"You called me," Jake said.

"You called me first. Five minutes ago," he said. "Who are you?"

Realizing it was the kidney broker, Jake said, "I'm anonymous, just like you."

The creepy sci-fi voice said, "How did you get this number?"

"Through trickery."

"Who did you trick?"

"Not going to say," Jake said. "No names. Seems like the best policy, all things considered."

"What do you want?"

"Help."

"What makes you think I can help you?"

"You helped someone I know."

"In the same way you need help?"

"Yes. Can we meet?"

75

"I'll call you back." The call disconnected.

***

The SWAT team packed up as CSI did their work on the murder scene, while a team from the L.A. County Sheriff's Department coordinated with local DEA reps on the pot farm side of the crime.

Detective Densmore and Agent Fuller were in the command center doing a post-mortem on the raid. Agent Fuller was searching the databases of the California Secretary of State and the County Recorder. "Well, it comes full circle," Fuller said.

Densmore was applying a fresh coat of lipstick. She dabbed her lips with a tissue and waited for more information.

Agent Fuller said, "One guess as to who owns our tacky and soon to be forfeited McMansion."

"I dunno," Densmore said, "I'll take Alphonzo Blount for a hundred."

"No. Try Shelton Birch."

"The toxic asset king?"

"Yep, seems he still has title on quite a few of the foreclosed properties whose mortgages he bundled."

"That's pretty brassy."

"Of course the deeds are in the names of various trusts and shell corporations," Fuller said. "You gotta hand it to him, really knows how to make a buck. From the looks of it, in the course of bundling all those mortgages, he would omit some of the properties from the inventory lists so when the creditors came calling, they'd get a list of several hundred properties and not know anything was missing."

"And then he repurposed them as grow houses?" Densmore nodded approvingly. "That's not bad."

"And he could just as easily have repurposed another one for transplants and another one for human trafficking."

"Diversification."

"He's a businessman," Fuller said. "Smart enough not to put all his eggs in one basket."

Densmore leaned toward one of the monitors where the coroner was wheeling the body to the meat wagon. "So what about fingerless Joe Jackson? Pretty clear from the YouTube video he was the freeway shooter," she said. "Can't really tell if he's the one in the hospital footage but he's the same height, race, and gender, so I'm going to guess he is. You think he worked for Birch?"

"I'd think he'd answer to somebody further down the chain, like Alphonzo Blount probably did. But Birch could be the one pulling the strings ultimately."

"Assuming Shelton Birch is the head honcho in this scenario you've imagined."

"Well, let's review," Agent Fuller said. "We already know Mr. Birch is the libertarian type who prefers not to suffer the heavy yoke of the government restricting his freedoms with its onerous laws against fraud and shooting newspaper reporters. And the missing eyeballs do a pretty good job of connecting the two murders."

Densmore pressed her lips into a fine red line. "If Birch is behind this, why would he have someone killed *here* of all places and left behind to be found? You're in enough trouble if we find your grow house, but one with a corpse in it? If you're smart enough to diversify, you're smart enough not to do that, right?"

Fuller mulled that for a moment. "Maybe they were going to move the body later. Maybe they got tipped on the search warrant and the SWAT team. Maybe Mr. Birch has connections on our side of the thing."

"That would suggest corruption within the system."

"The system that mysteriously dropped charges against Mr. Birch in the shooting of that newspaper reporter?"

"That's the one."

"No," Fuller said. "There's bound to be some other explanation that doesn't implicate any of our hard-working public servants."

10

Jake was sitting at his desk that night, surfing the Web while eating a grilled cheese. First thing he did was run a search on the kidney broker's number. Not surprisingly, it was spoofed.

Every now and then there was a 'ping' on the SCOPE page indicating an update in one category or another. *Ping*, a liver recovered in Long Beach was in transit to San Bernardino; *ping*, a potential new donor, a twenty-year-old male, six feet, one seventy-five, O-positive, pending next-of-kin consent; *ping*, someone in line for a kidney removed from list, deceased.

There was another *ping*. The update was good news for a number of people, especially Toby Castro, the death row inmate. He'd be getting his heart in the next day or two. Jake knew this could mean only one thing: a deal had been cut, non-disclosure agreements had been signed, and Keri Carr had finally given consent to 'donate' her son's organs.

Everyone who was logged into the SCOPE system got this information, as did the one person who had hacked in.

***

Jake slept in the next morning, rousing himself at ten. It was as close to being on vacation as he'd gotten. He was on his second cup of coffee when his phone rang. He recognized this number. It was the dialysis unit at Ascendant Medical.

"Hi, Jake, it's Megan." One of the nurses on the floor. "Sorry to bother you on vacation but Angel Ross is a no-show. I made some calls, found out her mom's in jail. Angel's not answering at home. You have any ideas?"

Jake was already putting on his jeans. "I'll see if I can track her down."

He was out the door in five minutes. He had a few ideas, places she'd mentioned that she liked to hang out.

It took him an hour. He tracked her down at Black Skwid Ink, a tat joint on Pico. He parked on the street and nearly got side-swiped by the Big Blue Bus servicing the Number Seven route.

He stopped in the doorway when he saw her. Not even noon yet and she had a beer in one hand, a cigarette in the other. Sitting next to her was the proprietor, a knuckle-dragging ink monkey who called himself 'Bones' who was trying to slip his hand under her shirt.

Angel swatted him away, irritated. "Cut it out, asshole."

Bones smirked and gave it another try. Angel swatted him harder. "I mean it!" When she stood to move out of his reach she saw Jake standing in the doorway. She stared at him for a second, trying to figure out what was wrong with the picture.

"What're you doing here?"

"Looking for you," Jake said.

Bones came up behind Angel, reached around with both hands, grabbing her. "Those are some sweet little titties."

Angel pulled away. "Jesus, Bones, would you quit? God!"

Jake stepped into the room. "Play time's over, Angel," he said. "Let's go."

"What?"

"Come on." Jake held his hand out. "Dialysis?"

"Screw that," she said. "Leave me alone."

"Let's go," Jake said. "I'm serious. This isn't how I want to spend my vacation."

"Yo, you heard her," Bones said. "Fuck off or you're gonna get hurt." He was a big kid, maybe twenty-five, and inked up like a Maori tribesman. He also had a chrome nose stud, black spikes in his ears, and a couple of snakebites in his lower lip.

"Bones, forget it," Angel said. "He's from the hospital, just leave him alone."

Bones glared at Jake. "He's the one came in here stirring up shit."

"Look, he's, like, a nurse or something," Angel said. "You don't need to prove anything."

"A *nurse*? Ain't that sweet," Bones said. He lit a joint and took a big toke. "I've never beat the shit out of a nurse. This shouldn't take long."

"That's for sure," Jake said. Over the course of two tours in Iraq, even with a surgical detachment, you learned a lot about fighting. Jake enjoyed the art of it. He'd seen smaller guys take out big brawlers simply because they knew what they were doing while all the brawlers knew was how to be violent.

"So what's up, nurse Nancy? You wanna get your punk ass out of here or what?"

"You got insurance?" Jake asked the kid.

"What?"

"Insurance, dipshit. You got any?"

"What, like car insurance?"

"Medical," Jake said.

"What do you care? I don't need insurance, nothin' wrong with me."

"Yet."

"Okay." Angel set her beer down. "Let's not do this."

"Oh, we're *gonna* do this." Bones made a big show of flicking the joint away. He started posturing, getting closer to Jake. Too close for his own good, but what did he know?

"Boner, if you're not out of my sight pronto," Jake said, "I might end up breaking some of your bones. It's always better to have insurance if you show up at the hospital like that. They charge, like, ten times as much to set a bone if you don't have insurance. Doesn't make any sense to me, but that's how the system works."

The kid said, "Who is this asshole?"

"He's… it doesn't matter. Just let it go."

"No way," Bones said.

"Don't be as stupid as you look," Jake said. "Pierced-up pussy like you ought to know when to tuck tail."

"Shit, I'm gonna mess you up."

The kid dropped his hands to his sides, one moving slowly toward his back. Jake just waited. Didn't matter if the kid pulled a gun, a knife, or a sap, Jake could tell from the way he was standing the kid didn't know how to fight. His feet were too close together, no balance in any direction, a bowling pin waiting to be knocked down.

Angel said, "Don't do it, Bones."

"You better listen to her," Jake said.

The kid pulled a knife, a pretty big one. But he was standing too close to use it, so Jake swept his right leg under the kid's feet and put an elbow to the side of his head. The kid went down hard. His head cracked the corner of a glass display case on the way and the knife skittered across the floor. Bones made a move for it so Jake kicked him in the ribs. He was rearing back for another when Angel pulled him backwards.

"Whoa, dude," Angel said, looking at Jake with newfound respect. "I think he's good." She leaned down to Bones. "You're good, right?"

Bones moaned and wiggled ambiguously.

"No? You need one more?" Angel kicked him in the balls, curling him up like an alarmed armadillo. "How you like my titties now, asshole?"

Bones moaned again and rolled onto his side, leaving some blood on the floor where his head had been.

Jake squatted and said, "Here's the takeaway, Mr. Boner. Don't play with knives. You could get hurt." He glanced at the cut on Bones' head then patted him on the shoulder. "Now don't worry, you'll live to be stupid another day, so you might want to look into that medical coverage we discussed earlier." He stood, and gestured toward the door. "Let's go. You're late for your appointment."

"What if I don't want to?"

"Angel… it's up to you," he said. "I can take you there or back home or wherever, but you don't want to be here when he gets up."

Angel knew Jake was right so she followed him out to his car and got in. They headed east on Pico. After a few blocks, Jake said, "You know what happens if you just stop doing the dialysis, right?"

"Yeah, I read the brochure," Angel said. "It sounds lovely. All the twitchy muscles and the itching and agitation and confusion."

"So you know the more crap you put in—"

"Dude, I know. I'll die if I don't go."

"Okay," Jake said.

She framed her gothic face with her hands. "But at least I'll look the part."

Jake gave her a dour look. Truth was, dialysis was only going to delay her death. She needed a kidney, and soon. "Where to?"

She stared out the window for a moment, then said, "Hospital, I guess."

"Good call."

After driving in silence for a while, Angel glanced over at Jake and quietly said, "Thanks."

"For what?"

"Nobody's ever fought for me before."

***

Once the deal with Keri Carr was struck, it triggered a flurry of activity in the Southern California transplant community. Surgical teams for recovery and transplant were put on notice while medical transport companies stood by to move the organs to hospitals throughout the region.

Somewhere in Los Angeles, the man who had hacked into the SCOPE system made a phone call. "The package will move from Valley Memorial to Ascendant Medical."

With Alex Carr on the table in the O.R., the attending physician called time of death at eleven PM on the nose. She split the sternum and pried him open like a reluctant oyster. She cross-clamped the ascending aorta and administered the cardioplegia, then removed the heart and handed it to a nurse who prepped it for transport.

Simultaneously, on the other side of the Hollywood Hills, a nurse was giving Toby Castro's chest a vigorous Betadine scrub while someone else draped him from head to foot, leaving only the surgical field visible. When he was ready, Dr. Mark Simmons made a perfect incision, parted the skin, and took the sternal saw to Castro's breastbone.

Back in the Valley, a nurse placed Alex's heart into a series of plastic bags and saline ice solution, then into a hard plastic beer cooler which she wrapped with duct tape, and handed to a young man who worked for L.H.O. Transport. He left in a hot trot heading for his car.

A few minutes later the SCOPE system posted the update, changing the status of the heart from 'Pending Recovery' to 'In Transit.'

The unauthorized man made another call to say, "The package is leaving."

The young driver for Living Human Organ Transport checked his traffic apps; the roads were wide open. He headed for the 405.

Dr. Simmons and his team opened Castro's chest, moving him to bypass so they could remove his damaged organ in preparation for the transplant.

The surgical resident watching from the observation deck was in touch with the transport driver. She came on the intercom to say the donor heart was twenty minutes out.

Castro's old heart was now in a stainless steel pan off to one side, still pulsing, but weaker with each beat, like a fish dying in the bottom of a boat. While the heart-lung machine oxygenated and circulated Castro's blood, Dr. Simmons raised a theoretical question about the legal ramifications of having a death row inmate die on the table. "I mean, what's their motivation to prosecute? Know what I mean? Maybe there was a little too much anesthesia, whatever," Mark said. "Happens all the time, right?"

One of the nurses said, "You're aware this is being recorded, right?"

"What? Of course, I'm just making conversation until we can give the gift of life to this man so the state can take it away the way God intended. Suction."

When the transport driver took the exit for the Medical Complex, he called to say he was five minutes out. A mile up the road he took the service entrance for Ascendant Medical. Ahead, there was a dark stretch where a couple of streetlights were out. Halfway through the darkness a black SUV, headlights off, pulled from a side street blocking the road. The transport driver slammed his brakes. Behind him, a black van stopped tight on his bumper.

No way out.

Things happened quickly from there. Two men, heads covered with black balaclavas, jumped from the van. A moment later there was a gun in his face, a black hood over his head and his hands were zip-tied to the steering wheel.

They grabbed the cooler and were gone. The whole thing took twenty seconds.

Dr. Simmons checked the time. Ten minutes had passed since the driver reported he was five minutes out. "Where's the goddamn courier?" he barked at a nurse.

She shrugged. How was she supposed to know?

Sitting in the steel pan, Castro's heart managed one more beat.

Dr. Simmons shouted up to the observation deck, "Find out what the hell is going on!"

After a minute the resident's voice came over the intercom. "L.H.O.T. can't raise the driver. Hospital security's on their way to see what they can find."

Simmons glanced back to the stainless steel tray. "Uh, somebody get that on ice." After which there was nothing to do but wait. Castro might survive for hours on bypass, or not. Either way, it wasn't a long-term solution. Dr. Simmons wondered if Castro's old heart was still viable. Then he started to wonder if he had any good options but to put the sorry thing back in.

A few minutes later the surgical resident came on the intercom. "Security found the driver. Said LAPD is on the scene."

"What for?"

"There was an incident."

"Not my problem," Simmons said. "Have someone hotfoot it up here with that damn cooler."

"There is no cooler."

"Say again?"

"Cops said somebody stole it."

11

By the time Detective Densmore arrived, they had floodlights illuminating the crime scene. She was finishing her interview with the L.H.O.T. driver when Agent Fuller arrived.

He approached with arms out wide, gesturing at the scene. "On my way over here I was wondering if you were going to treat this as a robbery or a homicide."

"Doesn't have to be an either-or proposition," Densmore said. "Currently it's just armed robbery. The man waiting on what is now stolen property is up there on a heart-lung machine." She gestured at Ascendant Medical. "But that can't last forever, or so I'm told."

"The L.H.O.T. driver have anything useful to say?"

"He said he thought I was hot."

"Good for you. Did he propose?"

"No, I told him he was too young for me," Densmore said. "Other than that he was useless. One minute he's about to deliver the cooler, the next he's got a black bag on his head. Said the whole thing didn't take thirty seconds."

"Sounds professional," Fuller said.

"Yeah, and…" Densmore's phone rang. "Hang on." She answered, listened for a few seconds, then said, "Okay, thanks." She hung up. "Now it's a robbery *and* a homicide. Patient just died."

Agent Fuller gave it a moment of silence.

Densmore glanced around at the scene. "Well, this is a first," she said. "Murder victim's half a mile from where the crime that killed him actually happened."

"That's your professional opinion? It was murder?"

"That's not my profession," Densmore said, "that's the D.A.'s problem, but it's a legitimate question. Technically it's a homicide. Don't know if it's murder or manslaughter. The theft did show reckless disregard of substantial risk resulting in another's death, but you'd have to show the thief knew the intended recipient would die." Densmore pointed to some broken glass on the street. "Looks like they shot out the streetlights in advance, so we've got premeditation. Besides, who steals a human organ on the spur of the moment?"

"Yeah, what's the point in that?" Fuller said. "You have to know what organ, what blood type and all that if it's going to have any value. Whoever organized this needed access to medical files at the donor hospital or the information on the SCOPE site." Fuller paused to entertain an alternate theory. "Somebody like your organ-procurement buddy."

Detective Densmore looked highly skeptical. "You think Jake Trapper is involved in this?"

"He'd have all the information to make it work."

"So would everybody else at SCOPE and UNOS and… anyway, why?"

"Money's the best bet," Fuller said. "Maybe he's got gambling debts, or he got blackmailed into it, or he's the mastermind of the whole thing, I don't know. I'm just saying he's in a perfect position to orchestrate something like this." Agent Fuller pulled his phone and hit a contact. "Yeah, I need a background check. Last name Trapper…"

***

The next morning Jake found himself staring at a three-day-old cinnamon roll, the closest thing to breakfast food in his kitchen. He was lamenting his lack of foresight when he noticed the half stick of butter in the dairy bin and realized all was not lost. While his coffee brewed he turned the bone-dry pastry in the melted butter until it reanimated.

He took the coffee and roll to his desk and called the dialysis unit at Ascendant Medical. They confirmed Angel had come in for her scheduled session. Maybe he'd brought her around. A small victory, perhaps temporary, but maybe all he needed if the kidney broker called back.

By force of habit he checked the SCOPE site. As expected, Alex Carr had been deleted after harvesting. None of his parts were listed, indicating they'd been transplanted. Clicking over to the *L.A. Times,* he glanced at the national stories as he scrolled down to local news. The headline *"No Clues on Hijacked Heart"* caught his eye. Three short paragraphs was all it took since no one had information beyond when, where, and how it happened. There was no mention of the donor's name or the intended recipient.

He called Mark Simmons but he was in the middle of a consult, unavailable. Before he could call Detective Densmore, his phone rang. He answered. The digitally altered voice said, "Glove compartment."

Click.

Jake went to his car. All his maps, title and registration, and the stethoscope were stacked neatly on the passenger seat. The only thing in the glove box was a pack of matches from a restaurant in the Marina. On the inside flap someone had written "Noon."

He went inside, changed into jeans and a dress shirt, then rummaged through his desk until he found Detective Densmore's business card. He headed for the Marina, calling Densmore on the way.

She answered by saying, "Can't talk right now, doing cop stuff."

"You know why I'm calling?"

"Yeah, but we don't know much."

"Can you tell me what you do know over dinner?"

She didn't hesitate. "Love to."

"It's a date."

Jake pulled into the restaurant parking lot. He'd driven past the place a hundred times but he'd never eaten there. It had a nautical theme, though it looked less like upscale Marina del Ray than like something the castaways on *Gilligan's Island* might have built if hungry tourists had arrived on their shore for an episode. You approached on a rickety pier tied to splintering wood piles linked by thick, knotted ropes. The interior was all dusty fiberglass dolphins and primitive fishnets draped on the walls.

Jake took a corner table and waited for the man with the digitally altered voice. He assumed it was the same man he'd seen talking to Scott Daniels and others in the dialysis unit. Sure enough, in he walked, looking very Marina del Ray in deck shoes, no socks, khakis, and a Hawaiian shirt, lightly tanned, like he'd strolled over from his boat. He walked straight to Jake's table and took a seat.

He said, "I know what you're thinking. What a dump, right?" He held up a hand. "Swear to God, best seafood in the Marina. I recommend the curried oysters." He smiled as he pulled what looked like some sort of remote control from his pocket and placed it on the table.

Jake noticed its blinking LED. "What's this?"

"Security," the man said. "In case you wore a wire, which you didn't." He put the device back in his pocket. "Can't be too careful."

"I get it," Jake said. "So, now that's out of the way, mister…?"

"Kaye will do."

Jake nodded. "Sure, fine." He got it. "K" as in "kidney."

The waitress came by, took their order. Jake got the calamari and ice tea. He hated oysters.

When she left, Mr. Kaye said, "We're very cautious. We do full background checks before we engage with anyone. I know who you are, where you work, your military background, the interesting comments you've made in the newspaper, all that sort of stuff, otherwise we wouldn't be here."

"Fair enough," Jake said.

Mr. Kaye chuckled. "By the way, you nearly gave Mr. Daniels a heart attack with that story about the goat kidney."

"Yeah, well, I had to tell him something," Jake said. "He wasn't giving you up."

Mr. Kaye didn't seem surprised. "He was especially worried about the, what was it, Mexican razor worms?"

"Guatemalan."

"Yeah, the Guatemalan razor worms. I loved that. I asked him where he got that crazy idea and he told me it was you, the SCOPE rep of all people. Naturally, my first thought was you're working with the police, but we asked around and found out you're not exactly a by-the-book kind of guy, not by a long shot. We found that reassuring."

"I've got a job, that's all," Jake said. "I don't agree with all of my employer's policies but my politics don't matter."

"Tell me anyway."

Jake shrugged. "People ought to be able to do what they want with their own bodies," he said. "The law against buying and selling kidneys is short-sighted, nanny-state legislation that results in a lot of unnecessary deaths."

"That's very libertarian of you," Mr. Kaye said. "So, cutting to the chase, I take it that you, ironically, need a kidney?"

"Not me. Someone else."

"Of course you understand we're not a charitable organization."

"Goes without saying."

"It's cash and it's not cheap. On the other hand, what's the cost of not doing it?"

"How 'not cheap' is it?"

"A hundred thousand and you're good as new."

"That's a lot of money," Jake said. "You don't have a sliding scale for the working poor?"

The man smiled, though not with any cruelty. "The working poor is where we tend to *get* our kidneys," Mr. Kaye said. "Closest we get to a sliding scale is to charge the one-percent crowd a bit more."

Jake appreciated his honesty and the fact that he stuck it to the rich, or at least said he did. "Do you guarantee a living donor?"

"Absolutely. Well compensated too. And only perfect matches."

"Who does the surgery and where?"

"I can't tell you that, as I'm sure you understand. Suffice to say that you are not the only person who disagrees with current laws. As Scott Daniels and others will attest, the facility is state-of-the-art and the surgeons and staff are all top notch."

"What if I can't afford it?"

"That would be a shame. But you wouldn't be alone, and there's always your list."

Jake thought for a moment then said, "Would you consider a trade?"

"What, like your car? No thanks. I've seen your car."

"I give you one of my kidneys. In return my… client gets one."

"It sounds like *you* are the charitable organization."

"I'm a charitable individual. What do you say?"

"I have another idea."

"I'm listening."

"What if you steer clients our way? What if you put me in touch with well-heeled dialysis patients who you think might be open to the gray market? For every client we get, we knock off, say, five grand of your debt. You keep your kidney, your client gets a new one, we get some business, everybody wins."

"Ten grand per client," Jake countered. "But I don't start until my client is on the mend."

"No, that's all in your favor. Seventy-five hundred per and we help you after you've steered us five clients."

"What if I can't find more clients after the surgery?"

"You either pay cash on the balance or we repossess." He gave Jake a hard look then relaxed into a smile. "I'm kidding," he said. "You either pay the balance in cash or we *will* take your kidney, up to you." He smiled again, and this time it was all business.

Jake thought he'd be able to hold up his end of the bargain, one way or the other. "I have to see the surgical facility first."

"Of course," the man said. "I'll be in touch."

***

Jake was driving home when he got a text from Detective Densmore.

<<When and where for dinner?>>

Jake replied quickly, meaning to ask, *Want anything special?* But it came out as, <<Want anything sexual?>> Not noticing, he hit send.

She replied, <<Slightly awkward. I'm guessing autocorrect, but maybe…>>

<<Specious! No, special! Anything special? Christ Albuquerque! Almonds! Almighty! God I hate autocorrect.>>
<<Amen! How about seafood?>>
<<Just had squish for lurch.>>

<<Que?>>
<<Squash for lynch. Dammit! Squid for lunch.>>
<<Ah. Maybe Tex Mex?>>
<<Sure. Rat at Taxi Nostrils?>>
<<No thanks, I hate rat.>>
<<Nexus Crust! Eat at Taco Bistro!>>
<<Ah, love Taco Bistro. BTW, how fat are your fingers?>>
<<Want me to pickle up?>>
<<Depends. Is your pickle as fat as your fingers?>>
<<Meant pick you up?>>
<<No, I'll meet you and your fat pickle at Taxi Nostrils for ratting. How's 8?>>
<<Gyrate!>>

Before Jake could correct that to 'Great!' he got a call from Mark Simmons. "Hey, what's up?"

"An interesting development in the heart department," Mark said.

"The one that was hijacked?"

"No, no developments on that, at least none shared with me," Mark said. "You asked your detective friend?"

"We're having dinner tonight. Hope to find something then."

"A date? So we've got lots to talk about. What time you two meeting?"

"Eight."

"What if we meet at ICU before that, around six? I'll tell you about this heart thing and give you the sex talk."

"See you there," Jake said.

ICU was a restaurant on the southern edge of the L.A. Medical Center. The place featured waitresses in skimpy nurse outfits and bartenders dressed like surgeons, serving drinks in specimen jars, that sort of thing. It was popular with the hospital crowd and medical fetishists.

Jake and Mark were sitting at an operating table waiting for their drinks and rehashing the Scott Daniels thing.

"The razor worm thing was brilliant," Jake chuckled. "He coughed up that phone number like it was a hot snail in his mouth."

"Yeah. Why, exactly, are you trying to contact a kidney broker? You got something you want to tell me?" He sipped his drink. "It's that girl, isn't it? I told you not to get involved."

Jake made up a story about Detective Densmore wanting to interview the broker. "Remember the dead guy with the missing eyes? Our detective thinks that might be connected to the black market organ crowd. When I told her I saw a kidney broker, she asked if I could track him down. Unfortunately the number he gave me wasn't working, probably a throwaway cell phone." The waitress arrived with a fried onion bloom smothered in chili, all served in a bedpan. "Boy," Jake said, "That looks authentic."

As the cardiologist shoveled the fried onion and braised meat down his gullet, Jake steered the conversation to the Toby Castro case.

"Mr. Death Row was prepped," Mark said. "Courier was five minutes from handing it over when he got jacked. I'm standing there staring into the chest cavity of a killer when the cops called and said someone stole the damn heart."

"What'd you do?"

"Same as any cowboy," Mark said. "Put the old one back in, tried to raise the dead. Hit it with two hundred joules, then three hundred, then four, but… nada. Considered trying again with five hundred but it was already starting to smell like meat on a spit or the electric chair so…"

Jake looked slightly aghast.

"All in a day's work," Mark said with a shrug. "Anyway, the reason I called in the first place is I heard from a colleague who said he'd just seen our Mr. Fontaine in regard to adjusting his anti-rejection drugs."

It took Jake a second to understand. "Fontaine got a new heart? Where?"

"I'm guessing it wasn't Dick Cheney," Mark said. "And my colleague didn't ask, so my second guess would be overseas, probably Egypt. All he could say was that the stitching looked good and so did Mr. Fontaine. Took him off Prograf, put him on Rapamune, then called me to gloat about taking my client."

"Egypt's what, a seventeen-hour flight? That's a tough trip for a man that age just had open-heart surgery," Jake said. "Makes you wonder." He checked his watch then slapped a ten on the table. "Sorry we don't have time for the sex talk, but I gotta go."

"Alright, but don't blame me if you do it all wrong."

12

Jake got to Taco Bistro a few minutes early. He could smell the carne asada and grilled onions half a block away. He made his way through the crowd and grabbed a pub table near the back.

A few minutes later Detective Densmore pushed through the doorway, all hips and lipstick. She stopped, casually surveying the room from a vantage point where she knew everyone could see her. More than a few conversations ground to a halt. He caught her eye and waved her to the back of the restaurant. Heads turned as she shimmied between the tables.

Jake stood when she arrived. "Nice entrance," he said, pulling out her chair.

She smiled. "Mom always told me, if you've got it, flaunt it." She stuck her leg out like a railway crossing gate, stopping a young waiter. "Some girls got legs, but I got gams, am I right?"

The waiter stared, mesmerized. "Yes you are, you do."

"Up here." Densmore snapped her fingers up by her eyes. "Thank you. Now, could we get two cold beers and matching tequila shots of the silver variety?" She lowered her leg and sent the waiter on his way. "Sometimes I swear I was born too late," she said. "I think I would have been a really good broad or a dame, back when they had those."

"I'm with you," Jake said. "Back then they got Mae West and Jayne Mansfield. What did we get? Kardashians."

"Life's unfair and then you die," Densmore said. "How's your vacation?"

"Kind of dull until tonight. Thanks for coming out."

"Thanks for asking," Densmore said. "Even though I know you're just using me for information." Their drinks arrived. "Just keep in mind there's a lot more to me than that." She hoisted her shot glass. "Salud!"

They downed their tequilas.

"So let's just get this out of the way," she began. "To date we've got nothing on the heart theft. Far as we can tell, it's the first time this sort of thing has happened."

"You think it's connected to the Yuri Petrov thing?"

"Alphonzo Blount," Densmore corrected. "Probably, is my guess." She took a pull on her beer, then aimed the tip of the bottle at Jake, saying, "Let me ask, the heart they stole, it wouldn't be good for just anybody, right?"

"Right. Great match for the man on the table, but not someone bigger or smaller or with a different blood type."

"Could you look at your heart lists and narrow it down to who would have been a fit? See if any of those people mysteriously dropped off the list without benefit of dying?"

"Yeah, sure, as long as... wait a second..."

"What?"

He was already shaking his head. "No, the timing doesn't work. Never mind."

"Tell me anyway."

"Transplant surgeon friend of mine told me one of his patients, too old to get on the heart list, suddenly showed up with a new one. But he wouldn't be ambulatory if he'd just gotten the one from Alex Carr. Way too soon. He probably went overseas for it, though I have my doubts about that too."

"Easy enough to find out," Densmore said. She pulled her phone and started tapping. "Immigration app," she said. The waiter stopped to take their order.

"Combo plate," Jake said. "You?"

"Make it two. And another round." She looked at Jake. "What's the name?"

"Fontaine with an 'e' at the end. Henry, middle initial J."

She pecked at the screen for a minute, pausing for the results. "Got three of 'em. Senior, junior, or the third?"

"Gotta be senior."

She selected him and a moment later said, "Bingo. Henry J. Fontaine, age, very old, hasn't been outside of the U.S. in the past four years."

"Interesting…"

"Yes it is, and I know a certain federal agent who will be keen to have a chat with this Mr. Fontaine regarding his new ticker."

"Fed like FBI?"

"No," Densmore said. "Department of Health and Human Services of all things, enforcement division or something. Bit of an oddball but tells interesting stories. He's looking into the Blount case from the black market angle. Oh, and you'll love this. The other night, we're at the scene of the crime speculating on whodunit and he reaches the conclusion that you're as good a suspect as any."

"He thinks *I* stole the heart? How does he even know who I am?"

"I mentioned you in passing," Densmore said. "I don't think he seriously considers you a suspect. He just pointed out you have access to all the information necessary to facilitate the crime."

"That's true but it's a pretty big leap."

"Yeah, he does that." Densmore told Jake about the raid on the grow house. "He got it in his head that it was a hospital for illegal transplants but all we found was a ton of weed and a dead man missing his eyes and fingers. The eye thing connects him to the Blount case and we guess the fingers were an attempt to thwart identification, but his tattoos gave him away. Turns out he was a man by the name of Thaddeus Dell, recently paroled from Carrizo State Prison where he once assaulted none other than Alphonzo Blount. We figure Mr. Dell is the one who killed Blount and took his eyes."

"Finishing what he started at Carrizo?"

"Don't think so. The assault at Carrizo was over chocolate pudding and painkillers," Densmore said. "The thing with the eyes suggests this was something else."

Their food arrived, stalling further speculation. They compared food notes. She liked the enchilada with the avocado-corn salsa, he preferred the carne asada taco with the roasted tomatillo sauce. They split a flan for dessert, then split the bill after a mock struggle.

"I'll let you pay next time," Densmore said.

"Next time, you say?"

"Don't you think?"

"Sure, but with less shop talk."

"I'm all for it," Densmore said, touching his hand. "We'll get all confessional and vulnerable and see where that goes. First, though, I need to ask a personal question."

"Go ahead."

"Are you married?"

Jake offered a sheepish smile. "I was. She left. A while ago."

Densmore waited to see if he wanted to offer more but he didn't. "So what's with the ring? You waiting for her to come back?"

"No," Jake said. "I broke a knuckle playing basketball. Now I can't get the ring off."

"A jeweler could cut it off."

Jake admired it and said, "I guess I didn't want it off that bad. I mean, it's a nice ring."

Densmore decided to leave it there. She waved a hand to erase that part of the conversation and ate the last of the flan. "Here's another question, less personal. Would you consider helping me on my case? From the transplant side of things, I mean."

"What, like a consultant?"

"Like that, except for the part where you get paid," she smiled. "Budget cuts and all."

"Why should I work while I'm on vacation?"

"What the hell else you gonna do?"

"Fine."

***

Densmore had parked illegally near the front of the restaurant. Her Crown Vic being obviously LAPD was safe from tickets and towing. Jake was half a block down in a No Parking zone with a Physician's Emergency placard in his window. He slid in behind the wheel thinking for a moment about that touch on his hand. He tried putting his key in the ignition, but it wouldn't go. There was something jammed in the slot.

It was a card with an address and the words: "Second floor. Midnight."

It was a parking garage in Culver City, not attached to anything, just a freestanding five-story garage that looked like it was built in anticipation of a development that never happened. He went to the second deck and waited. Ten minutes later, Mr. Kaye emerged from the stairwell and crossed the garage to Jake's car.

"You want to see the facility, now's the time," Mr. Kaye said.

"Fine with me," Jake said, only slightly drunk.

"Hands on your car, please." Jake complied and Mr. Kaye frisked him. "I will need your phone and you will wear these." He handed Jake a pair of headphones. "And this." A blindfold.

Jake did as he was told. "Now what?"

"Some culture." Mr. Kaye plugged the headphones into an iPod and hit the play button.

It was an opera. It began quietly enough that Jake could hear an engine cranking one floor up. A vehicle came down the ramp and stopped a few feet away. The exhaust was diesel. He had to step up into whatever it was, a van, a truck, he couldn't tell. Someone buckled Jake's seat belt and off they went.

Jake didn't know much about opera but he was pretty sure this was being sung in German, a language he didn't understand. Yet owing to the power of the composer, he still managed to get the sense this was the tragic story of a plus-sized woman being callously tortured by a sadist with a flugelhorn.

Jake was drunk enough to think that since he knew where they were starting, he stood a decent chance of figuring out where they were going. They drove on surface streets until the sadist began to employ kettle drums in his cruel plot, then they got on the freeway, though Jake couldn't tell if it was the 10 or the 405, let alone in which direction they were travelling. He was completely lost by the time the woman's tormentor finished her off with a chorus of bassoons. The vehicle then drove down a ramp and a moment later came to a stop. Jake thought they'd been driving for thirty minutes, and the best he could do was narrow down the location to a radius of roughly one hundred and twenty miles.

Someone helped Jake from the back of the vehicle. It drove away and a roll door closed behind it. The place smelled like a mechanic's garage, tires, oil, and brake fluid.

Someone took Jake by the arm to guide him. During a quiet passage in the music, Jake heard the sound of elevator doors opening. Someone led Jake on board. Once the doors were closed and the elevator was going down, Mr. Kaye removed the blindfold. They were in a hospital-bed elevator, large enough for a gurney, some medical equipment, and personnel. Doors on both ends.

Mr. Kaye took the headphones from Jake. "So, what did you think? That's one of my favorites."

"There's no excuse for what that man did to that poor woman."

Mr. Kaye looked amused. "He married her."

Jake was genuinely surprised. "I bet they divorce in act two," he said. "Or there's a murder."

The doors opened to a tile hallway buffed to a shine. Mr. Kaye led the way down the hall, past spacious hospital rooms, all private and comfortable as anything at the Four Seasons. Some were dark, others glowed with the blue light of television screens. By each door hung a wall-mounted medical chart-holder made of what looked to be walnut. Jake could hear the telltale sounds of monitors and pumps. They toured the facility, ending in one of the two operating rooms. All the equipment was state-of-the-art and sparkling. It was a five-star, underground boutique surgical center.

There was only a skeleton crew this time of night, and when they did see any of the staff, they were always hidden behind surgical masks, presumably to mask identity.

Mr. Kaye was leading Jake toward the staff kitchen when they passed a nurse wearing cat-eye glasses with little rhinestones in the corners. She said hello in passing and Jake could tell from the way the wrinkle in her mask changed that she smiled, so he smiled back.

After she passed, Jake said, "I'm gonna go out on a limb and guess this isn't what you call an accredited facility."

"No, we prefer not to have those sorts of noses poking around, given that what we do is, strictly speaking, illegal," Mr. Kaye said. "But we meet or exceed all standards set by the Joint Commission and the other accreditation outfits. Our surgeons and staff are all first rate."

"Yeah? Exactly how do you get quality surgeons willing to risk their licenses?"

"Look around." Mr. Kaye gestured grandly. "We've got the best equipment, a great support staff, and no bureaucracy," he said. "What else could you ask for?"

"Gobs of cash?" Jake said.

"Makes the world go 'round," Mr. Kaye said. "But that's not all of it. There's also politics and philosophy. You're not the only one who thinks there ought to be a market for kidneys. You know a lot of doctors, right? They don't all agree with AMA policies, or the medical board, or the reigning medical ethicists. They go along to get along. But a lot of surgeons think outlawing the kidney market is short-sighted, if not immoral."

"So it's surgery as political protest?"

Mr. Kaye smiled. "As for their license, there's really not much chance they'll lose it unless they tell on themselves. We're very strict about anonymity. Patients and surgeons can't identify one another. Charts have medical information but no names. That's another reason we don't have any problems finding surgeons. There's no chance of a malpractice suit. Our clients understand that going outside the system has trade-offs and the inability to sue is one of them. Everyone who comes and goes from here does it exactly the way you did it. Clients don't know who performed their surgery and have no idea where it was done. All they know is they have a new kidney and they feel like a million bucks."

"Well, nine hundred thousand after paying their bill."

Mr. Kaye held up his hands briefly. "Now, full disclosure, not everyone here is in good standing with the powers-that-be. We have some foreign surgeons not licensed in the states and we've employed the occasional doctor or nurse with license issues, a DUI here, a bit of pilfering from the pharmacy there, but we never hire anyone who lost a license for incompetence or negligence. We don't need to."

Jake had more questions and Mr. Kaye had good answers for all of them. In the end, Jake was satisfied, so they confirmed the terms of their deal and sealed their fates with a handshake.

***

Jake was trying to decide whether he should start steering clients to Mr. Kaye before asking Angel if she was willing to go down that road, or if he should ask Angel first to see if there was any point in proceeding. There were potential problems either way.

If he told Angel first that she'd be getting a kidney sooner than expected, and all she needed to do was be patient and stay on dialysis, that might buoy her spirits and keep her on track. But if she said something to someone who knew she hadn't suddenly moved to the top of the official list, red flags would pop. That was asking for trouble. Additionally, Jake had no idea how long it might take to find enough clients to make the deal happen. It might drag on long enough that Angel would lose faith in him, think he'd lied, decide she didn't want to go on. She might do something drastic and he couldn't live with that.

Or he could tell her the truth, that she could get a kidney, but only by breaking the law. Given her arrest record and general disdain for authority, Jake didn't think the legal aspect would enter into her decision. Maybe that was the way to go.

Jake's phone rang.

"I was wrong," Densmore said.

"About what?"

"Paying you, to consult."

"Don't beat yourself up," Jake said. "I assumed the consulting thing was just your way of trying to see me again. Slightly desperate, but sweet in an indirect way."

"You want the money or not?"

"Seriously? Where'd this money come from all of a sudden?"

"The Feds."

"You got federal money for a local homicide investigation?"

"The money's coming from Agent Fuller."

"The oddball from DHHS who floated me as a suspect?"

"Yeah. Apparently he's decided you're okay."

"What changed his mind?"

"Fontaine's new heart. When I told him, he nearly shot his wad. He's sure it's the break he's been waiting for. He wants to meet."

13

Angel laughed. "What do you mean, 'slightly illegal'?"

Jake shrugged innocently. "Well, let's say somebody finds out and brings charges. It's unlikely, but if it happened, they wouldn't come after you, unless it's to testify," Jake said. "If they go after anybody it'll be the people who brokered the deal."

"That's you, right?"

"Yeah, but don't worry," Jake said. "They only go after big-time brokers with ongoing enterprises. They don't care about people who facilitate one-time deals." Jake was making this up; he had no idea who prosecutors went after, but he thought this had the ring of truth. Given the urgency of the situation, he didn't think it mattered. Angel needed a new kidney, and soon.

The two of them were sitting on a bench in the shade of a pepper tree in the middle of the L.A. Medical Complex. Angel had just finished dialysis. Jake had a couple of grilled cheese and avocado sandwiches from one of the food trucks parked nearby.

"How am I supposed to pay for all this?" Angel asked. "I mean, it's not cheap, right?"

"That's taken care of," Jake said. "And the less you know, the better, trust me."

She looked at him like the frightened child she was.

"Do you trust me?"

Angel nodded. "Yeah, I do."

"Good. Here's the thing. Your mom can't know this is happening, all right? Seriously, she can't be trusted with this. She's—"

"I know."

"If she knew anything… and let's say she got in trouble with the cops for, you know, drugs or whatever, she might try to use this to save her ass. I'd be toast. Okay?"

"I get it. You're sayin' Mom's a screw-up."

"That's not my point," Jake said. "It's just, there's a lot at stake and—"

"Why are you even doing this?"

"It's my job."

"Your job's doing it legally," Angel said.

"Yeah, well, I'm branching out," Jake said. "This is a big decision, Angel. Just think it over. You don't need to answer now."

"Okay."

"Okay, you'll think about it?"

"No. Okay, let's do it. Dialysis blows."

"Alright, but only if you're sure."

"I'm sure."

"I'll get things started."

They sat there for a moment watching the people come and go.

"It's not her fault," Angel said out of the blue.

Jake shook his head, confused. "What's not whose fault?"

"Mom. She's not a bad person," Angel said. "She's just… she's got problems."

***

Two days later, Jake and Detective Densmore were in Agent Fuller's office in the Federal Building in Westwood. Jake was signing papers and asking how Fuller had convinced the DHHS to pay him for consulting on a criminal investigation.

"Simple," Fuller said. "All you do is use the T-words when you're filling out the forms."

"The T words?"

"Terror, terrorist, terrorism," Fuller said. "After 9/11 it's all you need to say if you want federal money or military equipment. In this case I said you had the expertise necessary to assist in the investigation of a potential transplant terrorism network."

"Transplant terrorism?"

Fuller shrugged. "We got the money, didn't we?"

Fuller still had his suspicions. He thought if Jake *was* involved in the black market, being close to him was better than not and a cash lure worked every time. He gave Jake a hearty pat on the back and handed him another sheaf of papers.

As Jake signed and initialed where he was told, Agent Fuller talked about his most recent lead. "Cop I know down in Harbor Division called me about half a dozen missing persons. Doesn't look to be a serial killer since no bodies are showing up. He thought I might want to look at it as a possible organ situation. Best lead he's got is a bartender telling a story about a man coming in near closing time one night offering to buy drinks for anybody who wants to join him at another place where he's going. Bartender says he never saw any of the men again, and they were regulars.

"So I join him one night on a rolling stake-out, cruising a bunch of skeevy joints down in San Pedro where all these guys were last seen. We're watching a place called the Rusty Compass when the door to the bar opens and we see a man leading a string of drunks out to his minivan. We follow, ending up at a warehouse near the waterfront where the drunks all pile out and follow the driver inside. We sneak over for a peek, but the windows are all blacked out. We try the door, but it's locked."

"What'd you do?" Jake said.

"We got in the car and drove through the door. And it's hard to say who was more surprised," Fuller said. "The people inside when we came crashing through, or us when we saw what was going on." Fuller leveled his gaze. "We couldn't believe it. Looked like something out of the Dickens' playbook. Forty bunks, most of 'em occupied with men, each one with a leg shackled to a bolt in the floor and a big bore needle sticking in their arms."

"What the hell was it?"

"It was a blood farm," Fuller said. "You should have seen these guys, they were… they were gray. I don't mean pale. These bloodless schmucks were the color of prison oatmeal. Thirty-seven men just laying there, emaciated and glassy-eyed, staring at the ceiling while they got bled day-in and day-out. Seems a couple of entrepreneurial lab techs had got tired of making small money at the blood bank. They had cartons of blood bags, stacks of certification stickers, bar codes, the whole nine yards. They were making a fortune."

"You're right," Jake said to Densmore, "he does tell a good story."

Agent Fuller assumed a wounded expression. "You don't believe that? Listen, stranger things going on out there than blood farms, you can trust me on that."

"Yeah," Densmore said. "Get him to tell you about the fat lab in Alabama and I don't mean a dog."

"Another time," Fuller said. "I've got to get on a conference call. Let's meet here tomorrow and we'll go see Mr. Fontaine."

***

From the moment Jake made his deal with Mr. Kaye, he had one person in mind as the first potential client. Harris Bunnel was an affable millionaire Jake knew from a private dialysis center in Brentwood. Straight out of college Harris had opened a foot massage place in a strip mall. Within two years he'd opened four more, followed by an upscale day-spa featuring Swedish, Thai, and deep tissue massage.

After reading a magazine article about exotic massage treatments, he added what he called the Aztec Tepezcohuite Body Drench to the spa's menu. It proved so popular clients soon had to make reservations a month in advance if they wanted to part with three hundred dollars in exchange for being vigorously rubbed head-to-toe with a pine bark mulch mashed up with aloe and mint.

Harris quickly realized the more exotic-sounding the treatment, the more demand there was and the more people were willing to pay. As quick as you could say 'a fool and his money' Harris was promoting Himalayan herbal salt scrubs, Porphrya red algae soaks, and manual lymph drainage massage. Lately they'd been promoting romantic couples colonoscopy weekend cruise packages. Sales were through the roof.

In any event, Jake had only known Harris for a month when the man asked if Jake knew how he might go about acquiring a living-donor kidney. He had the money and was happy to pay while looking the other way. Jake suggested transplant tourism, but Harris confessed to a fear of travel, said he was looking for something locally sourced. Jake said he couldn't help and Harris let it go.

But Jake assumed he was still interested.

He left the meeting with Agent Fuller and Detective Densmore and drove straight to the Brentwood clinic where Harris was undergoing dialysis.

"Mr. Bunnel, you remember some months back asking me how you might get… that thing you wanted?"

Harris perked up. "You bet I do. Name your price."

"Someone will be in touch."

"What do I owe you?"

Jake started to wave him off but thought better of it. "Well, you have, like, a gift certificate for a massage or something?"

Harris pulled a card from his pocket. "Carte blanche, my friend. Lifetime. Tell them I sent you and ask for the Muladhara Root Treatment."

"What is it?"

"It's not on the menu, you have to ask for it. You lay in this hammock made from gluten-free yak hair and you breathe sacred smoke from a Kemenyan temple. Then they work cinnamon and ground red ginger into your marma sockets while passing a vibrating bowl over your head to clear up your negative energy."

"Sounds a little new-agey for me."

"I'm messin' with you," Harris said. "Ask for a Muladhara Root Treatment and you'll get a ninety-minute Swedish deep-tissue massage and a happy ending."

"Now you're talking."

***

They were on a winding street in Pacific Palisades, Jake in the back of Agent Fuller's SUV.

"We're not going to his house?" Jake asked.

"Why would we?" Fuller replied. "Even if we got past his gate, the damn house is thirty-two rooms sitting on five acres. Old coot could play hide and seek with us long enough for his army of lawyers to show up."

"We're going for an ambush," Densmore said. "Some people get flustered when confronted by authority in public. We'll see if Fontaine's one of them."

Just past the monument sign for the Riviera Country Club, Fuller stopped at the guard-house and dropped his window.

The man on the gate stepped out with his clipboard. "Can I help you?"

"Special Agent Fuller, DHHS." He flashed his creds then aimed his thumb toward the passenger seat. "That's Detective Densmore, LAPD. We're here on official business."

"What the hell is DHHS?"

"Open the gate, please."

"Who's that in the back?"

"He's with us."

"You here to see someone in particular?"

"Yeah, the golf pro," Fuller said. "We've all got the yips. Open the gate, please."

The guard leaned down and took a good look at Densmore. "You're a detective?"

Fuller's window glided shut in the man's face, left him gazing at his own reflection. The guard tapped on the window. When it rolled down, he was looking at the business end of Fuller's Glock. "Open the gate, numb nuts."

They drove up the hill to the clubhouse and parked in the grand entry court. Detective Densmore and Jake were at the front door when they realized Agent Fuller was standing by the fountain taking pictures. "What are you doing?"

"What does it look like?" Fuller gestured at the building. "This is classic regional vernacular design. I love this stuff!"

Densmore looked at Jake. "Bit of an architecture fetish."

"Connoisseur," Fuller said.

Densmore tapped her watch. "Do you mind?"

"Gimme a second." He gestured at the building. "Look at the exterior arcades!"

"Yeah, and imagine what you'll see inside. Like, maybe a man with an illegally obtained heart who could possibly help us solve several murders."

Agent Fuller took one more photo then put his phone away and mumbled, "Philistine."

Once inside, they stopped in the archway leading to the spacious lounge. Agent Fuller nudged Jake. "You see him?"

Jake surveyed the room. "See those three men? Fontaine's the one sitting." He was relaxed on a plump leather sofa by the fireplace having a drink. Two of his peers had stopped to chat with him before moving to a table near the window overlooking the tennis courts.

Agent Fuller started toward Mr. Fontaine when Detective Densmore stopped him. "I've got this," she said. As she crossed the room, she popped a couple of buttons on her blouse. She stopped in front of the fireplace to warm herself and to give Fontaine a lingering rear view after which she turned to him, leaned over, and gave him an eyeful. "Hello, Mr. Fontaine."

He stared at her cleavage for several moments. "Hello," he said, finally looking up to her eyes. "Who are you?"

"Why don't you ask your friends?" Detective Densmore gestured at the two men Fontaine had been talking to, both of whom were already eyeing her. "They made the arrangements."

Mr. Fontaine looked over to his friends and winked. The two men responded with two enthusiastic thumbs up. Mr. Fontaine gave the sofa cushion a little pat. "Please, won't you sit?"

She slid in next to him and said, "It must be your birthday or something, huh?"

"Let's call it a new lease on life," Mr. Fontaine said. "And you are the perfect way to celebrate it. Would you care for a drink?" He reached for her leg but she deftly blocked him.

"You go ahead, I like to be clear-headed," Densmore said. "I know some girls get less inhibited the more they drink, but I'm dirtier when I'm sober."

Mr. Fontaine's eyes got bigger. "Oh, I like dirty girls."

"I bet you do," Densmore said as she put a hand on his thigh and squeezed it lightly.

Even from across the room Jake and Agent Fuller could see Mr. Fontaine's expression change when she touched him. He swayed just a bit and leaned into her.

"She's got quite a touch," Fuller said.

From where Detective Densmore was sitting Mr. Fontaine's response was even more obvious. His eyes fluttered and he made a moaning sound as he leaned over until his head was resting on her chest. His breathing hurried and all she could think was, *Oh boy, talk about premature…* She pushed him to an upright position and whispered in his ear, "So tell me about this new lease on life of yours. It sounds exciting."

Mr. Fontaine wobbled a bit, said, "Trezpluh," then he slithered off the sofa until he was crumpled, face-down, on the carpet.

Densmore gave him a moment then nudged him with her foot. "Mr. Fontaine? You okay?" He didn't respond. Densmore got down on the floor just as Agent Fuller and Jake arrived.

"Jesus," Agent Fuller said. "What the hell did you do?"

They rolled him over. Jake took one look, saw the drooping face. "Looks like a stroke."

Detective Densmore appeared slightly offended. "That's not going to help my reputation a bit."

Jake pulled his phone and hit 9-1-1.

14

The mood was pessimistic as they strapped Mr. Fontaine to the gurney. From what Jake could gather, the paramedics were offering two-to-one odds on Fontaine making it to the hospital.

On their drive back to the Federal Building, Agent Fuller, Densmore, and Jake discussed options on how else they might find out who had arranged or performed Fontaine's transplant. There was talk of subpoenas and bank records but they assumed that would all come to naught owing to the hourly rate of Fontaine's attorneys and the customer-first policies of the more popular offshore banks. Still, Agent Fuller had one other idea – an admitted long-shot – but they all agreed it wouldn't hurt to give it a try if the opportunity presented itself.

When they got back to Westwood, Agent Fuller went to make some calls and pull whatever strings might be necessary to set the long-shot in motion. Jake and Detective Densmore headed back to visitor parking.

Along the way Jake said, "You like Fuller's chances on this?"

"Assuming Fontaine doesn't make it, yeah, the Feds usually get what they're after," Densmore replied. "But I don't expect it'll lead anywhere."

"No, probably not," Jake said. "What if we had dinner? You think that might lead anywhere?"

Densmore smiled. "We won't know unless we try. You have some place in mind?"

"I'll text you."

"With your fat fingers?"

"They're all I have."

"Them and your big pickle." With that she ducked into her car and drove off.

Jake was still smiling as he got in his car, headed for Long Beach where he hoped to find some potential kidney clients. Merging onto the 405 he wondered what Densmore would think if she knew what he was up to. Would she care? Would she do something? What *could* she do? He wasn't committing a crime as far as he knew. He was simply asking people what they thought about the gray market, right? After that, Mr. Kaye stepped in and assumed the legal risks. Jake wondered if he could be charged with conspiring to violate some aspect of the National Organ Transplant Act. He knew some of the more brazen kidney brokers had been arrested in high-profile cases, but he'd never heard of anyone going to jail. For the first time since he started down this road he wondered if he should consult an attorney.

His phone rang, another area code Jake didn't recognize. He guessed it was Mr. Kaye on a spoofed number. Sure enough, the digitally altered voice said, "You're one for one, keep up the good work, maybe get a fancy massage." *Click.*

Jake figured this meant Harris Bunnel had come to terms with Mr. Kaye. Instantly, Jake felt like he was all-in on the deal. He was stacking up points towards Angel's transplant and all he needed was more. He called Scott Daniels' nephrologist to get his opinion on the quality of Scott's transplant. The man said it was as good as he'd ever seen, said Scott's kidney function was close to a hundred percent, and there was virtually no rejection. In other words, it was top-notch work done with a near-perfect match.

That sealed it. Jake merged to the fast lane and sped toward Long Beach.

***

By the time he left Long Beach, Jake had two more referrals. He didn't know if he was getting lucky or if the illegal kidney market was just badly underserved. He decided to test the theory by stopping at a dialysis center in Palos Verdes on his way home. He had another referral within the hour. Maybe it *was* this easy.

As he slogged up the 405, Jake started thinking about the money. If everything went well with Angel and all of his referrals, Jake wondered if he might land a permanent position. Even at Mr. Kaye's original offer of five thousand per referral, Jake would be able to supplement his income to the extent that his biggest problem would be how to launder the money.

A text from Densmore diverted his attention.

<<Tired of waiting for suggestion. How about Karma's Kitchen, Indian food, Hollywood?>>

Traffic was slow, so Jake took a shot at replying.

<<Sure, I love nuns.>>
<<Interesting. Catholic?>>
<<Naan! Not nuns.>>
<<You don't like nuns?>>
<<When?>>
<<Any time, day or night. They're just women in funny outfits, after all.>>
<<I meant dinner.>>

They met at seven, ordered chicken vindaloo, lots of naan, and a couple of beers. They had killed half an hour with small talk when Densmore asked Jake how he'd ended up as a transplant coordinator.

"I thought my medic experience would translate to paramedic work," he said. "But I failed to take into consideration the lingering effects of PTSD. Or, more likely, I thought, 'nah, that's not going to happen to me.'"

"I heard that."

Jake thought he heard some commiseration or confession in her comment, but he didn't press her. Instead he said, "Some of the situations were too much. I'd overreact if somebody didn't move fast enough or wasn't doing what I thought they ought to. Turned out my co-workers didn't appreciate being assaulted on the job."

Densmore nodded sympathetically. "What I heard is you know you've got PTSD if the last time someone crawled into your bed they were promptly sedated and taken back to their own ward."

Jake laughed. "How many soldiers with PTSD does it take to change a light bulb?"

"None," Densmore said. "They won't go near it, might be a trap."

"Ah, you know the classics," Jake said. "So, what's your story?"

Densmore picked at the label on her beer bottle. "After a year on the job I'd seen plenty of gore and all and handled it pretty good too," she said. "But my first murder-suicide with a shotgun? I thought I was going to lose it," Densmore said, staring at the table. "Could not get that scene out of my mind. Started with nightmares. Couldn't concentrate, got depressed. Standard PTSD reaction."

"Understandable," Jake said. "I mean that's hard. Your job always starts with somebody dead, somebody you can't help, it's always too late for that. In Iraq, at least we could save some of them."

"Yeah, but the ones you couldn't…"

Jake stared off into space for a minute. "There was this one time, we were in a little village and made contact with some insurgents. The squad I was with cleared 'em out pretty quick. When the shooting stopped, I looked across the way and saw a door open. It was… green." Jake seemed surprised he remembered that detail. "Anyway, this young girl came out of her house, I guess she was twelve, thirteen years old. She looked around to see if the fight was over and then she took off running across the street toward something. A second later she hit an IED. She was still alive when I got to her, but not for long, and there was nothing I could do for her. She looked up at me like she knew I was going to save her. I've never felt so helpless."

"What was she after?"

"Her doll," Jake said. "She just wanted to get her doll."

Densmore put her hand on Jake's. "I don't know how anybody comes away from that kind of thing with their shit together at all."

"Plenty don't," Jake said. "You see a therapist?"

"Oh yeah," Densmore said. "You?"

"Not as much as I used to. I learned to meditate, just take some quiet time, decompress. And, as the saying goes, if it fails with meditation, there's always medication." Jake made a funny face. "I wasn't going to cut it as a paramedic. Then somebody told me there was an opening with SCOPE and here we are, four years later, making jokes about our disabilities." Jake smiled at Densmore. "What's your story?"

She put her hand to her chest. "You mean how did a nice girl like me end up in a job like mine?"

"Do tell."

"I've got a better idea," Densmore said, touching him under the table. "Let's go back to your place and I'll tell you the whole story."

"I dunno." Jake gave her a skeptical look. "I saw what you did to Mr. Fontaine."

She rolled her eyes. "Christ, you give one guy a stroke and you're labeled for life."

Jake pushed back from the table and said, "Ahh, what the hell."

"Yeah, you only live once."

***

A few hours later Detective Densmore walked out of Jake's steamy bathroom with a towel wrapped around her. She was holding up a glass container in one hand. Jake was sprawled on the bed. "You have makeup remover?"

"I was a Boy Scout," Jake said. "They taught us to be prepared."

Densmore held up a piece of paper in her other hand. "You bought this yesterday."

"Yeah." Jake smiled. "I was feeling lucky."

Densmore was standing there without any makeup. This was the first time Jake had seen *her,* more than the lipstick. "What do you think?" she asked. "You like with or without?"

Unadorned, she was sweet looking. "I like both," he said. "You have a very pretty face. I like the whole innocent, girl-next-door thing you got going now, but I gotta admit, you're hot when you tart it up."

"Tart? I'm not going for tart. I'm going for bombshell or broad or dame!"

"Well, okay, you hit the trifecta on that."

"Thank you very much." Densmore dropped her towel and, as she climbed back into bed, Jake pretended to have a stroke.

***

Later, in the dark, Densmore asked the question that had been on her mind. "Why'd she leave?"

120

"Who?"

"Your wife."

Jake hesitated. "Not sure. She didn't leave a note."

"Did you see it coming?"

"Probably should've. I wasn't easy to live with when I got back. I did a lot of self-medicating. And she was impulsive, one of the things I liked about her actually. She'd just do things at the drop of a hat, like when we got married, totally spur-of-the-moment thing after we'd been dating a few weeks. We were in Vegas. She saw a chapel with a drive-up wedding window and she insisted, said it was what she'd always dreamed of, so that's what we did."

"And then what, you came home one day and she was just gone?"

"Yeah. Didn't even take all her stuff, just packed a suitcase and left," Jake said. "I tried to find her but she didn't want to be found, I guess. She told me once she wanted to try living in Europe, so maybe she's over there somewhere. I don't know. Wherever she is, it's for the best. I don't think we were meant to last."

***

The next morning Detective Densmore returned from her car with a fresh change of clothes and a makeup kit.

Jake said, "Talk about prepared."

"I was a Girl Scout."

"Love your cookies," Jake said. "Furthermore, I'd say you earned a merit badge for last night."

She went into the bathroom to change and do her face. "So, what's on your plate today?"

Jake didn't think he should tell her he planned to round up a few more kidney referrals, so he said, "A friend of mine gave me a gift certificate for a fancy massage, but I don't feel like I need one now."

"You're welcome."

"Don't really have anything on my schedule. You?"

"Looking into Thaddeus Dell's background," she said. "Trying to find a good suspect for that, you know, anybody with some loose fingers in their pocket. Also poking around to see if we can connect him to Shelton Birch or Randell Harlow."

Jake pulled on a pair of jeans and a T-shirt. "Are you free tonight?"

"Yeah, unless you want me to start charging for it. And frankly I wouldn't mind the extra money." She pursed her lips and applied a red cream lipstick.

"I'm going to an awards banquet thing," Jake said. "Hoping you'd be my date."

"What awards?" She blotted her lips on a tissue.

"The Grafties," Jake said. "Sort of the transplant industry equivalent of the Oscars."

She looked at him like she was waiting for a punch line.

"I'm serious. Santa Monica Civic Center. Red carpet, paparazzi, celebrities with liver transplants, the whole thing. Could be fun."

Densmore wiggled her eyebrows. "Tell me you got nominated for Best Supporting Organ. The Big Pickle Award!"

"Thanks," Jake said, "but they don't have a category for what I do. They act like the whole thing begins and ends with the surgeons. However, my friend Dr. Mark Simmons is up for Best Peripheral Artery Endovascular Stent Graft Placement for the fifth time."

"Good for him."

"Yeah, if he finally wins. He's sort of the Susan Lucci of vascular surgeons." Jake shrugged. "I like to be there for support, just in case. Plus it's open bar."

"I'm in," Densmore said. "How should I dress?"

"Bombshell."

15

Jake was in a fine mood that night. He'd hit Del Mar and Laguna Beach in the morning, picking up two potential referrals. At lunch, Mr. Kaye called to say he'd finalized three more of Jake's earlier contacts. That afternoon, Jake landed another three in Newport Beach.

His negotiations with Mr. Kaye having been inexact, Jake needed thirteen and a third referrals to cover the transplant, so his goal was fourteen. At the rate he was going, he'd get there within a week. As it stood, Jake was just one away from having Mr. Kaye start the process of finding what he promised would be a perfect match for Angel.

Now they were at the cocktail reception having drinks waiting for the awards program to start. Densmore was turning heads in a shimmering red gown and matching clutch, Jake and Dr. Simmons looked respectable in their rented tuxedos. Dr. Simmons was drinking scotch and waxing philosophic about his losing streak when a hand clasped his shoulder and a man said, "You've got to think positive!" It was Dr. Steven Brewer who continued, "There's no way you can lose six in a row. Nobody's that bad."

Mark made the introductions. "Dr. Brewer, this is Detective Densmore, LAPD."

He looked her up and down. "You're kidding."

"Robbery-homicide," she said, pleased at his reaction.

"And this is Jake Trapper from SCOPE."

Dr. Brewer paused a moment, then he pointed at Jake and said, "Oh, you're the one from the story, in the *Times*. "The girl who didn't get the kidney? Did you really say that?"

"Not exactly," Jake said.

"Even close?"

"I used some of the same words. Does that count?"

"I wouldn't worry too much," Dr. Brewer said. "As far as I can tell nobody reads the paper anymore."

"Apparently my boss still subscribes."

"Your frustration's understandable," Dr. Brewer said. "That's a hard enough job without having to navigate their arbitrary lines. Can't imagine having to ask a family member to donate their loved one's organs. That's got to be tough."

"Takes some getting used to," Jake said. "By the way, those five thousand kidney screenings you donated did a lot of good. That was very generous."

Dr. Brewer waved it off. "Doing what we can, that's all."

Detective Densmore asked Dr. Brewer if he was up for an award.

"He's getting the Humanitarian Award," Dr. Simmons said. "And well deserved. Dr. Brewer here started out as a general practitioner, left the profession after a few years to open a little business that he grew into what is now known as The Medicus Group. They essentially print money."

Dr. Brewer shrugged. "Business is good, can't deny that. But let's talk about you," he said to Densmore. "I bet your job's far more interesting than what any of us does."

"Some days *are* more exciting than others," Densmore said.

"Care to regale us with a tale?"

"You want a robbery or a homicide?"

"Definitely homicide," Mark said.

"Okay, let's see." Densmore thought for a second then said, "Oh, a recent favorite was this guy named Willie Love."

"This was a killer?"

"No, the victim," Densmore said. "Mr. Love was in bed with his fifth wife and they were rubbin' their fun bits when all of a sudden, BOOM! The door blows open and these four women bust into the room. But not just any women, mind you, these are his other four wives. And not previous wives, either, I should mention. Turns out ole Willie is still married to all of 'em. Keeps them in different apartments all around town and somehow they figured it out and got together on this thing."

"Uh oh," Dr. Simmons said.

"Uh oh is right," Densmore said. "One of them has a gun, two of 'em have lead pipes, and one has a damn machete. So Willie's thinking he's about to meet a sticky end and he starts to beg for his life and profess his unending love for all five of them."

"As you do," Jake said, admiring Densmore's command of her audience.

"But then, much to his surprise, he's given a choice. The women announce that the only way Willie lives long enough to reach divorce court is if he satisfies all five of them, right then and there."

"Not the worst thing I can think of," Jake said.

Densmore smiled. "Keep thinking. Willie's a big man, out of shape, but willing to give it a go if it means they don't chop him up and bury the parts in the desert. At trial, testimony revealed that after an hour or so Willie was three-for-three and making good progress on the fourth, a woman who liked to be on top. According to the transcripts she was riding him hard too, like she was grinding oats or something, when all of a sudden Willie's heart started to seize up. The wife in question didn't skip a beat," Densmore said, "just kept grinding until she got what she was after, all the while Willie's clutching at his chest and turning a new shade of blue. According to the M.E., Willie was still alive when number four hit her home run and number five stepped to the plate. So there's Willie, just lying there, not looking so good, and number five's standing by the side of the bed, slapping a lead pipe in her hand saying 'Willie Love, or won't he?'

"As you might imagine, Willie was unable to rise to the occasion. Unfortunately, number five took umbrage at the fact that Willie had let the other four take a bumpy ride on Captain Winky but was not going to service *her* needs. So, either insulted or jealous, or maybe both, she took the lead pipe to his head once or twice." For a visual aide, Densmore tapped Jake on the side of the head with her clutch.

The house lights dimmed twice so the four of them drifted toward the auditorium.

"So what happened?" Dr. Brewer asked.

Densmore shrugged. "Willie was dead when paramedics arrived. Autopsy said cause of death was a heart attack. Grand jury declined to indict the wives since they considered it Willie's spousal duty to keep 'em satisfied. They also believed Willie had no one but himself to blame for the fact he had five wives all demanding the same thing simultaneously."

"Jesus H. Jones," Dr. Brewer mumbled. "I'm surprised just having the five wives didn't kill the poor bastard."

"Hate to say it," Jake said, "but technically that wasn't a homicide."

"No, but it's a good story."

They showed their tickets at the door. The usher sent Dr. Simmons and Dr. Brewer down to the front and directed Jake and Densmore elsewhere. Once seated, Jake started to flip through the program. Densmore pulled her phone to silence it just as a text came in. She gestured at the program. "So who's favored to win in your friend's category?"

Jake considered the list of nominees. "The good money's on Dr. Glick. She's won the last two times." He looked up. "Why, you in a betting mood?"

"Could be. Might even take a chance on your Dr. Simmons."

"You sure? That's gotta be ten-to-one."

"Yeah, well, the odds-makers are taking a beating out there today."

"What makes you say that?"

She showed him the text. It was from Agent Fuller: <<Our long-shot came in. Meet at my office in the morning.>>

***

After dialysis and a forty-five minute bus ride, all Angel wanted to do was collapse into bed. But when she opened the door to the apartment, she saw that would have to wait.

She didn't even need to turn the light on. The smell told the story. Her mom had been partying again. Spilled beer, cheap wine, overturned ashtrays, the stink of crack and a hundred cigarettes smoked in a closed room left the air smelling like some combination of tar, cat urine, and a melted shower curtain. Tired as she was, Angel knew she'd never get to sleep if she nearly gagged with each breath.

She left the door open to air the place out. She looked in her mom's room to see if she was passed out there, but she wasn't. Angel opened all the windows, put in her ear buds, dialed up some Gothic metal, and got to work. She filled a garbage bag with the crap in the living room then moved to the kitchen.

More bottles and cans, dirty dishes in the sink, and a saucepan with something burned onto the bottom. There was a large can – chili with beans – open and empty on the floor next to the smoke detector, smashed. Angel looked up and saw the wires hanging from the wall. She guessed that Nikki or one of her guests had put the chili on the stove then wandered back to the pipe, forgetting all about it until the smoke alarm went off.

Angel took a knife and chipped at the saucepan until she realized she was wasting time and energy. She put some water in the pan hoping to boil it out. While that was on the stove she started on the other dishes.

She was listening to one of her favorites, Twisted Colon's debut album, Cream of Satan. The industrial din pumping into her ears would have made it impossible to hear a jet landing in the bathroom, let alone hear Bones as he entered the apartment and closed the door behind him, throwing the dead bolt. He peeked around the corner and saw Angel at the sink, washing dishes, lost in her music. He closed all the windows and curtains and slipped into the kitchen.

He was standing a few feet behind her when he pulled the stun gun from his pocket. He stepped forward, stuck the thing in Angel's back, and pulled the trigger.

She screamed and spun around, eyes wide and heart pounding.

"Goddammit!" Bones was cursing at the stun gun, shaking it, trying to figure out why it hadn't worked when it dawned on him that he'd failed to turn the thing on to begin with.

Angel was backing away, yanking her ear buds out. Her phone hit the floor. "What the hell are you doing here? Get out!"

"Not yet." Bones flipped the switch and pulled the trigger again. This time a nasty arc of voltage snapped between the probes. "There we go."

"What are you doing?"

"You're fixin' to find out, aren't you?" He lunged, but Angel dodged him. "You think you're just gonna kick me in the balls and that's gonna be the end of it?" Bones was waving the stun gun around. "You oughta know me better'n that. Now come here and take your medicine. Your little nursey friend's not around to help you this time." He started tossing the stun gun from one hand to the other. Unfortunately for Bones this required more concentration than he possessed so he didn't see the empty chili can on the floor. It skidded from under his foot when he stepped on it and he went down hard on his ass. He scrambled to his feet just in time to see the saucepan of boiling water coming toward his face.

It hit with enough force to dislodge the carbonized chili and put a nasty gash on the side of Bones' head. That plus the third degree burns on his neck and he let out quite a howl.

Angel lost her grip on the pan when it hit or she'd have done it again. It bounced out of reach leaving her unarmed. "Somebody help!" She thought her only chance was to bull-rush past him and hope he missed. She pushed off the counter and tried to stiff-arm him, but Bones got hold of her shirt. Angel punched his nose to break it, but he held on, blood trickling across his mouth now. He grinned as put the stun gun to her neck and pulled the trigger.

Once she was compliant, Bones tightened the zip ties around wrists and ankles, gagged her, and carted her out the back door.

***

Fuller, Densmore, and Jake met in a conference room in the Federal Building, all three having coffee. Agent Fuller had a folder on the table in front of him. He was spinning it around while he said, "As expected, Mr. Fontaine was DOA. Also as expected, within ten minutes of notifying the family, Mr. Chad Huntington Yardsworth had a court order preventing any sort of post-mortem work being attempted."

"Not that they've got anything to hide," Densmore said. "So what'd you do?"

"We complied," Fuller said. "Of course we were smart enough not to contact the family until *after* we'd done a laparoscopic biopsy on the heart and submitted tissue for DNA matching."

"So give." Densmore pointed at the file. "Who was the generous donor?"

Fuller shrugged. "Don't know yet. I was just told we got a hit…" he glanced at the door, "…still waiting for it."

"So what's in the damn file?"

"Huh?" Fuller slid it over to Densmore. "Oh, nothing, it's empty, it was just sitting here."

A minute later an assistant walked in with another file, handed it to Fuller. "Here we go."

He opened the folder and gave it the once-over. "And the winner is… one Scottie Moorehead, looks like an Aryan Brotherhood asshole, convicted six years ago on two counts of first-degree murder with special circumstances."

Jake tried to make sense of that. "And what, he escaped, got in an accident, and became an organ donor?"

Fuller read a little more. "Nope, last seen alive in an isolation cell at Carrizo State Prison."

"Well he can't be a donor, then, right?" Detective Densmore asked Jake if there was any scenario where Moorehead might be eligible.

Jake was shaking his head. "Couldn't even donate blood if he'd wanted to. Though ironically, if he *needed* a heart, he could have sued to get one."

"It gets better," Agent Fuller said. "According to records provided to the California Department of Corrections by McAfee Protective Services, the outfit that runs Carrizo, Mr. Moorehead was found in his cell two weeks *before* Mr. Fontaine had his transplant. Says here he hung himself."

Fuller and Densmore looked at Jake like he might have an explanation.

"Well, you can botch a hanging," Jake said. "End up in a coma, brain dead qualified, I've seen that happen, but… even then we know Fontaine didn't get his heart through the UNOS system, so I don't know."

"Nope." Now Agent Fuller was shaking his head. "No coma. According to the report, he was found dead in his cell."

"Reports." Densmore was getting a refill on her coffee. "Reports say whatever you need 'em to," she said. "I wouldn't put too much credence in the paperwork."

"Yeah that's crap," Jake said. "Even with the new warm-heart transports, a heart's not viable more than eight or ten hours. So, a couple of weeks doesn't pass the sniff test."

Agent Fuller stared out the window for a moment. "Wait a minute. There was a case a couple of years back. Guy killed his wife and three kids, up in Portland, I think. They tracked him down in Mexico. Sent him back to Oregon where he was sitting on death row when he suddenly decided he wanted to make amends by expediting his execution so he could donate his organs, save some lives."

"I remember that," Jake said. "And one like it in Ohio. Both said they'd drop all appeals, save the state some money, donate all their organs upon execution. Medical ethicists were crawling out of the woodwork to get CNN face-time on both of those."

"How'd it play out?"

"Didn't happen," Jake said. "Too public, nobody would touch it. Lots of philosophical talk but nobody did anything. Waste of good organs."

Agent Fuller said, "So maybe Moorehead had the same idea but decided to keep it out of the press. He wasn't interested in a public policy debate, he just wanted to get it done."

Densmore gave him a skeptical glance. "Anything's possible," she said. "But my experience is your white supremacists aren't that savvy."

"Okay, let's look at this," Fuller said. "There are two obvious options. It was voluntary or it was forced on him. If it was voluntary, someone had to propose the idea in the first place. I'll go out on a limb and say the idea came from outside since Moorehead doesn't strike me as an idea guy. But I can imagine a scenario where, for example, Moorehead's mama needs money for cancer treatment and they – whoever *they* are – go to him with cash in hand, tell him he can take care of his mama and do some good beyond that. I could see Moorehead's attorney hatching the plan or maybe someone else did, then approached the attorney."

"Raising the question: why Moorehead?"

Densmore said, "Maybe they were looking for somebody no one would miss."

"No," Jake said. "He had to be a match. Nothing else makes sense. You don't find a donor then go looking for recipients that happen to match, hoping they have the wherewithal to pay the bill." Jake paused as it dawned on him. "Well, okay, that's what SCOPE does, but if you've got people conspiring to harvest the organs of a prison inmate, they'll know the recipient first, then go find a match for him."

Fuller held up finger. "Here's another scenario…"

Densmore started to rub her temples. "Fellas, I'm getting a headache with all your scenarios."

"What do you suggest?"

"Start with what we know, go from there," Densmore said. "The man was in prison. Maybe he hung himself, maybe someone just wants it to look like he hung himself. And who's in a position to do that?"

"Guards," Agent Fuller said.

Densmore touched her finger to her nose. "Exactly. Problem is you can't just go marching through the front door of a semi-militarized institution and start asking incriminating questions about a crime they may have committed."

Jake said, "So what do you do?"

"Sneak around the side and peek in the windows first," Fuller said.

16

After scoring some coke Nikki headed straight home with a spring in her step. She wanted another drink and thought one more boost was just the thing to go with it. She'd watch a little Cartoon Network and have a few laughs before calling it a day.

She saw the garbage sack sitting outside the door and assumed, as usual, Angel had done a little clean-up and would no doubt give her a load of shit for leaving the mess in the first place. Then she'd get all up in Nikki's business about her friends and the drugs and being more responsible, and who needed all that crap after a hard day? She just hoped Angel wasn't home so she could enjoy her toot in peace. Who was she to judge anyway?

Nikki went to the kitchen to get a beer. She saw Angel's phone on the floor and picked it up, thinking it was unusual but nothing more. She took a bottle from the fridge and went back to the living room, pulled out the dime of coke, and grabbed the remote. She laid out a couple of rails and snorted one then glanced up at the television.

What the hell's that?

A big square blacked out in the middle of the screen. She turned on a lamp and crossed the room. She stared at it for while, trying to understand.

She stepped toward the hall and yelled, "Angel?" No response.

Nikki went back to Angel's room. She wasn't there. Nikki went back to the television and pulled the note from the screen. It was just like something from a TV show or a movie, all the letters cut out of a magazine and glued together to make new words.

I got angel. I want $500. Ill be in touch.

Five hundred bucks? Nikki wondered who the hell thought she could ever get her hands on five hundred bucks. Maybe her landlord had left the note, he was always badgering her for the rent. He had a key, could let himself in. Asshole. Then she thought maybe Angel had done it, faked her own kidnapping, the little bitch.

Oh, I see, leaving your phone on the kitchen floor, a little clue, make it look like something happened. I get it. How dumb do you think I am?

Nikki snorted the other line of coke and read the ransom note again. She stared at it for a while, her brain awash in a surge of dopamine. She smiled when the idea hit her.

***

That afternoon Jake went to a dialysis center in Santa Monica where he picked up a couple more kidney leads. Later he went over to meet Mark Simmons for some basketball. They played at an outdoor court on the western edge of the L.A. Medical Complex where you could always find a pick-up game.

Mark was already playing when Jake arrived. Jake got picked up by the team playing next, and now they were down to game point, Jake guarding his friend.

Mark set up in the low post and called for the ball. He dribbled slowly as he backed Jack under the basket. After three seconds in the lane, Jake started counting. "Four, five, six…"

At 'seven' Mark hooked his left arm around Jake and laid up the game winner.

"Game!" Mark shouted as he high-fived his teammates.

Jake laughed as he walked off the court. "Seven seconds in the lane *and* you have to hook me to get your shot? I'm embarrassed for you."

"Considering you're so famous for not following the rules, you're sure a stickler for others doing it," Mark said. "Now go cry somewhere else."

Jake flipped him off and headed for the water fountain when he noticed a man approaching him, well dressed, tanned, two-hundred-dollar haircut. The man gave a friendly wave. "Excuse me, Mr. Trapper? Do you have a second?"

"For what?" Jake was wondering if the man was a cop of some sort, investigating the kidney deals.

"Just want to talk," the man said. "I have a proposition, a business proposal."

"Do I know you?" Jake took a drink at the fountain.

"No, but we know some of the same people," the man said. "For example I'm sure you remember the late, lamented Alex Carr and his lovely mother, Keri?"

"Sure, I remember them." Now Jake was worried the guy might be investigating the off-the-books deal he initiated to secure Alex's organs for SCOPE. "Who are you?"

"I'm Mitchell Wick." He smiled modestly as if expecting Jake to be impressed.

Jake shrugged. The name meant nothing to him.

Wick seemed hurt but moved on. "The TV producer? I'd like to talk." He handed Jake a business card.

Jake glanced at the card. "About what?"

"An idea for a show. I want you on board."

Jake stared at him for a moment. "On board? Wait, back up. How did you know the Carrs?" Jake wiped his head with a towel. "You mind if we sit?"

Wick steered Jake to a nearby bench. They sat at opposite ends, facing each other. "Alex Carr tried to burglarize my house. He was doing some work on my property and that's where he got the idea to kidnap my Buddy."

"Who's your buddy?"

Wick registered genuine surprise that Jake didn't know. He pulled his phone and tapped the screen. *"Buddy.* The head judge on *One Hit Wonder*? Cute little black-handed spider monkey?" He showed Jake a clip from the show, Buddy covering his ears as a contestant sang a chorus of their song. "He's won three Emmy's. Surely you've heard of the show."

Jake just shook his head.

"Doesn't matter," Wick said, putting his phone away. "Anyway, Carr botched the kidnapping and, I don't have all the details, but he ended up in a coma on my living room floor. Flash forward a few weeks and I find his distraught mother camped out at the gate in front of my house. She starts by saying she just wants to see the last place her son was really alive. When I refused, she got around to her real pitch, a shakedown as ill-conceived as her son's kidnap plot. Says she's going to sue me for what happened, but because she was in a generous mood, she offered me the chance to make it all go away for a hundred grand."

Jake didn't know what to make of the fact that a television producer was trying to hire him for god-knows-what, but in light of the fact that he had recently attended a Hollywood-style awards show for transplant surgeons, he decided he'd stick around to see what was in it for him.

"Wait, she was threatening to sue you because her son tried to steal your monkey, then somehow ended up in a coma in your living room? How does that make any sense?"

"It *doesn't* make any sense, which is exactly what I told her. Then she got all weepy and, in her final ploy, launched into a sob story, telling me how she had hoped to make some money by selling her son's organs instead of just giving them away like most people do. I think 'idiots' is the word she used. In the course of things she mentioned your name as the person from SCOPE who got the ball rolling on the deal she eventually made, which she characterized as highway robbery."

"I have no idea what you're talking about."

Wick held up his manicured hands. "Of course not. You'd be nuts to say otherwise. But while I'm listening to this lunatic tell this story, I have an idea for a new reality show." He made a sweeping gesture and announced, *"America's Got Kidneys!* Or... I don't really have a good title yet. Or even a format, really. I mean, it could be a lifestyle change show or a fantasies fulfilled thing, but I'm thinking some sort of combination of those along with some playoff element, but it's a great idea."

Jake was dumbfounded. "What, like three contestants need a kidney and they're competing for the one you're offering as a prize?"

"Something like that, but tasteful."

"Of course."

Wick paused and looked past Jake at someone and said, "Can I help you?"

"Jake, you didn't tell me you had Hollywood connections," Mark said.

Jake aimed a thumb at Wick. "You know this guy?"

"I know who he is, sure." Mark held out his hand. "Big fan of your shows."

They shook hands. "Thanks," Wick said. "Your friend here doesn't seem to own a television."

"Yeah he's a pop culture mongoloid."

"Mr. Wick, this is Dr. Mark Simmons, you may have heard of him as the only doctor on earth who couldn't win a Graftie Award if he was the only surgeon nominated," Jake said. "Mark, Mr. Wick here has a monkey that's won three Emmys."

"It's an honor just to be nominated, as you know, Jake. Oh wait, that's right, you've never been nominated for shit, so you have no idea."

Someone yelled from the court, "Yo! Ball's up! Let's go."

"Nice to meet you, Mr. Wick. Give me a call if you need a Graftie-nominated heart surgeon."

Jake rubbed a sore leg muscle. "I've seen enough television to think it's possible a network would go for whatever the show might turn out to be, but the government won't."

Wick shrugged. "That's my problem."

"What do you want from me?"

"Your expertise," Wick said. "You know how it all works. I want someone to brainstorm with, someone to answer questions, explain the rules and regs and all that so I don't have to do the research myself. Saves me time. But look, I'm sure I can find someone else in your field who wants to make five thousand a week batting ideas around, so if you're not interested I could—"

"Whoa," Jake held up a hand. "I never said I wasn't interested."

***

After telling Mr. Wick he'd be in touch, Jake headed home for a shower. On the drive he was so preoccupied with the thought of making five thousand a week consulting for a television producer that he didn't notice the car following him until he was a few blocks from his house.

It was dark now and he couldn't tell what model car it was. He hoped it was Detective Densmore. Jake pulled into his driveway and the car stopped, blocking the drive behind him. He got out of his car and looked. It wasn't Densmore's Crown Vic. It was a top-of-the-line Mercedes. The passenger window glided down and the driver leaned over so Jake could see him. It was Mr. Kaye.

"You got a minute?"

"Sure." Jake walked over to the car.

"You're very good at this," Mr. Kaye said.

"Yeah?"

"We've already done deals with seven of your referrals and I'm confident of three others that I've talked to."

"Glad to hear it," Jake said. "I got a few more leads today. Feels like I've barely scratched the surface."

"Get me your client's medical records so we can start looking for a match."

"Wait here." He disappeared into his house, returning with a folder.

When he handed it over, Mr. Kaye said, "I've been thinking, perhaps we should explore the possibility of an ongoing relationship. After we take care of your client, that is. I think you would find it quite profitable."

Jake nodded. "I'll think it over."

"Good."

Jake gestured at the file. "How long do you think?"

"A week, maybe less," he said. "But the match will be perfect." Mr. Kaye put the car in gear. "I'll be in touch."

Jake stepped back and the car drove away. When the tail lights disappeared around the corner, he broke into a crazy grin.

What a day.

He'd secured a kidney for Angel and been offered two jobs at insane rates of pay. He'd keep his job with SCOPE, piggybacking his work for Mr. Kaye on those hours. All things considered, Jake couldn't think of a single reason to reject either offer.

He looked up at stars and thought that he was in one of those perfect, rare moments when all was right in the world. He figured the only way the moment could get any better would be if Detective Densmore dropped by for a visit.

And then, as if on cue, a car rounded the same corner where Mr. Kaye had turned moments earlier. The car picked up speed as it approached. It crossed the center line, veering toward Jake's property, screeching to a halt after hitting a neighbor's garbage can and jumping the curb with one wheel.

The door flew open. It was Nikki. She was waving a piece of paper and screeching, "They kidnapped my baby!"

***

Jake ushered Nikki into his house. "Calm down," he said. "What's going on? What are you talking about?"

"I came home and found this." She waved the ransom note.

He looked at the note, then at her. "Uh, you probably shouldn't be touching that, Nikki. Fingerprints and all that?"

"Oh, yeah," she sniffed and swiped at her nose with her sleeve. "I was so upset I didn't even think about that."

"It's okay," Jake said. "Put it on the table, let me see."

I got angel. I want $5000. Ill be in touch.

"Did you call the cops?"

"No! No cops! He said so."

"You talked to the kidnapper?"

Nikki hesitated and rubbed her nose. "Yeah, he, uh, he said he'd be in touch. Like it says in the note." She pointed at it. "And he called."

"What did he say?"

"He said no cops!"

"Yeah, I got that part. What else did he say?"

"Uh, he told me to get the money pronto and wait for him to… call again, on, uh, Angel's phone." She frisked herself and pulled it from a pocket. "That's how I found you. You're in her contact list." Nikki dropped herself onto the sofa, all pitiful. "I don't have five thousand dollars! What am I going to do?" She looked around Jake's place. "You have anything to drink here?"

Jake ignored her. "When was Angel's last dialysis session?"

140

"Her what? Oh, yeah, I don't know. She was handling that," Nikki said. "I been busy, working." She looked toward the kitchen. "You got a beer, anything?"

"You understand she'll get very sick if she doesn't get the dialysis? If she misses two or three, she could die."

"That's why I came to you! We need to get the money so we can get her back in time. Before it's too late, right? I don't have that kind of cash. I was hoping you did. I mean, I know you like her and all and you'd want to help her. That's why I'm here."

"Right." Jake examined the note more closely. He wasn't interested in the errors, the lowercase 'a' in 'angel' or the missing apostrophe in 'Ill.' And he wouldn't have thought twice about the lack of a comma in 5000 except for one thing. He didn't think *that* was a mistake.

"Nikki," he said, "I can't help but notice that all these letters and numbers are *glued* onto the page." He pointed at the *$5000.* "All except this one zero here that makes five hundred dollars into five thousand dollars." He folded his arms and stared at her.

"Huh." Nikki pretended to give the note a closer look while she thought of an answer. "I see what you're saying. I guess he just ran out of glue," she said. "So, you have that kind of cash on hand or we need to hit the ATM or something?"

"It's in the middle of the note, Nikki. See? Everything else is glued," Jake said. "That zero is taped on, like it was added later. By someone else."

She looked again, scratching at the back of her hand. "Well maybe the guy decided to raise the price after he'd run out of glue. That could happen."

"Nikki," Jake said. "You added the zero."

Her mouth dropped open. "I what? What are you saying?"

"And that's giving you the benefit of the doubt."

"What's that supposed to mean?"

141

"I'm assuming you didn't put the original note together and then go back and tape on the extra zero later," Jake said. "Jesus Christ. What's wrong with you?"

"You can't judge me!"

"I can't? Nikki, you're trying to profit from your own daughter's kidnapping."

Nikki paused long enough to work up some crocodile tears. "I know," she said. "It's the drugs." She wiped at her dry eyes. "It's not me, it's the disease. It's the drugs make me do bad things." She peeked to see if Jake was buying it.

But Jake was too busy wondering what kind of world-class moron demands a five-hundred-dollar ransom for a sick child, though he had a pretty good idea of the answer. "I'll be right back." He went to his bathroom and returned with a pair of tweezers that he used to pry up a few of the letters. He flipped them over and sure enough, partial images of tattoos, ads for tat parlors, that sort of thing, adorned the scraps.

Jake looked at Nikki and said, "You know that creep who calls himself Bones? Has a tattoo place on Pico?"

"Yeah, that's where Angel got some of hers done. So?"

"You know his real name?"

She shook her head.

"Give me her phone."

Nikki handed it over. "I need to use your bathroom."

Jake pointed the way then scrolled through Angel's contacts. He found 'Bones' and an address that wasn't on Pico. He went to his computer, looked it up. An apartment in Culver City. He looked up the phone number for Black Skwid Ink and called it. A woman answered.

"Yeah, Bones there?"

"He's working," she said.

"How late are you open?"

"Midnight."

Jake hung up just as the toilet flushed and Nikki returned. He tried to make eye contact with her, but she looked away. He held out his hand. "Let's have 'em."

"What?"

"The pills, Nikki."

17

Nikki handed over the pills she had pocketed, saying, "Well, they're past expiration. I figured you were just gonna throw 'em out."

"Just saving me the trouble, then?" Jake shook his head. "I need these, Nikki."

"Sorry, how was I supposed to know?"

"They're prescriptions! You don't just… never mind, of course you do." He left the pills on his desk. "Let's go."

On her way out, Nikki looked back over her shoulder. "You sure you don't have a beer or something in there?"

Jake led her out the door and parked Nikki's car in his driveway. They both got into his car and headed for the address in Culver City.

"What if she's not there?"

"We'll cross that bridge when we get to it," Jake said. He considered calling Densmore, to get some advice, but time was critical and he wanted to get Angel to dialysis as soon as possible. He thought if the LAPD got involved, they'd have to call the FBI, and they'd want to set up a command post and interview Nikki and the neighbors, and by the time they were ready to actually do something, he could have found Angel or at the very least eliminated the most obvious suspect.

Nikki started looking through the glove compartment until she noticed Jake staring at her. "Sorry, habit." She closed the compartment and shifted in her seat to face Jake. "How long does she have? I mean before she starts getting sick."

"Depends when her last session was," Jake said. "Depends if she's been following her diet and things like–"

Nikki's cell phone rang. She pulled it from her pocket and was about to answer when Jake stopped her.

"Wait a second," he said. "Who is it?"

Glancing at the screen she said, "Caller unknown. What do I do?"

"If it's him, stall. Say you're still trying to get the money together." He thought about how stupid that sounded, given the ransom was five hundred dollars, not five million. "Don't tell him I'm with you, okay? Put it on speaker."

Nikki answered, "Hello?"

"You got it?"

"Got what?" Nikki winked at Jake like that was a good stall.

"The money you stupid crack-head!"

"Hey, I'm not a crack-head. Who told you that?"

"I want the money."

"I want to talk to her."

"You can talk to her all you want when you see her. Now, get the money!"

"I'm working on it, asshole. It's not like I have that kind of cash just laying around," she said. "I'll have it in an hour or so. Where do I take it?"

"I'll call you back and tell you." He ended the call.

Jake told her to look up the number. She did and a minute later said, "It's that tattoo place all right. And he called *me* stupid."

The Culver City address took them to a shabby, thirty-unit apartment complex. They didn't know which one belonged to

Bones so they checked the mailboxes. Some had names, some didn't, and none said 'Bones' or 'Manager.' Half the apartments were dark, loud music was coming from one, a loud argument from another. Nikki went up the stairs and started peeking in windows.

Jake found an apartment with a mezuzah on the doorframe. He knocked.

A woman's voice behind the door said, "Who is it?"

"Sorry," Jake said, "You don't know me."

"Oh," the woman said. "You're a little early."

"Well, no, I'm not whoever you're expecting," Jake said. "I'm looking for somebody who lives in the building, hoped you might be able to help."

"Just a second." The door opened to reveal a nun, Sisters of Mercy from the looks of the outfit, starched white wimple, black serge pleated habit, and rope belt cinched at the waist. She also had a lit joint in her hand, which seemed a bit out of place.

Jake eyed the mezuzah. "Uh, slightly confused. Aren't you... Catholic?" He didn't know what to say about the joint.

"Oh god!" She snatched the mezuzah from the doorframe, ducked inside, then returned with a crucifix which she quickly hung on the front door. "Thank you! That would have been a disaster." Then, as if realizing her lack of hospitality, she offered the joint to Jake.

"No, thanks." In the apartment, Jake could see candles burning and what looked like an altar.

Nikki called down from upstairs, "Hey, I smell weed! Who's got weed down there?"

Just then car headlights swept across the front of the apartment complex ending like spotlights on Jake's back. A car door opened, followed by a man saying, "Everything okay?"

The sister waved. "Yeah, fine, just looking for somebody."

It was a priest holding a leather whip and a spreader bar. Jake looked back and forth between the priest and the nun. "If you don't mind my asking, what order are you with?"

146

The nun winked at him. "I'm Sister Spanks, that's Father Flagellation. We're a team." She smiled and showed Jake the back of her habit was a spanking skirt.

Jake admired her bare cheeks. "Well, Sister, you've been truly blessed."

"Thank you."

Nikki was coming down the stairs, saying, "Save me a hit, would you?"

The priest joined them at the door, gestured inside. "We need to get ready."

The nun shrugged. "New client coming."

"I won't keep you," Jake said. "I'm looking for a guy calls himself Bones. You know which apartment is his?"

Sister Spanks put her hands together as if in prayer. "Two oh eight."

Jake caught Nikki on the second floor landing. "Where's that weed?"

"Try to focus, Nikki. The question is 'Where's Angel?' And the answer is probably two oh eight." Jake led the way to the door. It was locked. The lights were off but the television was on pretty loud.

Nikki said, "You any good at picking locks?"

"Not bad." Jake reared back and kicked the door in.

Angel was tied and gagged on the floor in front of the television. She had a black eye and bruises on both arms.

The moment Angel was untied, Nikki folded her into her arms and soothed her, stroking her hair, saying, "You're all right, baby. I'm here."

Jake was surprised and touched by Nikki's instant and apparently sincere transformation from scheming druggie to loving mother, the sight of her child in danger triggering maternal instincts that hadn't been completely stamped out by the drug use.

Angel was emotionally shaken but, other than the bruises, she seemed to be all right.

"When was your last dialysis?" Jake asked.

"Yesterday."

"How do you feel?"

"Beat up."

"Did he do… anything else?"

"No, just put his hands all over."

"Okay. You're going to be fine." Jake called a friend who did dispatch for a non-emergency medical transport outfit. He arranged a ride for Angel and Nikki over to Ascendant Medical. He stopped on his way to the door. "Does Bones have a gun?"

Angel shrugged. "I've only seen him with that knife."

***

On his drive to the tat joint, Jake called Densmore. "Quick question," he said when she answered. "Do you get, like, points for arrests?"

"Stats lead to promotions, sure," she said. "Why do you ask?"

"Do you get more points for arresting, say, a kidnapper than a jaywalker?"

"Yeah," she replied, the skepticism growing in her voice. "Why, you know where I can find one?"

"As a matter of fact, I do."

Densmore paused, then said, "I'm going to need more details."

Jake told her the story from the original confrontation, to the ransom note, to the rescue.

"Is the girl okay?"

"Yeah, black eye, some bruises," Jake said. "Ambulance is taking her and the mom to the Med Center to check her over."

"And you're on your way to confront this creep?"

"I'm going to make sure he stays put until somebody with a badge shows up," Jake said. "If he comes at me with that knife again, I'll defend myself. But if he's smarter this time than he was last time, I'll just detain him."

"I'm glad to hear you say that because you don't really sound like you're in a *detaining* mood," Densmore said. "Tell me I'm not going to have to be there as a homicide detective."

"Only if he kills me," Jake said. "My plan is to keep him there for the cops, and I just thought if you got bonus points for the arrest, *I'd* get bonus points for getting *you* bonus points."

"Ah, so that's what you're after," Densmore said. "Where am I going?"

"Black Skwid Ink on Pico." He recited the address.

"Where are you?"

"Two minutes away," Jake said.

"Want my advice?"

"Whatever you got."

"Don't do anything stupid."

Jake parked on the street in front of the place. From there he could see an inked-up twenty-something at the front desk staring down at her phone. He couldn't see Bones or anyone else. Jake grabbed a tire iron from the trunk and stepped inside. The buzz of a tattoo gun was coming from behind a folding screen toward the back of the space.

The young woman looked up from her phone and she saw the tire iron. Jake put a finger to his lips. "Shhh." He smiled and gestured for her to leave.

She called into the back, "I'm going to grab a latte, you want anything?"

"Yeah, bring me some titties." Bones and another man laughed.

Jake slipped toward the folding screen that served as a privacy shield for clients. Edging around the right he wouldn't be able to see anything until he was fully exposed. Edging around the left, he caught a reflection in a mirror that provided him a view of Bones and the damage Angel had done to him: a nasty scar on the cheek, some blistered skin, and a swollen, crooked nose. Jake smiled. She was a tough little cookie.

Inching further, Jake could see the client, a twitchy, bug-faced creep who was picking at a needle scab while Bones jammed black ink into the back of his neck, what looked like the Nazi SS symbol.

Jake took a step back and said, "Hey, Boner, I hope you're spelling that tat better than your ransom note."

The buzzing stopped. "Who the hell is that?"

Jake came around the corner wagging the tire iron. "Also hope you took my advice regarding that medical coverage."

Bones, squatting on a stool behind his client, peered up at Jake like the slowest animal in the herd, aware of a present danger but with no idea how to deal with it.

The bug-face said, "Who's this asshole?"

Jake ignored that and kept wagging the tire iron in Bones' direction. "Boner," he said, "you are good and truly screwed. Angel is at the hospital and LAPD is on the way here. And they, along with the Feds, take kidnapping very seriously." To the bug-faced client he said, "I were you? I'd get my mangy ass out of here, lest they think you were involved."

"Kidnapping?" The skinhead bolted to his feet. "You dumbass! I can't be here when no cops show up looking for kidnappers."

Bones jumped up too, put his knife to his client's throat and yelled, "Shut up!" He stared at Jake. "You don't get out of my way, this man dies."

Jake shrugged. "That's his problem, not mine. Also, you might want to keep in mind that adding a murder charge to your current situation would be extra dumb but I'll leave that up to you." Jake cupped his free hand around an ear. "Hear that?"

When the bug-faced client heard the approaching sirens, he reached under his shirt, pulled a .22, and shot Bones in the foot. Bones dropped his knife and start hopping around on his one good paw, howling like a coyote in a trap.

The shot went clean through, but being a small caliber wound, was nothing compared to what Jake had seen in Iraq. "Oh, I bet that hurts," he said. "You probably ought to sit down and wait for the EMTs."

Bones took a wild swing at his client. "Why'd you fuckin' shoot me?"

"I got warrants, dumbass!"

Just as the creep raised his gun to shoot Bones again, Detective Densmore stepped in from the back, gun drawn, and yelled, "Drop it! LAPD!"

This got the creep's attention long enough that Bones took the opportunity to hop-skip as fast as he could toward the front door, knocking the screen over on his way out.

"Drop it!" Densmore stayed focused on the creep with the gun.

The creep looked her up and down. "You're a cop?"

"Now!"

The creep made the mistake of raising his gun. They fired at the same time. Densmore remained standing, her gun still trained on the creep, who was now sprawled on the floor, not moving.

Meanwhile, Bones was moving at a pretty good clip, hell-bent to get across Pico. The gunshots made him look back but they didn't slow him down, and he hopped directly into the path of a Number Seven bus going forty-five miles an hour.

18

"Wow." Jake was still staring out the front window toward Pico. "How far you think he went?"

Densmore wagged her head back and forth. "Couldn't say, never studied physics, but I'd guess he went a considerable distance."

Jake started for the front door to go see.

"Wait," Densmore said. "Don't move." She holstered her gun, pulled her phone, started taking video of the scene, explaining the extra levels of investigation that come with an officer-involved shooting. "It's a real pain in the ass," she said as she tossed the phone to Jake. "Take some from your angle, get my position, the victim, the folding screen, everything."

Later, they were on the street talking to one of the investigators as the paramedics loaded Bones into an ambulance.

The investigator said, "He was probably plastered to the wind-shield for a second while the driver tried to process what had happened. "She said she was doing forty-five when the man came hopping off the sidewalk. Typical reaction time for a trained driver's around three-quarters of a second. By the time she moved her foot from the accelerator to the brake, she'd already carried him fifty feet. Took another hundred and forty feet to bring it to a stop, after which the driver said your perp slid off the windshield like something from a Roadrunner cartoon."

A detective pulled Jake aside to get his version of what happened. Jake got the impression nobody was questioning the validity of the shooting. They had the skinhead's gun, found the bullet he'd fired at Densmore lodged in the doorframe. The detective kept Jake for an hour or so.

When he was finished, Jake found Densmore. She said she was going to be there for a while. "Go check on the girl," she said. "We'll talk tomorrow."

"Any word on Bones?"

"Paramedic said he's in a coma."

"Where they taking him?"

"County USC."

Jake nodded and started walking away, then paused. "Hey, you know if anybody checked him for an organ-donor card?"

19

After the shooting and seeing Bones get hit by the bus, Jake was too wound up to go home, let alone sleep, so he went by the hospital to check on Angel, but she'd already left. The doctor said she was okay, declined to be admitted, and went home with her mom.

Jake drove out to the ocean and went north on the coast highway, a half-moon leaving a white streak across Santa Monica Bay. He pulled over at Zuma and sat in his car, just looking at the water. He slipped off his shoes and walked along the beach until he found a good spot where he sat down and dug his toes into the sand. The rhythm of the waves was calming. He did some breathing exercises, tried to clear his head. Time well spent.

A couple of hours later Jake was turning into his driveway when a car pulled to the curb in front of his place. It was Densmore. She was exhausted and irritated from the interrogation she'd just endured.

"You okay?" Jake asked.

"Yeah, just don't feel like being alone."

"Me either."

"Got any scotch?"

"Come on in."

***

They slept until nine when Jake got up to make coffee. He checked his email and found one from Mitchell Wick, asking if he could come by that afternoon to consult on the reality show idea. After confirming, Jake turned his attention to food.

He was staring into his mostly empty fridge when Densmore came into the kitchen wearing his bathrobe. Jake said, "You have time to go out for breakfast or would you be okay with just mustard?"

She smiled. "Honey, I'm on administrative leave after the shooting. I got time for breakfast, lunch, *and* dinner."

They went to a funky little joint on Rose Avenue and were half-way through some huevos rancheros when Agent Fuller walked into the restaurant and crossed to their table. "I heard you two had a busy night," he said.

Jake looked up, surprised. "How did you know we were here?"

Fuller looked incredulous. "I'm with the Feds," he said. "Don't you read the news? We track your phones."

They stared at one another for a moment, Jake and Densmore wondering if he was kidding. Fuller slid into the booth next to Densmore. "So what happened?"

They gave him the blow-by-blow of the kidnapping and confrontation.

"The good news," Jake said, "is that Bones actually signed up as an organ donor, so his life will not have been a complete waste."

Agent Fuller nodded at Densmore. "What about the asshole took a shot at you?"

"Sadly, his life *was* a complete waste," she said. "But it's over now. You want some breakfast?"

"No thanks," Fuller said. "Just wanted to share some follow-up on the alleged suicide at Carrizo." He stopped a passing waitress and asked for coffee. Then he said, "The prison was built by McAfee Protective Services during the prison privatization boom in the late eighties. McAfee owns and operates twenty prisons in the U.S. Company was founded by an ex-FBI agent name of Hutch McAfee. He brought in a half-dozen of his old FBI pals and they got really good at securing government contracts. Started out like high-end rent-a-cops, but now they're all grown up and diversified, providing security for everything from construction sites to nuclear reactors and embassies. Company revenues are nearly three-quarters of a billion annually."

"Billion with a B?"

"Ain't no other way to spell it."

Densmore said, "Are the guards at Carrizo CCPOA?"

"No," Fuller replied. "Which is one of the many reasons McAfee makes so much money in the prison business."

Jake said, "What's CCPOA?"

"California Correctional Peace Officers Association," Densmore said. "Prison guards' labor union."

"Yeah and McAfee Protective Services is rabidly anti-union," Fuller said. "In fact, one of their services is union busting and strike breaking. They actually have a division for it."

"Get out."

"No kidding," Fuller said. "They're total mercenaries. The public interest is not in their mission statement." He unscrewed the salt shaker. "For example, let's say you've just had an environmentally disastrous chemical spill at your factory owing to your refusal to abide by federal regulations." He poured a pile of salt onto the table. "Now you're worried about witnesses or reporters getting to the scene, right? Well, McAfee will guarantee they won't."

"And they'll do it with non-union workers," Densmore said, wiping the salt off the table.

"Union thing's just a small part of it," Fuller said. "Private prisons get paid a set amount per prisoner, per day. Just like state prisons, inmates can get their sentences reduced for good behavior. But for *any* infraction, they get thirty days *added* to their sentence, and that means thirty more payments to McAfee. And guess what?

Prisoners at Carrizo are cited for infractions at a rate eight times higher than those in state prisons."

Densmore put a hand to her face and dropped her jaw in mock astonishment.

"Another cost-saver is they tend to hire the under-educated. If you're physically imposing and you have a GED, you have a good chance of getting hired."

"And they're guarding embassies and nuclear plants?"

"No, for the high-risk installations, they use more highly trained personnel, who also get paid better. A lot better in fact."

Jake said, "More highly trained like Special Forces or SWAT or something?"

"Yeah, plenty of them working for McAfee," Fuller answered.

Jake nodded. "So, guys who might be perfectly suited for hijacking a human heart from a courier with military precision and disappearing without a trace..."

"The thought crossed my mind," Fuller said.

"That's interesting," Densmore said. "Did you get the names of the guards on duty when Moorehead allegedly hung himself?"

"Didn't try to," Fuller said. "We still don't want to tip our hand. Besides, current employees have something to lose by talking to outsiders so it's unlikely we'd get any good information. My experience? You want an unvarnished version of how things go down at any given place of employment, you need to talk to someone who has nothing to lose by telling the truth."

"Like a former employee?"

"Yep." Fuller held up a piece of paper with a name on it. "Preferably of the disgruntled variety."

***

Fuller and Densmore left to track down the former prison guard while Jake went to a couple of dialysis centers to round up some potential kidney clients. He ended at Cedars-Sinai where he landed two more leads.

Mitchell Wick's company, Wiki-Wiki Productions, was nearby, its offices on the twelfth floor of one of the towers in Century City. Wick met Jake in the reception area and led him back to his office. "Come on in, meet the team!"

The office was modern and spacious with a glass-top desk, two plush sofas, a couple of leather club chairs, and an elliptical machine. The 'team' consisted of three twenty-something hipsters, lounging on the furniture. They were mid-conversation when Jake and Wick walked in.

A young woman, sprawled on one of the sofas, was saying, "Oh, please, I was steaming mine a year before it was cool."

Crossing to his desk, Wick asked, "What are we steaming?"

"Our vaginas," one of the guys said.

Wick seemed skeptical. "You steam your vagina? Is that a thing?"

She looked at him as if he'd just arrived from the eighteenth century. "Well, not anymore." She shook her head in disbelief.

"*So* last year," the guys said in unison.

"Good to know," Wick said. "Team, this is Jake. He's an actual transplant coordinator. He'll be consulting on this." Wick gestured at the hipsters. "Jake, this is the team. Ansel, Lazlo, and Bijou."

Jake waved to the group, who appeared not to notice.

"Oh, check this out." Wick picked up the silver tray from his desk and held it out to Jake. "You have to try these."

Jake saw a dozen brown, marble-size spheres that looked like something a dung beetle might find tempting. "What is it?"

"These are single-origin, conflict-free, artisanal, biodynamic chocolates made by a gender-fluid cooperative in Topanga Canyon. The cacao was grown in soil irrigated with quartz-infused water." Wick popped one into his mouth.

"They're totes amazeballs," the girl said.

"I'll pass, thanks." Jake took a sip from his water bottle.

"Alright then," Wick said. "Let's get started…"

***

The former Carrizo State Prison guard, a man by the name of Ronnie Brooks, was working security at a pot dispensary in the middle of the Valley. He told Densmore and Fuller he had quit the job at Carrizo owing to the constant harassment.

"From the inmates?" Densmore asked.

"From the company."

Agent Fuller said, "That's McAfee Protective?"

"No, McAfee just owns and operates the prison, it contracts everything out," Brooks said. "Guards and supervisors all worked for a company called American Incarceration Management, that was the name on my checks anyway."

"What sort of harassment?"

"If you complained about anything that went on, they'd cut your hours or move you to overnight shifts. It wasn't just that, though. It was the total lack of professionalism. Most of the guards only had a high school education, bunch of big goons, ex-jocks, bullies for the most part, making crap wages, so that's bad enough. But there was virtually no training for dealing with inmates and that's just a recipe for disaster," Brooks said. "You ever see that documentary on the Stanford Prison experiments?"

Fuller and Densmore both nodded.

"It was like that," Brooks said. "You give a bunch of assholes absolute power and control over a bunch of other assholes, it gets ugly fast. Psychological abuse, torture, you name it." He thought for a second. "The place was essentially… I don't know, medieval. Like one thing they did was called Gladiator Night where the guards would—"

"Sorry," Agent Fuller interrupted, "that's Roman Empire."

Brooks looked confused. "Excuse me?"

"Gladiators were a thing during the Roman Empire. You said medieval. That's different."

"Boys, we're getting off the subject," Densmore said.

"Well, small thing," Fuller said, "but the Middle Ages were a few centuries after the Roman Empire. Their architecture was derivative. They brought nothing new to the table."

Densmore said, "Don't get him started."

"Those pointy cathedrals and all the flying buttress crap, Jesus."

"Yeah, okay, whatever," Brooks said. "So anyway, Gladiator Night, guards would pick two inmates and pit 'em against each other. Winner got extra rec time, loser went to solitary. It was brutal, like dog fighting. One inmate told me he saw a man nearly chew the eyeball out of another inmate's face. Saw another one carted out in a coma."

Fuller and Densmore exchanged a glance when Brooks said 'coma.'

Densmore said, "You ever see these fights?"

"No, they only happened on days they replaced regular shift guards with this other crew," Brooks said. "One inmate told me they were ex-military, always talking shit about getting their training at Abu Ghraib."

"Nobody reported this?"

"Nobody who wanted to keep his job," Brooks said. "Besides, the only person you could report it to was the supervisor who was making book on the fights."

"Why not go to a law enforcement agency?"

"I talked to somebody at the state attorney general's office," Brooks said. "They said they had more important things to worry about than convicts getting into fist fights."

***

Jake and Mark Simmons were sitting at a corner table at ICU. Jake was describing his first day as a TV consultant. "I swear," he said, "for a minute they seriously considered making it a contest where dialysis machines were hooked to generators connected to stationary bikes. Contestants – and by 'contestants' I mean people with failing kidneys – had to peddle to power their machines. First one to complete an entire dialysis session wins a kidney."

"What?" Mark looked confused. "I mean, how?"

"All-expenses-paid to Mexico!" Jake held up a hand to swear on it just as the waitress delivered a plate of appetizers with a couple of hemostats instead of forks.

"Here's a better idea," Mark said. "What if everybody's hooked up just like you said but they don't know if they're powering their *own* machine or someone else's? You can quit peddling in the hopes of stopping someone else's treatment but you do it at the risk of doing it to yourself."

Jake smiled. "That's not a bad twist."

"I can't believe they're actually paying you for this."

Jake pulled a folded check from his pocket and snapped it open for Mark to see. "Not for nothing do they call it Hollyweird."

"Wow." Mark shook his head in disbelief. "Meanwhile, back in the real world, you'll be happy to hear that your pal Mr. Boner made good on his pledge to give the gift of life. We harvested this morning."

The comment gave Jake some pause, a somber look crossing his face.

"What?"

Jake offered a slightly guilty look. "I can't help feel some responsibility for his death."

"He's the one who ran in front of a bus," Mark said. "It's not like you shoved him."

"Yeah, but the whole thing might have gone different if I'd stayed out of it. I mean, sure, he was a creep and an asshole, but—"

"But nothing," Mark said. "Eight good people will have lives now, somebody's father doesn't die, someone's wife survives, someone's kid gets to grow up, and there's one less douchebag out there kidnapping sick children and peddling tramp stamps."

Jake shook his head. "I don't know…"

Mark sighed. "If you're going to take responsibility for the one life lost, you also have to take credit for the eight lives saved. Am I right? I'd take that all day long."

Jake shrugged. "I guess I can live with it."

He and Mark finished their food in a less jovial mood than how they'd started, paid their bill, and called it a night.

When they got up to leave, a man sitting at the bar called for his check. And just as he'd done when Jake came in, Agent Fuller followed him out.

***

Back at his car, Jake found a card jammed in the ignition again. This time it was an address on Manchester, down in Inglewood. He had thirty minutes to get there, which was doable this time of night.

Fuller stayed back so Jake couldn't see him. The phone tracking was all he needed.

The address was a strip mall in a distressed neighborhood. The usual lineup: a nail joint, a liquor store, check cashing, low-cost neighborhood clinic, video store, donut shop. Jake parked, got out, looked around, and thought, *Who rents videos anymore?* He assumed he was waiting for Mr. Kaye to show up and tell him where they stood.

Fuller parked across the street and watched Jake go into the donut shop and come back out with a chocolate-covered glazed. He walked along the storefronts, waiting for something or someone. Jake finished the donut, tossed the wrapper, licked his fingers, and wiped them on his pants. He was looking in the window of the video store when his head slowly turned to the right as if hearing something.

It was a pay phone ringing. Jake hadn't seen a pay phone in years but there it was. The phone continued to ring. No one else seemed inclined to answer, no apparent drug dealers or pimps or whoever might be using pay phones these days. So Jake went over and picked it up.

"Hello?"

The digital voice said, "We're ready. Day after tomorrow. Three P.M. Both of you." *Click.*

Jake went back to his car and wrote down the address. On his drive home he called Angel, told her the plan, reminding her not to tell Nikki.

Angel understood. She'd be ready.

Agent Fuller followed until he saw Jake was heading home. He decided to do the same. On the drive back to his place, the call at the pay phone nagged at him. It didn't prove anything but it shored up his belief that he was on to something.

20

The next day they met as scheduled at the Wilshire Federal Building. Densmore was standing at one end of the room by a white board propped on an easel. Agent Fuller sitting there with his arms folded, seemed agitated.

Densmore aimed her marker at Jake. "Brooks said only a couple of inmates disappeared while he was at Carrizo. Does that sound like enough to supply an ongoing transplant enterprise?"

"If it's a small enterprise, sure," Jake said. "Helps 'em stay under the radar."

Fuller was skeptical. "McAfee owns and operates twenty prisons," he said. "If the same thing's going on at all twenty of them at the same rate as Carrizo? That's a lot of parts."

"A lot of unnecessary risk too," Jake said.

Fuller seemed offended by the comment. "What do you mean by that?"

Jake shrugged. "I don't know what the suicide rate is for prisons but if this is going on at twenty of them, all run by the same company, and they call it a suicide every time, someone's bound to notice and look into it, don't you think? Why take that chance?"

Agent Fuller looked as if Jake had questioned his manhood. "You got a better explanation? Where do you think all the organs are coming from, Jake? Because we know for a fact it happened."

"We know it happened once," Jake said, casting a sideways glance at Densmore.

Fuller leaned on the conference table. "Why are you suddenly defending what goes on at McAfee's prisons?"

"Defending?"

Densmore said, "I don't think he's defend—"

"I thought we were on the same page here," Fuller interrupted. "We know Moorehead didn't kill himself and we know his heart ended up in Fontaine's chest, right? And I thought we'd agreed that whoever hijacked that heart were most likely ex-military goons in the employ of McAfee, just like the guards who took over the night Moorehead disappeared, so—"

"Whoa," Densmore said, her hand in the air. "Other than the fact Mr. Fontaine ended up with Moorehead's heart, the rest is speculation. I think we should—"

"Fine." Fuller held up his hands. "Alright, let me ask you, Jake. How would *you* do it? You're our organ-procurement consultant, after all, so let me ask, if you were going to control the illegal organ transplant business in Southern California, how would you do it?"

"Me?" Jake glanced at Densmore again. She looked as perplexed by Fuller's belligerence as Jake did. "Well, okay. First, can I ask why you're assuming there's only a single player at work?"

"Why not? Seems to me the transplant business scales nicely," Fuller said. "Demand is there and once you've invested in a facility, all you need is a steady supply of parts, right? You hire the right people, you get there first, and you corner the market. What am I missing?"

"There's, like, twenty-two million people in Southern California," Jake said. "And not all of them Boy Scouts. Hard to believe there's no competition out there in illegal transplants. I mean, why should this be different from other criminal enterprises like drugs or prostitution?"

"That's a fair question," Densmore said. "Just because East Side Gangstas move a lot of meth in the city doesn't keep White Nation Disciples from doing the same."

Agent Fuller gave her a look of disbelief. "You think the illegal transplant business is divided by turf wars? Gangs of vascular surgeons protecting territory with drive-by syringings?"

"All I'm saying is, whenever there's money to be made doing something illegal, there's always competition for it."

Jake said, "What if the market was divided by organ?"

Fuller stared at Jake for a moment. "Divided by organ?" Like it was the dumbest thing he'd ever heard.

"Why not?" Jake said. "If I was going to do this – and I think that was your original question – the answer is, I'd specialize."

"In what?"

"Kidneys."

"Why kidneys?"

"Risk-reward ratio," Jake said. "As long as the sellers are compensated, the recipients get off dialysis, and the insurance companies save money. Who's going to complain, let alone file charges? And if you're running a profitable kidney transplant business where consenting adults do nothing more nefarious than engage in phony directed donations, you'd be crazy to expand into other organs, especially hearts, and run the risk of murder charges."

"That doesn't explain Scottie Moorehead or the hijacked heart, does it?" Fuller asked, his tone confrontational.

"Precisely," Jake said, keeping his cool. "Maybe one party has the kidney market sewn up, or maybe it's two or three parties, leaving hearts and lungs for somebody who's more risk-tolerant."

Densmore smacked her hand on the white board, startling the men into silence. "You two mind if we get back to the subject?"

Jake and Fuller both shrugged.

Densmore wrote 'McAfee' on the board then drew a rectangle around it. "McAfee Protective Services is traded on the New

York Stock Exchange. Sixty percent of the stock is controlled by the McAfee family and the original partners. McAfee contracts everything out at the prisons they own and operate. So who are the contractors?"

She drew a line out from 'McAfee' then wrote 'A.I.M.' and circled it. "American Incarceration Management, a limited liability corporation, has the guard contract," Densmore said. "But the guards on duty when Moorehead disappeared worked for a McAfee *subsidiary* called McAfee Special Services." She drew another line out from the rectangle then a circle with 'M.S.S.' inside. "These are the guards who usually work the high-value targets like nuclear reactors and embassies."

Shaking his head, Fuller said, "The guards couldn't just choose inmates at random. They need to know blood types, all that."

"Exactly," Densmore said. She drew another line ending with a circle and wrote 'M.S.S.' inside it.

Now Jake was shaking his head. "You've already done M.S.S."

"Nope, this is a company called Medical Staffing Solutions, a professional limited liability corporation," Densmore said. "Different contractor. The initials are a coincidence. They have nothing to do with McAfee other than having the medical contract for the prisons. *This* M.S.S. provides doctors, nurses, and administration for the prisons. They do a full medical work-up on each prisoner during intake."

"In other words," Jake said, "everything you need to match unwitting donors to recipients' needs."

"So, either the guards are getting unauthorized access to medical records or they're in cahoots with someone from Medical Staffing Solutions."

Densmore nodded as she continued charting the contractors. "Next up is Correctional Medical Supplies."

As Densmore drew another line and another circle, Jake started to wonder if Mr. Kaye was, in fact, solely in the kidney business. He had believed it at first but over time he'd entertained the possibility that Mr. Kaye dealt in other organs as well, only to convince himself later that, no, the smart money was in the kidney business. Low risk, high reward. Now Jake considered the possibility he was only rationalizing on the chance Mr. Kaye was involved in more serious business.

But it was a moot point at this stage. Jake could only let things play out until Angel got her kidney.

***

"Jake?"

He looked up and saw Densmore and Fuller standing at the door. "Yeah?"

She aimed her thumb at the hallway. "We're heading for lunch, driving over to Sawtelle for some Japanese. You coming?"

"Uh, no thanks." Jake checked his watch. "I've got a thing."

Five minutes later they came up the ramp from underground parking, Fuller at the wheel. He stopped when he saw Jake getting into a limo. He nudged Densmore. "You see this shit? What kind of thing's he got where a limo's picking him up?"

"He told me he got hired to consult on a reality show about organ transplants."

"And you believed him?"

"I do now." A little closer to Sawtelle, Densmore stuck her elbow out the window. "I couldn't help but notice you were a little worked up this morning, talking to Jake. What's up with that?"

Fuller didn't answer, apparently not feeling the need to explain himself. She let it go.

Then he said, "You seriously think he's consulting for television?"

"Yeah, why not?"

Fuller looked straight ahead. "I'll tell you over lunch," he said. "You want sushi or noodles?"

"I'm good either way." Wondering what the big mystery was.

"I feel like noodles," Fuller said. "Maybe a big thing of udon, some tempura on top, or maybe ramen." A minute later he pulled to the curb.

Once they were in the restaurant, he chose a ramen bowl with pork; Densmore went with dipping noodles topped with a soft-boiled egg. They took a two-top and settled in. Fuller put his phone on the table and tapped his way to a site, then rotated the phone so Densmore could see.

"What's this?" she asked.

"What I want to show you." He scrolled down through a series of charts and graphs. "Part of what we do is monitor regional organ-procurement organizations, like SCOPE. We run analytics looking for trends, anomalies, whatever. The other day I ran a report, found an unusual number of people going off the kidney list in this region." Fuller showed the graph indicating the expected number versus the actual number. "I looked a little closer and found an interesting pattern of facts," he said. "How're those noodles?"

"Good," she said. "What sort of pattern?"

"First, none of the people who dropped off the list has died, which usually explains deviations like this. Second, none of them have travelled out of the U.S. in the past six months, so transplant tourism's off the table. Third, every one of them is what you'd have to describe, demographically, as 'high wealth' individuals."

Densmore studied the graph for a second. "Directed donations explain it?"

Agent Fuller shook his head. "It would be a world record."

Densmore knew it meant something that Fuller was bringing this up now instead of an hour ago, in the room with Jake. "Has Jake seen this?"

Fuller smiled enigmatically.

She paused, noodles dangling from her chopsticks. "You think he's involved? Seriously?"

"I think he's got some explaining to do," Fuller said. "His cell phone records show he's been near every one of the dialysis centers where these wealthy folks were getting their blood scrubbed. Beverly Hills, Newport Beach, Palos Verdes."

"His job takes him there," Densmore said.

"I thought he was on vacation."

"Maybe he's checking up on patients he's made friends with."

"He's got no friends in South Central? Pacoima?"

"Okay," she said. "Anything else?"

"Yeah. Here's the kicker. Since this all started after Jake was forced to take vacation, I decided to follow him, see if anything interesting happened. That's how I ended up across from a strip mall in Inglewood around eleven last night."

"What was he doing there?"

"I don't think he even knew at first," Fuller said. "Looked like he'd been directed to go there and wait. One minute he's standing around eating a donut, next thing, the pay phone's ringing and he picks it up, has a conversation." Fuller leveled a look at Densmore. "You tell me, does that sound like something legit?"

"No, I'm with you," she said. "That's sketchy." Densmore had to admit the facts made Jake look guilty of something but she had to keep in mind that Agent Fuller had launched a full-blown SWAT assault on a grow house that he would have sworn was a black market organ transplant hospital, so maybe deduction wasn't his strong suit. "You don't really think Jake's behind all this, do you?"

"No. He's a small fry is my guess," Fuller said. "Whatever's going on has been going on longer than Jake's been on vacation, but I'm sure he's involved, at least with the kidney part of it." He aimed his chopsticks at her. "Needless to say, this is strictly between the two of us."

Densmore made the gesture to zip her lips.

21

The limo took Jake to the studios where they taped *One Hit Wonder*. The driver told him Mitchell Wick was at Stage Sixteen.

Jake was heading that direction when an alarm sounded and red lights on the exterior walls began to flash. He thought this meant they were about to start shooting on the set until the stage door burst open and a broad-shouldered chimpanzee wearing a cowboy hat and a red vest charged out, screaming as he looked back at his pursuer.

The chimp made a beeline for the studio's main entrance. Ahead, the guard at the gate, sensing an opportunity for promotion, dropped his clipboard and came running toward the hundred and twenty pound primate, arms spread wide as if he could corral the thing like a runaway toddler.

Jake was watching with unbridled fascination until the stage door burst open again. This time it was a man with a bolt-action tranquilizer gun running as fast as he could, chanting, "Oh shit, oh shit, oh shit…" as he tried to load a pink feathered dart into the long-gun's chamber.

Ahead, the ambitious guard broke down into a football stance, preparing to tackle the charging primate.

The man with the tranquilizer gun stopped and took aim.

As it approached the guard, the chimp leapt into the air, reaching for a tree branch. The guard raised up to his full height grasping at the chimp's leg just as the tranquilizer dart left the barrel of the gun.

It hit just below the sternum. The guard looked down at the pink feather as the dose of ketamine entered his blood stream and dropped him like a dirty diaper. A moment later, three golf carts of security guards came gliding around the corner of the soundstage.

One of them called to Jake, "You see where that monkey went?"

Jake pointed up to the branches as the chimp brachiated from one to another until it reached the studio's perimeter wall and disappeared over the side.

Jake took a moment to process all this, watching the parade of golf carts humming out the front gate. Mitchell Wick strolled from the soundstage, a bemused look on his face. He waved when he saw Jake.

"What the hell was that?" Jake asked.

"Last audition of the day," Wick said.

"For what, *Animal Planet*? I thought you did some sort of a musical talent search thing."

"Yeah, and we need a new head judge to replace Buddy," Wick said. "Fortunately we saw a capuchin this morning with some real potential." He steered Jake toward the waiting limo. "I'm starved. The Ivy okay?"

Outside the studio gate there was no sign of the fugitive chimp, just a bunch of security guards scratching their heads, looking around, waiting for Animal Control.

Wick said, "We got some good news today. Found a telegenic sixteen-year-old who needs a kidney."

"Those aren't that hard to find," Jake said.

"No? How about a telegenic sixteen-year-old whose mother is a senior network executive?"

"Probably a shorter list."

Wick clapped his hands together. "Damn right it is! How lucky can you get? Now we just need to parlay that into an order to pilot."

"Are we meeting 'the team' for lunch?"

"No, I fired them," Wick said. "We're going a different direction, a little outside their wheelhouse."

"What direction *are* we headed?"

"I think with this new development we need to go documentary style. Treat the whole thing with some gravitas and emotion," Wick said. "So how do we do it?"

"How do we treat a life-saving organ transplant seriously?"

"How do we make it look like one of those directed donations is my question."

"'Look like'?"

"Yeah, you said it's just paperwork, right? Everybody swears no money changed hands."

"Well, yeah, but here's another idea," Jake said. "What if you really tried to find a qualified donor?"

Wick looked surprised. "I produce reality shows. We just stage these things. It's quicker, gives you more control. But okay, let's say we tried it your way. How would you find a qualified donor?"

"Start with the family," Jake said. "Have they been tested?"

Now he looked shocked. "Are you crazy? She's a network executive! She's not going to… wait a minute. That's good," Wick said, seeing the possibilities. "Open with the diagnosis. The kid's scared, the family's concerned, everyone wants to help. Doctor spouts some medical gibberish, insert some X-rays or cat scans or whatever. Then lots of grim talk about the waiting list, the cadaver organs, all that. End of first half-hour has the family pulling together to agree to get tested, see if they're candidates for donation. I like that.

"Third quarter-hour is the loving family being tested, everybody's nervous, and we cut to commercial before we get results. Come back from break and we get the bad news, nobody matches. The big gloom sets in before redemption, right?" Wick clapped his hands again, excited by a new idea. "Oh! What if they discover someone in the family has a previously undiagnosed disease? Caught just in the nick of time, wouldn't that be fantastic? A cancer spinoff from the first episode, I mean, if we're lucky."

"Yeah," Jake said, "fingers crossed."

"At the end of the pilot we're in a tight spot. Nobody in the family is a match, so now we have to go looking for a Good Samaritan. As credits roll we do a long, slow pan over the L.A. Basin, voice-over wondering if there's an altruistic donor somewhere in that sea of humanity. Something like that. So where do we look? Craig's List?"

Jake thought for a moment. "I've got a better idea."

"Great, hit me."

"What's your budget?"

"What's it need to be?"

"Could be as high as a hundred grand."

"That's doable."

"Let me talk to somebody."

"Atta boy!"

22

On the drive back to Agent Fuller's office, Densmore couldn't stop thinking about the call at the pay phone. That's the thing that stood out. That needed an explanation. Was Jake really involved in this? She found it hard to believe, though not impossible. She was going to ask Fuller a question when both of their phones rang.

She answered, "Densmore."

"Detective, this is Special Agent in Charge Delano with ATF, you got a minute?"

"Sure, what's up?"

"We're sitting on a guy, name of Randell Harlow." He waited to see if it rang a bell.

"Never heard of him."

"Mid-level weapons dealer," Delano said. "Got his tit in a wringer and he's asking to talk to you. Says he's got info on a homicide that's on your plate."

"Where are you?"

"ATF Field Office, Wilshire Federal Building."

"On my way. Five minutes." She ended the call.

Agent Fuller was still talking. "Right. Yeah, call SWAT. I can be there in half an hour." He clicked off and grinned like he'd just scored the game-winning touchdown.

"Sounds promising," Densmore said. "Another grow house?"

"Picked up some phone and internet chatter," he said. "Word combinations included 'life-saving transplant,' 'outside normal channels,' and best of all, 'no waiting list.'" Fuller nodded solemnly. "This could be it."

Densmore had her doubts but kept them to herself. Fuller dropped her in front of the Federal Building then rushed off to follow his latest lead.

Special Agent in Charge Delano met Densmore at the elevator and escorted her to the office, offered coffee but she declined. They were standing outside the interrogation room looking through the mirror at Randell Harlow, late forties, well dressed, a little jowly. Sitting there, chatting with his attorney. Didn't appear particularly worried over his situation.

Densmore said, "Whadja get him for?"

"He and his co-defendant, a Customs and Border Protection officer, were scheming to ship arms to the Philippines for some unauthorized end-users." He handed her a sheet with the particulars. Two dozen Barrett .50 caliber long-range semi-auto rifles, some FN 'SCAR' assault rifles, and several thousand rounds of body-armor-piercing ammo.

"I take it you're not supposed to do that."

"Violates the Arms Export Control Act."

"How deep's the shit he's in?"

"Three to five. Depends on his lawyer and if any of his claims pan out."

"What's he saying?"

"Swears it's all legit, administration and CIA-approved."

"What're they saying?"

"Same as you. Never heard of him. Attorney says it's all just a paperwork snafu, happens all the time. But they thought in the meanwhile, being law-abiding citizens, they'd offer to help us solve a homicide."

"It just occurred to them they have this information?"

"Funny how that happens."

***

Densmore entered the room, amused to see both men sit up straighter when they saw her. Sucked their stomachs in too.

"I'm Detective Densmore, LAPD," she said. "You two like *Mission Impossible*?"

The two men exchanged a confused look.

"C'mon, really?" Densmore said. "The CIA has disavowed all knowledge of your actions."

"Of course they did." Randell shrugged, all nonchalant. "CIA's same as anybody else in a situation like this. They'll throw you under the bus pronto if you're gonna make *them* look bad."

Densmore put the sheet onto the table. "How would this business make *them* look bad?"

"My guess," Randell said, "is they found out, or think they found out, that the *ultimate* buyer for the shipment was some Southeast Asian terrorist group, and they think I'm the one making the arrangements."

"But you're not selling to the end-user?"

"I'm *supposed* to be but I got no control over a bunch of jarheads halfway around the world, do I? I mean, if they turn around and sell to—"

"You're selling to the Marines?"

"I use the term loosely," Randell said. "My client's a company called McAfee Special Services. They're a private security, military contractor outfit. They hire lots of special-ops types, working all over the world. I been dealing with them for years without any trouble."

"Well, there's trouble now," Densmore said, taking the seat opposite him. "So, this homicide. Why'd you ask for me?"

"My attorney said you're the one assigned to investigate the murder of a guy named Yuri Petrov, the man who had the eyes popped out of his head?"

"Petrov's not his real name, but yeah, so?"

"So," the attorney said, "we thought Mr. Harlow could help you out with that and you could maybe help Mr. Harlow with this situation."

"We've already got Petrov's killer," she said. "But thanks. Is that it?"

"No," the attorney said. "There's more."

Randell said, "What if I could tell you who killed Thaddeus Dell?"

"What if you could but didn't?" She looked at the attorney. "That's what, obstructing justice? It's at least impeding a police investigation."

"But if I did, could you put in a good word for us?"

"That's all federal, but since it's merely a 'paperwork snafu,' I'll see what I can do. All depends what you've got."

"Where should I start?"

"Beginning seems like a good spot."

"Alright. It started when I sold this Mac-11 to a guy by the name of Bryce Weeks, eight hundred cash, no problem."

"That's the same Mac-11 Shelton Birch used to shoot that reporter?"

"The same," Randell said. "A week or so later Weeks comes back and buys a few more things, nearly twelve grand's worth, but he's only got four grand on him, says he'll have the balance in three days. We're doing the deal at his place so if things go sour I know where to find him, right? Plus I get the sense he's good for it. Cut to four days later and I've heard nothing. So I go back to his place. Guess who's moved?

"I ask around and get this address in Rancho Grandes," Randell says. "So I go over, carrying my nine 'cause I know what he's got, but I can't tell if anybody's home, damn windows are all covered in foil. So I'm creeping around back when somebody squeezes off a couple of shots, sounded like a .45."

"He shot at you?"

"No, this is all staying inside the house," Randell said. "Whoever's shooting has no idea I'm right outside. The kitchen door's unlocked. I let myself in expecting to find somebody holding a gun but instead I find Weeks with some pruning shears in his hands. The .45's on the counter, still smoking, so I've got the drop on him, not that it mattered."

"Is Petrov or Thaddeus Dell in this story somewhere?"

"I'm getting there," Randell says. "Mr. Weeks had my money and he handed it over with an apology, said he got sidetracked finding Mr. Dell, who I then noticed was duct-taped to the chair and bleeding out from the gunshot wounds. I might have noticed him earlier had it not been for the sight of that acre of weed growing in the house."

"Did Weeks say why he killed Dell?"

"Yeah, not that I asked," Randell said. "He's a talkative son of a bitch. Said Dell was supposed to kill this Yuri Petrov but screwed it up and in the process got a video of the botched hit put up on YouTube." That prompted a chuckle from Randell and his attorney. "Weeks said Dell made up for it by going to the hospital to finish the job by hand. Also took the man's eyes, according to Weeks, but I'm not sure what that was all about. Anyway, whoever wanted Petrov dead in the first place was now worried that Dell was a liability since he'd got his face on the Internet. So Weeks got the job of taking out Dell."

"Why was Dell at the grow house in the first place?"

"Weeks said he knew Dell from a stint at Carrizo State Prison. Weeks loaned him the Mac-11 for the Petrov job, so Dell was returning what he'd borrowed, unaware that Weeks had been hired to kill him."

"Any idea why somebody wanted Petrov dead?"

"According to Dell, Petrov was stealing from whoever he worked for and got caught selling the stolen goods, which turned out to be, like, human ligaments or some shit like that." Harlow grimaced. "Christ, what is wrong with people?"

"I ask myself every day," Densmore said.

"When the cops caught Petrov trying to sell these… parts, the man he was working for got worried Petrov might roll over on him so the man sent Dell to make sure that didn't happen. That's what led to the botched shooting on the freeway."

"Did Weeks say who Petrov and Dell were working for?"

"No, one of the few things he *didn't* say. Next thing I know, he's pruning the fingers off this Dell guy and sticking him in that walk-in fridge. Two days later, CHP is asking me who I sold the gun to and I handed over the name and the Rancho Grandes address, as any law abiding citizen would."

"Without mentioning the dead body or the weed."

The attorney said, "My client, understandably, feared for his life, what with Mr. Weeks being a cold-blooded killer."

"You know where Weeks is now?"

"Don't know and don't care," Harlow said. "But I can tell you that wherever he is, he's well armed."

***

The next day, Jake waited near the bus stop where he was meeting Angel. He parked in front of a Korean BBQ joint that wasn't opened yet.

A few minutes later the bus came and went, leaving passengers on the sidewalk. Jake scanned the crowd but didn't see her at first. He was looking for her dark Gothic eyes and tattered black leggings so it took a moment to recognize the girl wearing plain jeans, no makeup, and a pink Hello Kitty backpack. She looked years younger and nervous, until she saw Jake.

As she crossed the street Jake saw she had modified the backpack with a variety of decals: skulls where Kitty's head used to be, a pentagram, and stickers saying things like 'Goth Girls Rule,' 'Don't Touch me!' and 'I put the fun in funeral.'

After she got into the car, Jake looked at her for a moment longer than he should have.

She said, "What?"

He smiled. "Nothing." He put it in drive and pulled from the curb.

On the drive Jake told Angel how it worked and why they couldn't know where they were going. Angel said she wasn't afraid. She trusted him.

A few minutes later Jake pulled into the parking garage, never noticing Densmore had been following the entire time. She parked on the street.

He parked on the second deck of the garage and waited. After a minute, Angel said, "I need to give you something." She unzipped one of the pockets of the backpack, pulled out an envelope, and handed it to Jake. "Don't open it."

"May I ask what it is?"

"It's my will," she said. "You know, just in case."

"Your will?"

Angel nodded. "People die during surgery all the time," she said. "I think it's the anesthesia that does it more often than the operation. I thought I should be prepared, like I said, just in case."

"Angel, you're going to be fine," Jake said. "But okay, I'll hang on to this."

"There's also one of those advance directives in there," Angel said. "I do *not* want to be left on machines if somebody screws up." She took Jake by the arm, looked into his eyes, and said, "Pull the plug. Got it?"

"You've been on the interwebs, haven't you?"

"I'm serious," she said. "Promise me you'll pull the plug. I am *not* vegetable material."

Jake held up a hand to make the promise just as the stairwell door opened in the southeast corner. It was Mr. Kaye with a Macy's shopping bag. He crossed to where they were, handed the bag to Jake. He held out a hand. "Phones?"

Jake and Angel handed over their cell phones. In the bag Jake found blindfolds and headphones. Angel was relaxed, letting Jake blindfold her. She felt like she was in a spy movie. The opera on the headphones was the first she'd ever heard. It was gothic and she liked it. A few seconds later she smelled diesel exhaust and someone was helping her up into a van or something.

They drove for forty minutes, then parked. Someone helped them out of the vehicle and to an elevator. Once inside, Mr. Kaye indicated they could remove the blindfolds and headphones.

The door opened onto the gleaming hallway. "Follow me, please," Mr. Kaye said. He led them down the hall. There were others there, nurses and attendants, all wearing surgical masks, coming and going from patients' rooms. As they walked past a scrub room and an operating room, Angel gave Jake a look of approval. They rounded a corner to another hallway of private rooms.

Mr. Kaye ushered them into one. "You can leave your things here."

A nurse came into the room pushing a wheelchair. It was the nurse with the cat-eye glasses. Her surgical mask wrinkled and Jake smiled back. She handed a hospital gown to Angel. "Come on, honey, let's get changed, then we'll get you prepped." Jake and Mr. Kaye stepped into the hallway as the nurse closed the door.

"Surgery's in a couple of hours," Mr. Kaye said. "You can wait if you'd like."

"I'll come back," Jake said.

"Up to you." As they headed back toward the elevator, Mr. Kaye said, "Have you considered my job offer?"

"I have," Jake said. "And I accept."

They stopped to shake on it, standing just outside the O.R. "Excellent," Mr. Kaye said.

"Let me ask you a question," Jake said. "How flexible is your business model?"

"What do you mean?"

Jake explained the deal with Mitchell Wick.

"For a reality show?" Mr. Kaye seemed amused by the idea. "You're serious?"

"Their budget's serious."

"Ah." That sparked his interest.

While Mr. Kaye was mulling it over, Jake noticed something odd in the O.R. He was looking at it, wondering why it was there, when Mr. Kaye said, "I tell you what. I'll arrange for you to meet with someone who is a match and willing to sell but you'll have to take the ruse to Ascendant or some other hospital, sign all the documents, and have the surgery done there."

"Fair enough," Jake said. "How much?"

"Sixty thousand," Mr. Kaye said. "I'll pay the donor out of that and take my fee."

Jake said he'd get the medical info so they could find a match. Mr. Kaye escorted Jake to the elevator, handing him the blindfold and headphones. As he stood waiting for the doors to open, Jake thought about what he'd seen in the O.R., and it made him wonder about the people he was now in business with.

23

By the time Jake got back to his car and the driver returned his cell phone, he had missed two calls and a string of texts from Densmore:

<<We need to talk.>>
<<Hello?>>
<<You there?>>
<<Where the hell are you?>>

He replied: <<Sorry. Battery died. Just noticed. Taxi Nostrils in an hour?>>

She responded immediately. <<Yes.>>

Densmore got there first. She waved Jake over to her table. There were three shots of tequila lined up in front of his seat. Densmore had her own. The moment he sat down she said, "You might want one of those."

Something was up and it wasn't good. He downed one of the shots, waiting for an explanation.

Densmore said, "Did you know you're being followed?"

He looked over his shoulder, then back at her. "What? I mean, who?"

"Agent Fuller," Densmore said, no nonsense in her expression.

"Well, damn." Jake knew that 'being followed' wasn't as bad as 'being indicted or arrested,' but it wasn't good. Being followed meant Fuller was suspicious of something but couldn't prove anything. It might mean complications that could jeopardize Angel. Jake also felt that his only ally was sitting across the table from him, otherwise he'd still be in the dark. He downed a second shot, took a breath, and asked, "What does he know?"

Densmore ticked off the evidence Fuller had shared, including the late-night call at the pay phone. "I was willing to give you the benefit of the doubt on the kidney stats, thinking it could be explained by some combination of the coincidental and the circumstantial, but the pay phone thing I just couldn't explain away," Densmore said. "You care to enlighten me?"

"I'm trying to help somebody," Jake said.

"The girl?"

"Yeah." He told her the whole story, from Angel's diagnosis and abysmal family situation, to tracking down the kidney broker, to his deal steering clients to Mr. Kaye.

"Mr. K, as in kidney?"

Jake shrugged.

"Cute. Are you committing any crimes?"

"Don't think so," Jake said. "But I don't really care. Angel was going to die if I didn't do something. I did what I had to."

"I don't suppose you know where they do it."

"No idea. They're very careful." He told her about the blindfolds and headphones.

"You sure they only deal in kidneys?"

"As far as I know, yeah." While that was true, the equipment he'd seen in the O.R. at least introduced the possibility of heart transplants. But he didn't want to bring that up until Angel was home and safe.

"You didn't think you could tell me?"

"Had no reason to," Jake said. "I don't have any evidence Mr. Kaye's connected to the murders you're investigating and I didn't want to do anything that might interfere with Angel getting the transplant."

"What if this Mr. Kaye is the guy Fuller's looking for? What if you're working with the people who hijacked the heart and killed Scottie Moorhead?"

"Then the good news is you've already infiltrated the organization and I'm your man on the inside."

"Willing to help?"

"Once Angel is safe."

***

The next morning, Detective Densmore walked into the Office of Inspector General carrying a copy of the *Los Angeles Times*. She told reception she was there to see Agent Fuller and was directed to his office.

He was at his desk doing paperwork on his previous day's expedition when Densmore walked in waving the newspaper. "Nothing in here about you uncovering a clandestine organ transplant organization," she said. "What happened?"

Agent Fuller glared at her and pointed at a brown thing glistening on his desk. "Shit happened, that's what." It was a remarkably realistic, though fake, human turd. "Gift from my associates here in the office."

Densmore sat across the desk from him and asked, "So all that Internet and phone chatter was bogus?"

"No, it was legit," Fuller said. "Just not what we thought it was." He pushed back from his desk. "We get this address, a place down around Cloverfield and Twentieth, nothing on the building's frontage to indicate what the place is. We look around the side and the first thing we see is a big biomedical waste containment area."

"Encouraging."

"Right? Then, around the back, we get to a door with a nice little sign next to it says, 'Stercoraceous Transplants.' We're looking at each other like we can't believe how brazen they are, not that anybody knows what stercoraceous means, but they're advertising transplants right on the sign. There's no armed security and the door's unlocked so we go in." Agent Fuller shook his head. "Turns out it was an illegal FMT clinic and stool bank."

Densmore stared at him blankly. "Say again."

"FMT," Fuller said. "Fecal microbiota transplantation. Hot new therapy for Crohn's disease, clostridium difficile colitis, and some other gut problems."

"Did you say, stool bank?"

"Yeah, like an eye bank but stinks," Fuller said. "Anyway, we get past the receptionist and in back we find patients in exam rooms and somebody going room to room with a box of turkey basters and a beaker full of what looks like beef broth."

"Ewww, you're making this up."

"Nope. FMT's legit therapy," Fuller said. "FDA approved it a year or so ago, but you need to file an investigational new-drug application and get permission before you can administer the shit."

"So to speak."

"Yeah. You also need to be an MD to get the necessary license. When we mentioned this to the guy with the turkey basters, he said he didn't recognize the FDA's authority in the matter."

"Was he a doctor?"

"Wasn't even a homeopath," Fuller said. "Called himself a clinical ecologist, said he refused to deny patients treatment because of some regulatory agency. When we explained we were the criminal investigators for the DHHS, he tried to run. After we cuffed him, we went into the next room and found the staff filling triple-0 gelatin capsules with a freeze-dried version of the product, called them 'crapsules.' They were shipping the stool across state lines."

"You say that like it's illegal."

"Damn right it's illegal," Fuller said. "Now that FMT's a government-approved therapy, the FDA has classified shit as a drug, if you can believe it. And you can't ship drugs across state lines. So we put a stop to that."

Densmore hesitated then said it anyway, "A crappy job but someone's got to do it."

"Yeah, nobody's said that yet." Fuller picked up the gag poop and dropped it into the trash. "So that's how my afternoon went. How did yours go?"

"Much better," Densmore said. "I had a good long talk with Randell Harlow and got some answers on my homicides."

"Harlow's the gun dealer who put us onto the grow house with the corpse in it?"

"That's him," Densmore said. "Also the guy who sold guns to Shelton Birch who owned the house, leading you to speculate Birch was involved in the black market transplant business."

"I still think it's a viable theory," Fuller said. "You got something to support it?"

Densmore grinned. "I did a little poking around, discovered Birch is not only a major player in residential real estate, he's also a big swinging dick in commercial real estate, one of the city's major landlords."

"Leasing to any hospitals?"

"Not that I found," Densmore said. "But one of the buildings Birch owns happens to be the world headquarters for McAfee Protective Services."

"You don't say."

She cocked her eyebrows. "How you like me now?"

***

When Jake returned to see Angel, the nurse with the cat-eye glasses met him at the elevator. "Hello again," she said.

188

"How's the patient?"

"Doing fine, she's a sweet kid," the nurse said. "She thinks you're pretty great too, what with you being a virtual stranger and all, doing what you did. Most people won't stick their necks out like that."

"Somebody needed to," Jake said.

"Well, you're a good man, Charlie Brown, or whatever your name is. And don't tell me because I'm not supposed to ask."

They got to Angel's room and the nurse's mask wrinkled up again. "See you later."

Angel looked better than she had in a month. She smiled when she saw Jake, gave his hand a little squeeze, said she felt brand new.

"How's your pain?"

She nodded. "Really good drugs."

Jake told her to enjoy them while she could, then gave her a sermon on what he would do if he found her falling back into old habits, promising to personally reach into her abdomen, remove the new kidney, and give it to somebody who appreciated it.

"You are so sweet," she said in a dopey voice. "I think I'll go back to sleep now."

Mr. Kaye met Jake outside Angel's room, told him the surgery went fine, and said they would discharge her in a few days. He also said he'd received the info on the network executive's kid. "I'll have a match for you soon," he said. "Meanwhile, you should set up a social media page soliciting for a donor, so it looks like a legit directed donation. That has to be up before there's any contact between the parties in case anybody looks into the chronology of events."

Jake agreed then said he wanted to hang around and visit with Angel again when she was more alert. "Where should I wait?"

"Down here," Mr. Kaye said, escorting him. They walked down the hall discussing Angel's immunosuppressant therapy. "The induction phase will be shorter than normal since the match was so good. After that, you know the drill."

"Yeah," Jake said. "Maintenance and monitoring."

Mr. Kaye showed Jake into a room. "When you're ready to leave, a security guard will arrange transport. Oh, and there's this." Mr. Kaye pulled a slip of paper from his pocket, handed it to Jake. It was a series of typed numbers and instructions. "That's your Zipcoin wallet and the mix exchange number," he said. "For your payments. You know how it works?"

"I'll figure it out." Jake slipped it into his shirt pocket. Crypto-currency was fine with him. He'd always wanted an off-shore bank account.

"You mind if I ask why you did it?"

"Why I helped the girl?"

"Yeah."

Jake thought of the girl in Iraq he couldn't save. He said, "She needed it."

"Sure, but why her? Why not any of a hundred others?"

"You really care?"

"No, not really."

**

Agent Fuller and Detective Densmore combed through public records trying to understand the extent of Shelton Birch's real estate empire. Birch Realty Partners seemed to be the primary corporate entity but he also controlled Verdugo Property Management, Workman Real Estate Network, Bel-Air Land Development, Eagle Rock Acquisition Enterprises, Montecito Leasing Solutions, Del Ray Real Estate Resources, and Palisade Property Advisors.

Each was dedicated to a specific type of real estate; one handled office buildings leasing to law firms, accounting practices, insurance companies, and the like. Another dealt with medical office buildings, a third handled light industrial and warehouses. And so on.

"Let's split them up and see what we've got," Fuller said.

"Fine with me, but what exactly do you think we're looking for? I mean, this place where they're doing the transplants, how do you see it?"

"Don't know," Fuller said. "It's got to be big enough for an operating room, recovery room, maybe a lab, rooms for patients. I'd say they'd need at least ten thousand square feet."

"I'm going to guess most of the buildings in the inventory are candidates," Densmore said. "That's a lot of search warrants."

"Yeah, but I like the medical office buildings better than the law firm and accounting buildings, so I'm starting there."

Densmore went with Verdugo Property Management, which turned out to be an entity that owned and managed the garage where she had followed Jake the day before. "We can scratch Verdugo," she said. "It's all parking lots and garages."

They looked up when a college intern knocked on the door. "Agent Fuller? That cell you had me tracking has been dead for a couple of hours."

"Where'd it go dark?"

"Somewhere in Culver City," she said. "You want me to keep monitoring?"

"Yeah, let me know when and where it comes back on."

When the intern left, Densmore said, "Tracking Jake?"

Fuller nodded. "He keeps looking better and better, suspect-wise. I mean, who disables their tracking like that?"

"Maybe he's at a movie, set it to airplane mode or something."

"It's not that simple. What we track is embedded below root level and deeply encrypted. Jake is somebody who wants to disappear now and then and knows how to do it. He's not just flipping the sleep button."

Densmore took the opportunity to mess with Agent Fuller's fevered imagination. "Maybe it's somebody else, somebody who knows how to disable it."

His head snapped sideways, looking at her. "Somebody else like who?"

She lowered her voice secretively. "What if I told you he's working for an FBI task force looking into human trafficking from the organ angle?"

A look crossed Fuller's face. "Keep talking."

With a casual shrug she said, "He mentioned something but didn't go into details other than the consulting money's better than what you're paying."

"Son of a bitch." Fuller slapped a hand on his desk. "He's double-dipping and the Feebs are trying to horn in my case. Christ, you can't trust anybody."

"You can trust me," Densmore said. "If Jake gets anything, I'll pass it on." She gestured back to her computer. "Meanwhile, Shelton Birch? We should look for outpatient surgical centers."

"Good thought," Fuller said.

Five minutes later Densmore was staring at a name on her screen. It was familiar but she couldn't remember from where. It was listed under 'Tenants' for one of the buildings leased by Del Ray Real Estate Resources. It was the corporate headquarters for a company called The Medicus Group.

24

Jake looked around the room while he waited for Mr. Kaye to leave the building. The room had all the standard monitoring equipment and wall ports, a rotating and telescoping bed, hands-free sink. In the closet he found some hospital gowns, clean towels, a box of latex gloves, and stacks of surgical scrubs with caps and masks.

Jake found his size and put on a full set of blue scrubs, thinking he'd be able to get a better look around if he was dressed like everybody else. He stepped into the hall. A nurse and a patient were coming the other way, the patient holding on to a rolling IV stand as she walked. They didn't pay him any mind.

All down the hall, the doors were open, patients in bed reading, watching television, or doing post-op physical therapy. An orderly pushing a laundry cart nodded at Jake as he went by. Around the corner, it was more of the same until Jake came to a closed door. He peered in the window and was surprised to see a patient on a ventilator, being fed by IV, as if in a coma.

What Jake couldn't see from his angle was that the man's eyes were wide open and desperately searching the room. Jake pushed on the door and found it was locked. He pushed harder, rattling the deadbolt.

"Can I help you?"

It was a security guard who didn't sound like he wanted to be helpful. His uniform was generic so Jake couldn't tell if he was with McAfee Protective Services or A-l Rent-a-cop.

"I'm all turned around," Jake said. "Trying to find a patient. Teenage girl, lots of tattoos."

The guard pointed the opposite direction. "Room eight."

"Thanks." Jake went down the hall as directed. Behind him, the guard checked the door to make sure it was still locked.

***

Detective Densmore and Jake were at the bar at ICU waiting for their drinks.

"You told him I'm working for the FBI?"

"It was more of an insinuation," Densmore said. "If he asks, just be vague and let his mind go where it will."

The bartender, dressed like a surgeon, brought their drinks, Bloody Mary for Jake, something called a Code Blue for Densmore.

"Why'd you tell him that?"

"I was just messing with him," Densmore said. "Also thought it might get him to stop thinking of you as being involved with the whole transplant thing."

"I *am* involved with it."

"Yeah, but just kidneys, and just until the girl's okay, right?"

Jake looked a bit sheepish, like he had a confession. "Well…"

Densmore paused, her glass an inch from her mouth, waiting for Jake to finish what he'd started to say.

But Jake had lost his train of thought, or rather the train had jumped to a different track entirely. He could only stare at Densmore's ruby lips parted just so and those green eyes hovering over the shimmering blue cocktail. He couldn't wait to be with her again.

"Jake? What're you saying?"

"Let's go back to my place."

"Maybe later," she said. "Right now I need you to finish what you started to say.'"

"They have a bypass machine in the O.R."

She held her hands out in confusion. "I don't know what that means."

"You don't need a bypass machine if all you're doing is kidneys," Jake said. "Bypass is for open heart surgery and transplants, nothing else. So, there's that." Then he told her about the patient he'd seen in the locked room. "All the other rooms are open, patients are all ambulatory, but this one's on a vent and IV feeding."

"Which means what?"

"He's either in a coma or persistent vegetative state."

"Like your Mr. Blount, what did you call him?"

"A beating heart cadaver," Jake said. "Yeah, like that. I didn't have a great angle so I couldn't see everything, but I saw that much."

Densmore sipped her drink, thinking. She said, "Where does one even get a bypass machine or a ventilator? They have, like, hospital supply stores?"

"Sales reps pitch their equipment to hospital buyers."

"They'll sell a bypass machine to anybody?"

"Sure, it's not like they're regulated or anything." Jake picked up his phone and did a search. "You want new or used?"

"You can buy a *used* bypass machine?"

"Yeah, here's a Sarns 7400."

"How much?"

"No idea. Says here financing's available though."

"Let's say I want a new one," Densmore said. "What's the first place I call?"

"Around here, you'd probably go through The Medicus Group. They're the region's largest supplier of medical equipment," Jake said. "You met the owner at the Graftie Awards, remember? Dr. Steven Brewer?"

"Oh, right, tall guy with the paunch?"

"That's him," Jake said. "He's a big shot. Medicus Group is huge."

"I knew I recognized the name from somewhere," Densmore said. "What's his story?"

"The way I understand it," Jake said, "he came from a long line of respected physicians, and was expected to follow the family tradition. But the doctor gene apparently skipped his generation. Brewer couldn't get into the worst medical school in the country, and he ended up at some doctor mill in the Caribbean where he finished near the bottom of his class, yet he somehow managed to pass the boards and get a license to practice in California. Of course, the only job he could find was working as a GP in low-income neighborhood clinics where he misdiagnosed an aortic dissection as heartburn. After that and a few other doozies, he and the state Medical Board got together and agreed Dr. Brewer's calling was in some other field.

"And they were right. Next thing you know he starts a retail medical supply business, bedside urinals, adult diapers, walkers, that sort of stuff. And the thing takes off. One store becomes ten, then fifty, then a hundred, all over the Southwest. It keeps growing as the Boomers retire and he expands to the wholesale business. He ends up on the cover of *Forbes,* a huge success. And he gives back. Donates millions to kidney charities and other stuff." Jake paused. "What led you to Medicus Group in the first place?"

"Long story," Densmore said.

Jake waved two fingers at the bartender. "Another round, please."

Densmore recounted her interview with Randell Harlow. "If he's to be believed, a guy by the name of Bryce Weeks killed Thaddeus Dell."

"Dell's the one you think killed Petrov?"

"Real name's Blount, but yeah. Dell's the guy we found dead in that grow house, missing his fingers and his eyes."

"And where's this Weeks character?"

She sipped her drink. "Disappeared. Hasn't been home, hasn't used credit or debit cards or his phone, nothing."

"What's this got to do with The Medicus Group?"

Densmore connected the dots between Thaddeus Dell, Randell Harlow, and Shelton Birch, including Agent Fuller's theory that the transplant hospital might be in one of Birch's properties.

"You believe it?"

"Doesn't matter," Densmore said. "It got us looking at Birch and that led to the discovery that his company leases office space to both McAfee Protective Services and The Medicus Group."

"Interesting, but maybe coincidental if he's that big a landlord."

"Maybe," Densmore said. "And if you like coincidence, you'll love the fact that another one of Birch's companies owns that parking garage where you went with the girl."

That hung in the air for a second. Finally Jake said, "What?" He looked wounded. "Now *you're* following me?"

"It's not like I didn't have good reason," she said. "Fuller's evidence made me suspicious. And let's face it, he was right."

"I suppose there's that."

"So what do we have?" Densmore said. "McAfee providing the occasional inmate for organs as well as special-ops teams to hijack organs in transit, Medicus providing all the stuff to equip the hospital, and Birch providing the building? And your pal, Mr. Kaye, recruits the medical staff. That sound like it?"

"Mr. Kaye!" Jake reached into his shirt pocket and removed something. "I almost forgot. This is for you." He held it out to Densmore.

"A latex glove, how… sort of creepy."

"It's inside." Jake got a pair of hemostats from the bartender and pulled out the slip of paper Mr. Kaye had given him. "Don't touch."

"Whatcha got there?"

"Mr. Kaye's fingerprints," Jake said.

***

The next morning, Detective Densmore was leaning against the counter in Jake's kitchen, wearing his robe and sipping coffee while Jake searched his cabinets for something he could pass off as breakfast.

"I've got some powdered donuts," he said, checking the expiration date. "Oh, never mind."

"Why don't we just—"

The doorbell interrupted her.

"Hold that thought," Jake said. He went to the front door where he found a young woman with a small pink box in her hands.

She smiled and said, "I understand you're looking for a kidney."

Jake looked at her, then at the package. "You didn't bring it in that box, did you?"

"No." She opened it to reveal a warm slice of banana bread and a blueberry muffin. "I'm a pastry chef," she said. "Mr. Kaye sent me."

Jake wasn't sure what to make of that but if Mr. Kaye had sent her he thought he should find out why, plus she had food. "Come in."

She followed him to the kitchen.

"It's probably better if you don't hear this conversation," Jake said to Densmore. "I'll explain later, or not, depending." He handed her the box. Densmore took the muffin and excused herself.

Jake took a bite of the banana bread. It was spectacular.

The woman explained that she wanted to open her own bakery and needed seed money. The banks said she was too young and inexperienced and wouldn't give her a loan so she was selling her kidney. "The baked goods are a token of thanks for your help."

She was a perfect match for the network executive's kid and Mr. Kaye had sent her over to get instructions on how to proceed. Jake told her how the directed donation ruse worked and then he gave her Mitchell Wick's phone number. "I'll tell him to expect your call."

Jake showed her to the door and wished her luck.

"Who was that?" Densmore asked, walking into the kitchen.

"An entrepreneur," Jake said. "How's that muffin?"

"Fantastic," she said. "She's going door-to-door to drum up business?"

"Not exactly," Jake said. "Remember the reality show thing I mentioned? It's part of that. Probably better if you don't know the details."

They were in the living room finishing their coffee when Detective Densmore got a text. "Fuller wants to meet."

***

Ramon Recendez was hardworking and tough. He put in sixteen-hour days, starting at dawn doing roofing; at night he parked cars at a restaurant until it closed. His employers liked him because he always showed up. He didn't call in sick, no matter what. Ramon knew they could always find somebody else. Whenever he got sick, he simply bought something over-the-counter and rode it out.

But not this time. This time he had to see somebody.

The Pacoima Family Clinic was in a dusty, low-income neighborhood in the northeast part of the San Fernando Valley. Wedged between a liquor store and a check-cashing joint in a depressed strip mall, it was marked by a large red cross on a sign advertising services in Spanish. It stressed *No seguro necesario.* Which was good, because Ramon didn't have any.

He was in a room with a nurse. She was white but spoke Spanish well. She had taken his blood pressure, temperature, and medical history by the time the doctor came in.

He was friendly, had a good manner. He shook Ramon's hand.

The nurse said Ramon was presenting with pain in his abdomen, some nausea, and a low-grade fever. The doctor nodded, an easy call: appendicitis. Ramon recognized the word and nodded as if concurring with the diagnosis.

Ramon explained, apologetically, that he had no insurance and very little money. The doctor told him not to worry. He asked about family and friends. Ramon said he had come here alone and hadn't been here long, so, no, he didn't have anyone to help pay.

When the issue of his legal status came up, Ramon indicated he was suddenly starting to feel a lot better and why didn't they just forget the whole thing?

The doctor put a reassuring hand on Ramon's shoulder and told him not to worry about it. There would be no police, no problems. "You need a little operation," he said. "We'll take care of you. You'll be fine." The doctor shook Ramon's hand again, then said to the nurse, "Why don't you get started on the blood and urine work…"

25

Densmore and Jake walked into the conference room at the Office of Inspector General. The white board was still up with Densmore's diagram showing the connections between McAfee Protective Services, American Incarceration Management, Medical Staffing Solutions, and Correctional Medical Supplies. Added to that was the list of Shelton Birch's companies that Densmore and Fuller had compiled.

Agent Fuller was at the far end of the table, bleary-eyed and jittery from too much coffee. His suit looked like a wilted plant.

Densmore said, "Weren't you wearing that yesterday?"

"I pulled an all-nighter," Fuller said, rubbing his face with both hands. "Was it worth it? I have no idea," he said with an air of hopelessness. "Maybe. But that's the problem. Every time I think I've found something, I end up at a blood farm or a stool bank."

"Or a grow house," Densmore said.

"Yeah, thanks for reminding me." Fuller cast his gaze at the ceiling. "Rumor has it they're starting to have their doubts about me upstairs. If I don't find something soon, they'll have me taking phone tips on the Durable Medical Equipment Fraud hotline."

Jake sat down. "Did you find *any*thing?"

"Found another one of Birch's companies, but that's it," Fuller said. "Pico Property Strategies, leasing space to a company called

Golden State Interment, a chain with two dozen facilities around Southern California." He shrugged. "But I don't see what that gets us."

"I might," Densmore said.

Agent Fuller perked up, looking for any help he could get.

"When Alphonzo Blount, aka Yuri Petrov, got arrested for selling human ligaments, he told investigators they were legit, claimed he worked at a funeral home or something. Maybe it was Golden State Interment."

"Well, for what it's worth, GSI is strictly mortuaries," Fuller said. "No funeral homes."

"There's a difference?"

"Funeral homes do more hand-holding," Jake said. "They're big on ceremony and expense. Mortuaries, not so much. Also, most funeral homes don't have cremation facilities, mortuaries do."

"So maybe Blount was telling the truth."

"I don't think so," Densmore said. "When I interviewed Randell Harlow, he said Blount was stealing the ligaments from whoever he worked for, and whoever that was got worried Blount might roll over after he got caught. Question is: Why would you worry that someone might roll over on you if you're engaged in legal activity?"

"In other words," Fuller said, "the ligaments had to be obtained illegally."

"Seems like there are two scenarios then," Jake said. "Either they were taken from bodies at the mortuary without permission from the families or they were taken from bodies used in the black market organ transplants."

"Or both," Fuller said. He got up and stood in front of the white board, looking at all the names, trying to make sense of it. "I bet it's right in front of us and we can't see it."

After staring at the board for a moment Jake said, "What else did you find out about Golden State Interment? I mean, family-owned business? A corporation?"

Fuller went back to his computer and looked it up. "Golden State Interments is a DBA for a company called BMB Enterprises." He did another search. "And BMB is a subsidiary of something called The Medicus Group."

Jake and Densmore exchanged a look.

Noticing this, Fuller said, "You've heard of 'em?"

"Yep," Jake said. "They're in the medical supply business."

"And their corporate office," Densmore added, "is in a building owned by Birch."

***

Ramon Recendez sat in the room, pressing a cotton ball to the vein where the nurse had taken a couple of vials of blood. The nurse asked if he was in any pain.

With his hand Ramon made a circular motion around his abdomen and described it the best he could.

She understood. Poorly localized meant only mild inflammation, which meant the peritoneum wasn't yet inflamed. They still had some time.

"On a scale of one to ten," the nurse said, "with one being no pain, and ten being severe pain. How bad is it?"

"Cuatro, tal vez cinco," Ramon replied.

The nurse smiled. She knew he was just trying to cling to his masculinity. "Mr. Recendez, with the way you are holding yourself I'm guessing it's more like six or seven?"

Ramon shrugged. Maybe it was. But he didn't want to be any trouble. He could take the pain if it would save money.

"It's all right. I'm going to give you a little something to make you feel better." She prepared the shot, a syringe filled with a clear liquid.

It worked quickly. Ramon felt better, warmer, relaxed. He felt safe.

The nurse said they were going to take him to the hospital. She asked again if there was anybody they could contact for him.

He said there was no one. They were still in Honduras. It was hard to keep his eyes open.

They led Ramon out the back where an ambulance was idling, one of those non-emergency medical transport types. It said Good Shepherd on the side.

Ramon was drowsy but able to climb into the back. He laid down on the gurney and someone strapped him in. They shut the double doors and the driver put it in gear.

Half a mile later, Ramon was out.

***

Densmore flipped the white board around. Across the top she wrote: McAfee Protective Services, Birch Realty Partners, and The Medicus Group. Under those she wrote the names of the CEOs: Hutch McAfee, Shelton Birch, Dr. Steven Brewer. Below these she listed the subsidiaries they knew of and drew lines to show how they all connected. In the end it looked like a spider's web.

Densmore considered it for a moment, then rolled her eyes. "Birch, McAfee, Brewer. BMB Enterprises. Duh."

Agent Fuller got two techs from the I.T. department, had them searching everything from SEC filings, to federal tax returns, to the records of offshore registry agents.

Most of the businesses were incorporated in Delaware, the go-to state for organized crime and corrupt politicians worldwide who wanted to evade taxes, launder money, and otherwise hide who they were, what they were doing, and where they were doing it.

Ownership of the various entities was concealed in a series of shell corporations and holding companies, a dozen different trusts, several foundations, and further obscured by a passel of proxy owners.

"You gotta hand it to 'em," Densmore said. "They take this hide-and-seek shit seriously." She paused. "Try saying that three times quickly."

They discovered The Medicus Group was the parent company of Correctional Medical Supplies. Medicus also controlled Medical Staffing Solutions, which had contracts to provide personnel not only for McAfee's prisons but also for a chain of medical clinics in the poorer neighborhoods of Los Angeles and San Diego, a chain whose ownership traced back to Medicus and whose buildings all belonged, ultimately, to Birch.

Cross-referencing members of the various boards of directors, they came across another Medicus Group subsidiary: Good Shepherd Ambulance, one of Southern California's largest non-emergency medical transportation companies.

For a moment they thought they had it figured out: where donors came from, how they were matched to recipients, how they were moved, and who provided supplies and personnel.

"This is all supply side," Jake said. "What's the demand side look like?"

After staring at the labyrinth of names for a minute Densmore said, "Is there a way to find out who arranged all this? Like an agent for service of process, something along those lines?"

Fuller looked at the I.T. techs. "Well?"

They pulled up the site for the Delaware Division of Corporations. "Says here you can purchase direct web access to their corporate information only through authorized vendors."

"That's not why we hired you," Fuller said.

"Are you authorizing us to rootkit our way to a backdoor?"

"What do you think?"

"You need to say it."

"Fine," Fuller said. "You're authorized, now would you please—"

"We're in," the other techie said with a smirk. "*That's* why you hired us."

With a few keystrokes a string of names scrolled up the screen, except it wasn't a string of different names.

"Look who got sloppy," Densmore said. It was the same name again and again: Chad Huntington Yardsworth, Esq.

"Representative for the late Henry Fontaine, if I'm not mistaken," Fuller said.

"Makes sense," Densmore said. "The one-percent crowd's a small circle. They probably share this sort of information like insider trading tips."

"This is all great," Fuller said. "Only problem is if we start a formal investigation or a grand jury or anything else, Yardsworth is well enough connected that he'll get word and they'll shut the whole thing down. What we need is to find where they do it and catch them in the act," Fuller said. "We have to get inside."

That hung in the air for a moment until Jake said, "Yeah, I might be able to help there."

Densmore flashed him a look as if to say, *What are you doing?*

Agent Fuller stabbed a finger at Jake like he'd just confessed. "You're involved with it, aren't you? I knew it!"

Jake looked around as though he were about to start spilling State secrets. He gestured for Densmore to close the door. He lowered his voice and said, "Alright, I'm going to level with you." He picked up a pen and a pad.

"What are you doing?"

Jake put a finger to his lips, a silent shhhh. He wrote on the pad, *Safe to talk here? Other ears?*

"What?"

Jake put the fingertips of one hand on the table and moved them like a five-legged beetle.

Fuller studied it for a moment. "Spiders?"

Jake rolled his eyes and wrote on the pad, *Bugs!*

"What? No." Suddenly unsure of this, Fuller looked around in suspicion. "I don't think so."

Jake leaned over to him and whispered, "Okay, but they're in the building, right?"

"Who?"

"The FBI."

"Yeah, they're up on seventeen."

"Exactly! They could have come down here and, oh, never mind." Jake cast another paranoid look around the room. "Look, this is classified, and I am in it deep if they find out I said anything."

Densmore played along, looking at the underside of a lamp and behind the wall art as if checking for hidden microphones.

"Who are *they?*"

"The guys up on seventeen! I'm working with them on this," Jake said. "They approached me right after you did, wouldn't let me say no. They had me approach a man they suspected was a kidney broker, thought I could infiltrate by offering to steer kidney patients their way. I didn't have any choice," Jake said. "And it worked. I'm in."

"Jesus! Where is it?"

"No idea," Jake said. "I'm always blindfolded when they take me."

Fuller pointed at the ceiling. "They know I'm investigating this, right?"

"Hell yes, and they don't want you to get there first," Jake said. "They want this feather for their cap."

"Those *pricks.*"

"I'm with you," Jake said. "So look, I'm going to stall them as long as I can while we try to figure this out. I want this win for you but here's the hiccup. I've got an asset inside. She was my way in and I'll need to get her out before we do anything."

"When are you planning to go in next?"

"As soon as possible."

***

Jake made arrangements to visit Angel that afternoon. The process was the same: parking garage, blindfold, headphones.

But this time he wasn't the only one in the elevator going down to the hospital. This time he found himself next to a man on gurney who appeared to be coming out of a mild general anesthetic. He was Hispanic, wearing work pants and a T-shirt from a Honduran soccer tournament seven years earlier. Tucked in on the side of the gurney was the man's medical records.

There were two other men, both in full scrubs and masks, one on either side of the gurney. No one spoke on the short ride down.

When the doors opened, Jake let the men wheel the gurney out first. When he stepped into the hall, the nurse with the cat-eye glasses was waiting.

"Did you get, like, assigned to me?"

"Luck of the draw," she said. Her mask wrinkled at Jake and he smiled back.

The men pushed the gurney down the hall, past a wealthy-looking couple standing outside one of the rooms. They appeared to be giving strict instructions to a nurse. As the gurney disappeared around a corner, Jake said, "A little busier than usual."

"Yeah, some muckety-muck's kid came in this morning," the nurse said. "Very big deal apparently." She led Jake in the other direction, toward Angel's room.

"I thought everybody here was a muckety-muck."

"Some are muckier than others," the nurse said. "And luckier too. The kid's AB-negative but a donor just turned up. Now they're hustling some hotshot surgeon in from New York Presbyterian to do the transplant at daddy's insistence and on his private jet." She shook her head. "You ever wondered what it would be like to have that kind of money?"

"Sure," Jake said. He also wondered what this woman thought about what went on here. Did she know all the details? How could she not? Did they pay her enough not to care? Did she think the heart donors were all death row inmates and she had no problem with that?

The nurse stopped outside Angel's room, pulled the file from the wall-mounted chart holder, glanced at it quickly. "Good news," she said. "Your girl's been cleared for discharge."

It took Jake by surprise. "What, today?"

"It's up to you."

Jake needed to buy some time. Angel was his only excuse for being allowed inside the place and that access gave him the best chance for discovering its location. He also wanted to find out what was going on with this new patient and the Hispanic man on the gurney.

"That's great," Jake said, "but is there any way we can delay, like do a late checkout? I hired somebody to help but she's not scheduled until—"

"No worries," the nurse said. "How's tomorrow?"

"I think I can do that," Jake said. "Thanks."

"I'll let them know." The nurse walked away.

26

Jake went in to see Angel. She looked happy.

"They told me I'm good to go."

"I just heard." Jake went to the closet and pulled out a set of scrubs. "You think you can stand it here one more night? I need to make some arrangements for where you'll stay." He stepped into the bathroom, out of her sight.

"You have something in mind?"

"Just need a day to set it up." Jake came back into the room wearing scrubs. "C'mon, we're taking a stroll."

"What?"

"It'll be good for you, plus I might need your help." Jake told her the plan he'd just come up with. It was rudimentary to say the least.

"That's not a plan," Angel said. "That's, I don't know, bad improv or something."

"It's all I got," Jake said. "C'mon."

Angel shook her head. "You are crazy if you think I'm getting out of this bed, walking down the hall in this stupid gown, my whoopee cakes out there for everybody to see."

"Whoopie cakes?"

Angel shook her head. "Not gonna happen."

"It's a hospital, don't be so self-conscious."

x

210

"You can forget it unless you get me a robe or something."

There was no robe in the closet, so he handed her another hospital gown, told her to put in on backwards and tie it in the front.

"Hang on to my arm and remember what I said."

The hallways formed a square with a line down the middle. They went left out of the room, walking slowly, Angel being careful, Jake looking for exits other than the elevator. They turned at the first corner, heading for the room with the locked door. Jake could see the man still in the bed, on the vent and IV feeding. The door was still locked. They continued walking the square, now heading for the room with the muckety-muck's kid.

The wealthy couple had stepped inside, talking to someone in scrubs.

Jake whispered, "Now."

"Oooh, wait," Angel said, reaching for her stitches.

The couple in the room glanced up, then continued their business.

Jake said, "You okay?"

"Yeah, just give me a second," she said.

"Take your time." It gave him long enough to look into the room, see what was there, overhear some conversation. No one paid him any mind.

Jake said, "You need a wheelchair?"

"No, I'm okay," Angel said. They moved down the hall and turned again.

Halfway down this corridor was the lab. Inside, a nurse was doing a blood draw from the man on the gurney.

"A little more this time," Jake whispered. "But be careful."

Angel doubled over and moaned with surprising conviction, getting the nurse's attention. Jake held Angel up as she started to go down to her knees.

"You all right? Angel?" He called to the nurse who was drawing the blood. "A little help?"

The nurse came out and took Angel's other arm. "Where does it hurt?"

Angel motioned toward her stitches

"Hang on," Jake said. "I'll get a wheelchair." He ran into the lab, Angel turning so the nurse couldn't see what Jake was up to. He pocketed a vial of blood, grabbed a wheelchair, and returned to the hall. They helped Angel into the chair.

Angel played it perfectly, said it was a bad cramp or something and asked if that was normal. The nurse said it wasn't unusual, said it would get better. Angel gushed some thanks and expressed surprise at how quickly the pain went away. "I think I'll go lie down now."

Jake wheeled Angel back to her room. "I think you've got a bright future running cons," he said. "Now get some rest. I'll be back tomorrow to get you out of here."

***

Jake walked into the Federal Building carrying a canvas bag. Densmore was waiting in the lobby, a magazine rolled up in her hand. As Jake approached she held it to her mouth like a megaphone and said, "Attention K-Mart shoppers…"

"Blue Light Special?"

"Right here on page thirty-eight," she said, unfurling a back issue of *Forbes,* the one with Dr. Brewer on the cover. "Full color photo of the good doctor, along with his close friends Shelton Birch, Hutch McAfee, and some other members of the Club for Green."

Surprised, Jake said, "They're environmentalists?"

Densmore rubbed her finger and thumb together. "Different kind of green," she said. "It's an anti-tax, anti-regulation, anti-union, lobby group."

"They're not pro-anything?"

"I think they're pro-slavery, essentially, though they can't put that on the website." They crossed to the elevators where Densmore pushed the call button.

Jake thumped the photo with a finger. "I gotta say, Dr. Brewer could benefit from a few sit ups."

Once in the elevator, Densmore said, "You'll be further impressed to know that I got a hit on Mr. Kaye's fingerprints. His real name came up as Ed Volman."

"You dig up anything interesting on him?"

"Yeah, he died nine years ago," Densmore said. "Laid to rest by Golden State Interment."

"Any theories?"

"During the recession a lot of families stopped claiming their dead relatives' bodies because they couldn't afford the funerals, forcing L.A. County to do the cremations. Demands on the county crematorium got so high they stopped accepting bodies from the coroner. So the coroner's office contracted with two private crematories to handle the overflow."

"And one of them was Golden State Interments."

"I assume Mr. Kaye, whatever his real name is, was working there when the unclaimed body of Mr. Volman came in from the County. Mr. Kaye handled the cremation, put his own fingerprints on the paperwork where the deceased's prints were supposed to go, then filed it with the County."

"Why?"

"Same as Alphonzo Blount," Densmore said. "Say you leave your prints at the scene of a crime. Investigator puts them in the system, sees they belong to someone dead for years, they'll assume the prints were there prior to the crime and go look for someone else."

Agent Fuller walked into the conference room carrying a small box, asked if he'd missed anything. Densmore explained The Club for Green connection and Mr. Kaye's fingerprint situation. Jake recounted his afternoon visit to the hospital.

"First of all, this kid isn't on dialysis," Jake said. "There wasn't even a machine in his room, so he's not there for a kidney. And I heard them mention the kid's ejection fraction." He nodded. "It's a heart transplant, and I suspect the guy they were drawing blood from is the donor."

"Because?"

"Well, not to judge by appearances," Jake said, "but the man didn't look like the sort who could afford their services. If they just needed a few units of his blood, they'd drain him elsewhere. Plus he's AB negative, like the kid. You don't find one of those every day."

Jake pulled the items from his bag, setting them on the table. The vial of Ramon's blood, along with a rapid assay kit consisting of test panels, a container of sample diluent, and some capillary tubes. Jake transferred a drop of blood to the test panel, added the buffer solution, then set it aside and started a timer.

"He was wearing a ratty T-shirt for a Honduran soccer team from a tournament seven years ago. That's not the sort of souvenir you pick up at the Bradley Terminal when your flight lands. My guess is he's from Central America," Jake said. "So I'm testing for Chagas."

"Which is what?"

"Deadly, for the most part," Jake said. "If he's got it, his days are numbered. And if they give that kid any of his blood or his heart, the kid's future ain't so bright either."

"You don't think they're testing for it?"

"Maybe," Jake said. "But it's not automatic. I know of several deaths caused by Chagas transmission via transplant in major L.A. hospitals."

"Let's say he's got Chagas," Agent Fuller said. "Then what?"

Jake shrugged. "Depends. If they've already done the transplant, it'll be too late to do anything. If they haven't done it, all I can do is suggest they test for it. If they find he's positive, there's no way they'll give that kid the heart."

"You know when they're doing the transplant?"

"Based on what I heard, I bet it's tomorrow," Jake said. "I hope it's tomorrow anyway, since it's the last day I'll have an excuse to be there visiting."

"So it's the big day," Densmore said. "You go in to get the girl, try to save the rich kid, maybe the poor donor, and expose their location."

"Yeah," Jake said. "And exactly how do we plan to do that?"

"A tail probably won't work," Fuller said. "I'm guessing their drivers are trained, watching for that, taking evasive maneuvers as a matter of course." He looked at Jake. "Do they frisk you?"

"Usually," Jake said. "But they always take my phone."

"Okay." Agent Fuller pulled something from the box he'd brought. It was the size of a small candy bar. He walked it over to Jake. "You'll have to smuggle it in."

Jake considered the meaning of the word. "I'm supposed to swallow this thing?"

"No," Fuller said. "Stomach acid would ruin it." He handed Jake a tube of petroleum jelly. "This goes in the other end."

Densmore chuckled. "Oh boy."

Jake glared at her, then at Fuller. "You better have a Plan B."

"Sure." Fuller pulled an unusual looking pistol from the box, walked over to Jake, and shot something into his arm.

Jake nearly jumped out of his skin. "Jesus! What the hell was that?"

"A tracking device you don't have to stick up your ass," Fuller said. "It's a transponder. Not quite the range as the other one, but it's better than nothing."

Jake rubbed his arm like he'd been stung by a two-pound wasp, felt the lump under his skin. "Why not let me smuggle that instead of shooting me with it?"

A look of bafflement crossed Fuller's face. "Hadn't thought of that," he said.

Jake shook his head. "You ever given a thought to informed consent?"

"Oh yeah, I got that earlier," Fuller said. "You remember the consulting contract you signed? You agreed to this and a whole lot worse." Fuller launched an app on his phone and tapped a button.

Jake twitched and looked at his arm. "What was that?"

"The transponder," Fuller said. "I send a signal. That activates the transponder, which sends back your location. As long as you feel that vibration every now and then, you know we're with you."

"What's the range on this?"

"Depends on the terrain, mountains, buildings, microwave transmitters, stuff like that, but it's rated at a half-mile."

"So if their highly trained drivers manage to get a mile away, you'll have no idea which direction we've gone and no way to find me."

"Relax," Densmore said. "I don't think it's possible to get a mile away in L.A. traffic."

"Just playing devil's advocate here," Jake said. "But if a miracle occurs and you do lose the signal, then what?"

"We'll start a grid search, hope for the best."

Jake looked at Fuller as if he were moderately brain-damaged. "You'll do a grid search of greater Los Angeles?"

"Well, we'll have two cars," Fuller said in his defense.

"Oh, so just two hundred and fifty square miles each?"

"Yeah," Fuller said. "Just sit tight, we'll find you."

"You're a federal agent, right?"

"Yeah."

"And the penalty for assaulting or killing a federal agent is more severe than the penalty for assaulting or killing, say, me, right?"

Agent Fuller took a step back. "Yeah, so?

"So give me a badge."

"What? Why?"

"First time I met with Mr. Kaye, he scanned me with some kind of electronic thing to see if I was wearing a wire."

"RF detector," Densmore said.

"Yeah," Jake said. "And for all I know I go past one every time I get off the elevator at this hospital. Maybe not. All I'm saying is they're careful." He glanced at the lump in his arm. "This works with radio frequencies, right?"

"Yeah."

"If they find out I've got this thing in my arm, having a federal badge might make them hesitate before they do anything we can't undo."

"I can't give you a badge."

"Why not?"

"You think I've got a drawer full of them?"

Jake held out his hand. "Give me yours."

"Fine." Agent Fuller handed it over just as the timer chimed on Jake's phone and they gathered around the test panel.

Jake gestured at the result. "Looks like the game's on."

***

Jake and Mark were back at ICU, having a drink. Mark stared at Jake in disbelief.

"That's the plan? You're working with a federal agent preparing to break up a major underground transplant operation along with an LAPD detective working a series of murders and *that's* your plan?"

"Well, technically, Detective Densmore's still on administrative leave, so she can't really do much," Jake said. "But Agent Fuller's got a SWAT team on speed dial."

"Which is great except you don't know where to send them."

"Yeah, there's that."

"So the plan is you hope that the bad guys, the ones you say are ex-Navy Seal specially trained security force thugs, *hope* they don't notice they're being followed so your pal can swoop in with his SWAT team and keep them from killing you for setting them up?"

Jake peeled his sleeve back to show the bump under his skin. "There's also this transponder thing."

"Are you kidding? For all you know that's a Radio Shack transmitter with a range of fifty feet. Christ, you're a goner." Mark signaled for another round of drinks.

"What are my options? I got Angel in there," Jake said. "And now I'm going to get her out, or die trying."

"Fine," Mark said with a heavy sigh. "Give me your best case scenario."

"They follow me there, wait for me to get the girl, they go in, do their thing."

"Exactly. Nothing goes wrong. You don't need a plan for when nothing goes wrong," Mark said. "You need a plan for when everything goes sideways. Let's say you're almost out the door with the girl when they realize you've set them up."

"How are they going to figure that out?"

"I don't know, maybe they detect the radio frequencies coming from that thing in your arm. If they do, you need a plan to get out, right? Because your Fed buddy and his SWAT team are *outside* waiting on you. They can't help. They don't even know you *need* help, so you need a plan to help yourself." Mark grabbed a napkin and a pen. "What's the floor plan of this place? How big is it?"

Jake drew the floor plan to the best of his memory, indicating the locations of the patient rooms, the ORs, the lab, and the elevator.

Mark studied it for a second and started to shake his head. "No way that's the only exit," he said. "Place that size? What if there's a fire? You think they're going to leave all those billionaires in there 'till they're well done?"

"You're probably right," Jake said. "Bound to be some sort of emergency exit, but I can't go room to room looking for it. And I doubt anybody's going to show me if I ask."

"That's it!" Mark slapped his hand on the table. "The best way to get them to show you the emergency exits is to have an emergency."

Jake considered that for a second. "You want me to start a fire?"

"You just have to make them *think* there's a fire." Mark stood. "Come on."

"Where we going?"

"Hardware store," Mark said. "We're going to need some stump remover."

27

It was three-thirty that afternoon and cool out. It would be dark by five.

Agent Fuller was watching the two exits on the west side of the parking garage. Detective Densmore was on the east side on the phone with Fuller, saying, "He drove in a couple of minutes ago. You still got a signal?"

"Hundred percent."

"Great."

"Wait."

"What?"

"I lost it," Fuller said.

"What do you mean lost? You're half a block away."

"Maybe the garage is a Faraday cage."

"A what?"

"Wait, never mind," Fuller said. "It's back. Good signal. We're okay. I just hit the wrong button."

One of the gate arms went up on Densmore's side. "Okay, here we go," she said. "I've got a Good Shepherd Ambulance coming out."

"Uh, me too," Fuller said.

"Oh great," Densmore said. "I got a second one, now a third, all going different directions."

"Same here," Fuller said. "Which would be a good strategy if we didn't have the transponder," Fuller said. "Just sit still, let 'em go. We'll know soon enough which one is Jake's."

When all the ambulances were out of sight, Fuller said, "I've got him heading east on the Ten. I'll follow, you go parallel on Washington."

They stayed with the ambulance for five miles without a hitch. Traffic on the interstate was moving like an accordion, squeezing together to a slow crawl, then expanding to the speed limit. Surface street traffic was moderate, allowing Densmore to get ahead for a minute, then fall behind. The ambulance maintained a half-mile lead the whole time.

A minute later Fuller said he was at a dead stop, just short of the Figueroa Exit.

"I'm ahead of you," Densmore said. "Approaching the One-Ten overpass, but it's starting to crawl, and now I see why."

"What is it?"

"A busted water main," Densmore said. "You can't see that? Must be shooting forty feet in the air, north side of the interstate."

"Big rig's blocking my view," Fuller said. "Wait a second, the ambulance is moving again, and fast. Oh hell, they must be going up the shoulder with their lights."

"You following?"

"Can't," Fuller said. "I'm blocked by two lanes of dead traffic. Looks like they're getting off around the convention center. Can you get there?"

"Doubtful," she said. "I'm hemmed in and going about one mile a decade." The app on her phone showed Jake's ambulance was moving east, near the convention center, then the screen went blank. "Damn, I lost the signal."

Fuller had the same problem. "I'll try to get a visual on it," Fuller said. He got out of his sedan and slid across the hood of the car in the next lane, then jumped onto the hood of another.

The next thing Densmore heard on the phone was a car horn blaring and a man yelling about some asshole who better be getting his ass off the hood of this car pronto. This was followed by Fuller announcing that he was a federal agent. The horn stopped, a car door slammed, and a man's voice said, "Yeah? Let's see your badge."

"Oh shit," Fuller said. "Hang on a second! Wait! What do you think—"

Then the call dropped.

***

Riding in the back of the ambulance, blindfolded and listening to something that made the '1812 Overture' sound like a lullaby, Jake started to think everything might just turn out fine.

Angel had her new kidney and Jake thought this scare might put her on a better path. Fuller and Densmore had given him reason to believe his name wouldn't have to come up in any prosecution of the black market business, saying they could argue that the discovery of the entire enterprise sprang solely from their investigation of Alphonzo Blount's murder. Jake was still an overpaid consultant on Wick's reality show, and he had a good feeling about the thing he had going with Densmore.

Topping it all off, every minute or two he felt the odd and reassuring vibration of the transponder activating in his arm, reminding him that someone had his back.

Until it stopped.

He flexed his arm then poked at it, wondering if he'd switched if off somehow. He held his arm at different angles and swiveled around in his seat but nothing happened except that his unseen escort said, "What are you doing?"

"Just stretching," Jake said, glad that for once in his life he'd taken Mark's advice and had a backup plan.

When the ambulance doors opened, he was escorted to the elevator as usual. On the way down, the guard frisked Jake and found the thing in a plastic baggie in his jacket pocket.

"What's this?"

"Peanut butter sandwich," Jake said. "I don't like jelly."

The guard sniffed it. "Smells funny."

"Yeah, it's organic peanut butter," Jake said. "Smells like stump remover if you ask me, but it's gluten free and I've got celiac disease, so… well, actually they're not a hundred percent sure it's celiac, there's still some debate, it's quite controversial," he said. "I don't know if you're following that story but it could be what they call non-celiac gluten sensitivity but, whatever, I'm stuck eating this crap." Jake held it up. "You want a bite?"

The guard declined and escorted Jake to Angel's room where he said, "Wait for the nurse, she'll escort you out."

Jake stepped inside and was nearly hit by Angel, who was zipping around the room in an electric wheelchair. "Whoa, dude! You gotta get me one of these." She whirred over to the bed, skidding to a sideways stop next to her Hello Kitty backpack.

Jake was already in the bathroom changing into scrubs.

Angel didn't like the looks of that. "Wait, what're you doing? We're leaving in a second."

"We've got to do something first."

"I'm ready to get out of here."

"All right, listen. I've got to tell you something," Jake said. "I need you to know what's going on."

When Jake finished, Angel stared at him in disbelief. She said, "Wait, they're just going to kill the guy?"

"If they haven't already."

"Did they kill someone for me?" She was aghast.

"No," Jake said, though he had no way of knowing.

Angel pointed at the lump in his arm. "And you're still not feeling anything?"

He shook his head.

"So they don't know where we are."

Another head shake.

Angel picked up the thing in the plastic bag. "And you think this is the best way to get their attention?"

"It's all I got," Jake said.

"But if we wanted, we could just leave when the nurse gets here?" She pointed at the thing in the bag. "Instead of doing that."

Jake nodded sympathetically. "We could. Is that what you want to do?"

"No." Her expression hardened. "I want to help."

"Okay," Jake said. "Here's what I'm thinking." He laid out his plan. At the end, Angle's dumbfounded expression prompted Jake to say, "I'll admit, it's a little sketchy."

"A little?"

"It calls for some improvising, that's all. You're smart. You'll know what to do." Then, something occurred to him. "You have any matches?"

Angel smiled. "Of course I do."

There was a polite knock at the door and Jake slipped the baggie underneath Angel's Hello Kitty bag.

The nurse with the cat-eye glasses stepped in. "Okay, Angel, you all packed and…" She looked confused, gesturing at Jake. "Why are you in scrubs?"

"I need to talk to Mr. Kaye," Jake said.

"You don't need scrubs for that." She turned her head and gave a mischievous smile. "You were going to go sneaking down the hall looking for him, weren't you?"

"I need to tell him something," Jake said. "It's important."

"He's busy," the nurse said. "You can tell me on the way out, I'll pass it on when I get back." She tried to herd them to the door but Jake stood his ground.

"Might be too late then," he said.

"Sounds serious." The nurse folded her arms. "What is it?"

Angel wondered how this was going to play out. Wondering if she'd be able to help in whatever way Jake needed, when he needed it, the way he'd helped her. She owed him that for sure.

"Listen," Jake said. "The kid down the hall, have they done the transplant?"

"The muckety-muck? Not yet." She checked her watch. "Pretty soon though, why?"

"We can't let it happen."

"What? Why?"

"Because the donor, the man down there, has Chagas."

"How could you possibly know that?"

"Doesn't matter how," Jake said. "I know. And that man's going to die either way, but the kid's going to die too if he has the transplant. If we stop it, he has a chance."

The nurse looked at Jake like he was a child with an overactive imagination. "Look, I'm sure they know what they're doing. They wouldn't put a client at risk like that. Now, you want to change back into your clothes?"

"You know what goes on in this place?" Jake asked.

"I know I'm paid very well not to ask too many questions" she said. "And I know it's the place where your girl here got a new kidney. Isn't that enough?"

"All right," Jake said, "here's the deal." He pulled out Agent Fuller's credentials and flashed them at the nurse. "I'm undercover with the Office of Inspector General. They're going to kill that man and that kid, and you can either help me stop them and get some consideration from the prosecutor, or you can go the other way."

She put her hand to her mouth, shaken. "Oh my god. Okay, okay, I'll help, of course I'll help. I was just… I can't believe this is happening." She smoothed her scrubs. "C'mon, I'll take you to Mr. Kaye."

"I'll just wait here," Angel said.

***

Densmore was parked by the Convention Center, pinging the transponder and getting no response. In the rearview, she saw Fuller park. He walked over and leaned in the passenger window, revealing a newly acquired black eye.

Densmore smirked. "The hell happened to you?"

"Disagreement with a fellow motorist," Fuller said. "Big fella too, and a car enthusiast. Drove a seventy-three Ford LTD with a candied up pearl-blue paint job he said set him back four grand. Didn't appreciate my jumping on the hood." Fuller held up his phone, the screen a total spider web. "Busted this too, so I guess I'll be riding shotgun." He got in Densmore's car and gestured at her phone. "You have any luck?"

She started the car. "Nope. Which way?"

"Go down Pico. Last I saw, the ambulance turned onto Broadway."

Densmore handed her phone to Fuller and pulled away from the curb. "What do you think, ever widening circles?"

"Your guess is as good as mine." He pinged the transponder again. Nothing.

28

The nurse walked Jake down the hall and past the operating rooms where they could hear someone testing a sternal saw. "Don't worry," she said, "we've got plenty of time." She ushered Jake into a room. "Wait here, I'll go find Mr. Kaye." She closed the door behind her.

When Jake heard her lock it from the outside he realized the flaw in his strategy.

From down the corridor, Angel saw the whole thing, peeking around the corner. She decided it was time to improvise. She spun her wheelchair one-eighty and whirred into action.

Jake was locked in a supply room. He frisked the cabinets, pocketing items that might come in handy if he ended up in a tight spot, which was starting to look inevitable.

He poked at the transponder again, but it was still dormant. He heard a key in the lock, then Mr. Kaye appeared, standing in front of a burly security guard. "Jake, I'm disappointed."

"I know how you feel."

"I thought we were on the same page."

"We were when it was just about kidneys"

"I never said that's all we did," Mr. Kaye said. "You just convinced yourself that's what you were involved in. I understand."

He stepped back into the hall, gesturing for the guard to grab Jake. "Let's go."

"Where we going?"

"I need to keep you secure until this surgery's over," Mr. Kaye said. "Then I'll decide how to deal with you."

Jake could hear the sternal saw again, and this time it was being used, not tested. "That man has Chagas."

"So you've said. I think you're bluffing so we don't take the heart. I'm surprised you're so squeamish."

They were heading toward the locked room where the comatose man was kept.

"By the way," Mr. Kaye said, "if you're working undercover, you're much better off not revealing it until you're... safe."

"Yeah, well, I'm new at this."

They stopped outside the locked room, waiting for the guard to find the right key. "It's a shame about the girl," Mr. Kaye said. "The two of you could've just strolled out of here, happily ever after. Now?" He shook his head. "I'm surprised you'd put her in this situation but, like you said, you're new at this."

Jake slumped, put his hands in his pockets, shrugging like it was too late to change that, like he'd quit and had no fight in him at all. But in truth he had a good grip on a scalpel and he was about to put it to Mr. Kaye's throat when the fire alarm sounded, loud and disorienting. Up and down the hall flashbulb-bright strobe lights flashed urgently.

They stood there, looking around, caught off guard, half-expecting the noise to stop any second, like it was just a drill.

From the opposite corner of the hospital someone yelled, "We need to evacuate these rooms, now!"

By the time the guard got the key in the lock, they could smell the smoke. Mr. Kaye told the guard to lock Jake in the room, then hustled down the hall toward the commotion and the smoke. "Somebody turn that damn alarm off!"

Jake let go of the scalpel in his pocket and got a grip on a three-inch cardiac needle. He slipped off the protective cover. When the guard put his hand on Jake's shoulder, Jake jammed the needle into the guard's thigh then hammered it once with his fist.

The guard's scream was lost in the din of fire alarms and staff members yelling at one another.

"Open the exits!"

"Move the patients!"

Jake shoved the guard into the room, locked the door, and went looking for Angel.

He ducked into the first open room he came to and grabbed a surgical cap and a mask from the closet.

The middle age man in the bed said, "What the hell is going on out there?"

"Nothing to worry about, sir," Jake said. "Somebody burned a bagel in the staff lounge. They'll be here soon to remove your spleen."

"What? No, I'm here for a kidney!"

"Good luck!" Jake put on the cap and mask and slipped into the chaos, indistinguishable now among the others. He rounded a corner, the place so thick with smoke he could only see half the length of the corridor. A few steps ahead an orderly moved a section of wall sideways like a sliding glass door on tracks revealing another elevator. Two nurses appeared, coughing as they pushed a patient on a gurney through the smoke and onto the elevator.

The orderly yelled at Jake, "Go help on the north hall! If they can walk, send them up the stairs by room sixteen or by O.R. two. If they can't walk, get them to one of the elevators!"

Jake ran into the smoke-filled hallway calling for Angel.

He'd told her to set the smoke bombs anywhere she could get away with it, then wait to see where the exits were. "If you can get on an elevator, do it," he said. "If you see stairs and you can make it up a flight, do it. Don't wait for me. I'll find my way out."

"You won't leave *me* behind but I can leave *you?*"

"If they figure out what I'm up to, they'll grab you for leverage. You get out any way you can, as fast as you can. I got out of Iraq, I can get out of here."

Now, as he worked his way down the smoke-filled corridor, Jake didn't know if Angel was already out, if she was hiding, or if they'd grabbed her. He decided to make one round of the floor looking, then he'd try to stop the surgery and get out himself.

In the distance he heard Mr. Kaye again, "Somebody turn off that goddamn alarm!"

Jake made it three-quarters of the way around the perimeter, checking the patients' rooms and the lab, but he couldn't find her. Angel had set the smoke bombs in roughly opposite sides of the floor plan, near the corners. Jake was approaching the hall that ran down the center of the square when the alarm finally stopped. He wanted to call for Angel but knew it would give him away.

From behind, Mr. Kaye said, "I've got the girl, Jake."

He turned around.

It was a bluff, and Jake had given himself away falling for it. Mr. Kaye was fifteen feet away, his gun leveled on Jake. "You made a mess here. A big one."

"It's why I can't have nice things," Jake said. He thought his best move was to bolt for the center hallway, assume Mr. Kaye wasn't such a marksman that he'd hit him on the move. But it would put Jake in the smokeless hallway where he'd be an easier target.

Mr. Kaye was bringing the gun up to aim when something emerged from the smoke behind him. It was Angel, gliding fast and silent in the wheelchair, leading with a stainless steel I.V. pole like a jouster's lance. She caught Mr. Kaye in the back of the legs, buckling his knees. He hit the floor hard and fired a shot that missed Jake by a mile.

Angel smacked Mr. Kaye's head with the pole while he was still down then, quickly and silently as she had approached, she reversed into the cloud of smoke and disappeared.

"Get out of here!" Jake yelled. He bolted for the center hallway and was almost to the operating room door when Mr. Kaye took another shot, this time much closer. Jake burst into the first operating room, startling the transplant team as they prepared to open the kid's chest. "No time to explain," Jake said as he raced through, knocking trays of surgical instruments to the floor.

In the adjoining O.R., the surgeon had just placed Ramon's heart into a sterile basin. A nurse was walking it to the next room when Jake burst in, took the heart like a handoff, and kept running.

Crashing out the O.R. door, the stairwell was straight ahead. Jake never broke stride, taking the steps up two at a time. The metal door at the top was fitted with a crash bar that Jake hit with his forearm. It blew open, putting Jake in a warehouse that was the service garage for the fleet of Good Shepherd Ambulances. Across the way were the elevators and several gurneys with blindfolded patients being tended by nurses.

Jake sprinted across the warehouse, heading for an exit, when he heard the metal door crash open behind him. He didn't look. He knew who it was.

Mr. Kaye fired twice, both times missing Jake, but the bullets tore holes through the door ahead of him.

In the alley outside, a rat twitched and looked up at the shafts of light now beaming into the darkness. The door blew open, launching the rat into the brick wall across the way. Jake burst into the alley, wild-eyed and hyper-alert, scrubs stained with blood.

He skidded to a stop, trying to control his panic. He considered his options, left or right, trying to decide which way to safety. Problem was, he'd never been out this door. He'd never left this building except blindfolded in the back of a van.

He had no idea where he was.

Two more shots. The first missed, the second caught his shoulder. A little blood, a little flesh, maybe some muscle, but he'd live.

Assuming he got away.

Jake broke left, hoping for the best. He sprinted for the street ten yards ahead. As he ran, he glanced over his wounded shoulder. Bad idea. He clipped a Dumpster and nearly went down. It spun him around but he maintained balance, kept running.

He'd been in worse situations. During his time with the surgical detachment, he'd dodged down ancient Iraqi streets so narrow Helen Keller could hit you on the run. Here, at least he had room to dodge and weave.

Jake was almost to the street where he hoped to catch a break and flag down a passing car, get some help. He'd given up on the transponder.

Behind him, Mr. Kaye burst into the alley followed by a couple of security guards. Mr. Kaye waved them in opposite directions as he continued in the direction Jake had gone.

Jake couldn't believe his luck when he got to the street. It was the warehouse district, after hours. There was no traffic, not a soul in sight. All he could do now was find a place to hide, a fire escape, a manhole, anything. But all he could see were barred windows, padlocked roll doors, and alleys.

The alleys were his only hope. If he went down the street he was an easy target. If he made it to one of the alleys he might have a chance, forcing Mr. Kaye and the others to check all the options.

Jake took the alley to his right. He was pretty sure he made it without anyone seeing which way he'd gone, so they'd have to guess. Fifty-fifty.

***

Densmore and Fuller had circled their way to Chinatown looking for the transponder signal.

Fuller pulled some cash from his wallet. "Fifty bucks says he took the easy way out, left with the girl, and they're on their way back to the parking garage, leaving us hung out to dry."

"Hanging *us* out to dry? We're the ones supposed to have *his* back."

"He's the one who wasn't willing to use the bigger transponder."

"Yeah, imagine that," Densmore said. "What about the transplant?"

Fuller pulled a few more bills. "Another fifty says he was either too late to stop it or he just let it go 'cause it was easier."

Densmore sneered at Fuller. "Two hundred says you're full of shit on all counts."

The radio squawked a call for a squad car to assist LAFD Station Four. *"Report of a warehouse fire on Jesse Street."*

Densmore consulted a mental map. "Station Four's downtown," she said. "Little Tokyo, I think." She nodded in that direction. "Couple of miles that way."

"So?"

"I thought he was joking."

"Jake?"

"He said if all else failed and we weren't there for him he'd call the Fire Department."

"You seriously think—"

"Reports of shots fired."

***

The alley was dim. Jake couldn't tell if it went through to the next street. He checked the doors and windows as he passed but everything was locked. He reached a dead end and looked around. A couple of Dumpsters and some loading docks, their downward sloping ramps piled high with wooden pallets and trash, that was all. Limited choices: stand and fight, or hide. Unarmed, Jake knew there would be no fight. He'd just be a target.

Jake didn't like the idea of dying in a Dumpster so he slipped down one of the loading ramps and concealed himself with wooden pallets and bags of trash. Now he had to catch his breath so he didn't give away his position.

Jake listened. All around, voices echoed in the streets and alleys. Men shouting, fanning out, hunting. He heard sirens in the distance but he knew they could be for anything so he didn't take any comfort.

Jake's huffing breath fogged in the cold air. He tried to slow his breathing.

Calm down.

He was out of options.

Breathe.

He'd made his last move until they either gave up or they found him.

Stay calm.

Now, footsteps coming down the alley, moving slowly as a hunter's eyes adjusted to the darkness. The hunter stopped now and then to listen, then continued, coming closer.

Mr. Kaye whispered, "Are you there?"

Jake couldn't believe he'd ended up here. He'd just wanted to help Angel. Jake wasn't a religious man, but as Mr. Kaye got closer, Jake looked up to the heavens. Then he looked down at his hand, where he held Ramon's heart, steaming in the cold night air.

Mr. Kaye stood ten feet away, listening for a clue, but all he could hear were the sirens in the distance. He cocked an ear but couldn't tell if they were getting closer or not.

Jake felt something move among the trash, scratching and clawing.

Mr. Kaye looked more closely at the pile. "Jake, is that you?"

A rat emerged from a wet sack, scurried down Jake's leg, and out from the pile of trash. Jake's heart was racing as Mr. Kaye tensed, ready to shoot, until he saw what it was. He lowered the gun and turned to head back up the alley.

Jake breathed easier. He thought he'd made it, started congratulating himself for maintaining his cool. Then the transponder finally vibrated in his arm, and he yelped.

Mr. Kaye spun around, gun trained on the pile of trash. "Ah, you *are* in there," he said. "Why don't you come on out?"

Jake assumed if he didn't cooperate, Mr. Kaye was more likely to start shooting into the pile than he was to try digging him out. Jake also knew help was coming and he wanted to stay alive long enough to see it arrive, so he said, "Okay, give me a second, I need to dig myself out."

While Jake worked to extricate himself, Mr. Kaye said, "By the way, clever exit strategy back there. I'm guessing smoke bombs?"

"Yeah, all you need is a little sugar and some stump remover," Jake said as he emerged from the pile, still clutching Ramon's heart.

"That's no good to me anymore," Mr. Kaye said. "Might as well leave it for the rats."

"He had Chagas," Jake said. "You'd have killed that kid."

"Well, if that's true," Mr. Kaye said, "if he really had Chagas, then thanks. You did me, the kid, and his parents a favor. But I have to ask, if he hadn't had Chagas, then what? You'd have let us go ahead and kill the man?"

"We'll never know." The transponder vibrated again. Jake just needed to stall. "So now what? Sounds like the cavalry's coming."

Mr. Kaye smiled. "When the fire department arrives, they'll be on the other side of the warehouse where my guys will explain that we had a small fire resulting from some gas-soaked rags and an errant cigarette. They'll say it's all under control, and send them on their way."

"And then what, you'll just kill me and move on?"

"Noooo. I don't like wasting things," Mr. Kaye said. "You remember the old saying that the whole is greater than the sum of its parts? Well, in this case, that's not true. Fact is, your parts, taken separately, are worth far more than the whole of you."

"You're not worried they're going to shut your place down?" The transponder pulsed again. He had to keep Kaye talking…

"Unlikely," Mr. Kaye said. "But in any event, it wouldn't matter. We'd just rebuild."

A car squealed into the alley, beams on bright, blue lights flashing in the grille. Densmore and Fuller jumped out and took positions behind the car doors, guns leveled.

"Federal Agent!" Fuller shouted. "Drop the weapon!"

Mr. Kaye calmly turned around, his arms at forty-five degree angles from his body. There was nothing threatening in his movement, but he didn't drop the gun.

Densmore and Fuller came from behind the doors and approached on opposite sides of the alley, both aiming for center mass. Densmore yelled, "LAPD! Drop the weapon!"

Mr. Kaye leaned forward slightly, squinting into the lights. "You're a cop?"

"Drop the weapon!"

"I'd do it if I were you," Jake said. "I saw her kill a man just last week."

"I guess we'll find out how good I am," Mr. Kaye said.

"Before you do," Jake said, "let me ask, have you signed your organ donor card?"

236

Mr. Kaye laughed and then made his move.

Jake dove down the loading ramp as Agent Fuller and Detective Densmore got off eight rounds in four seconds.

Mr. Kaye fired once, hitting a brick wall on his way to the ground.

Epilogue

They found Angel in the hospital. In the smoke and confusion, she'd doubled back and hidden in the closet of the first room the staff evacuated. No one ever came back after getting the patient out. She was quite pleased with her improvisational skills. Jake called in his favor with his boss. She let Angel stay at her place while she healed, no questions asked.

***

The comatose man in the locked room turned out to be Bryce Weeks.

After Fuller's SWAT assault on the grow house and the discovery of Thaddeus Dell's body, Mr. Kaye decided Bryce Weeks knew too much and had to be dealt with. They brought him to the hospital under the guise of delivering a bonus for his work. Once there they drugged him, putting him into a medically induced coma to hold until they found perfect matches for all his organs.

A couple of days later Mr. Kaye realized he was wasting good money on the expensive hypnotics keeping Mr. Weeks in his coma, so he switched Weeks to a cheap paralytic, leaving him wide awake, fully aware of his fate, but unable to move.

When the police took Mr. Weeks off the Narcuron, he was in a mood to talk. He explained how the thing worked at the McAfee prisons. When a prisoner was found to be a match for a client, they moved the prisoner to isolation and dosed him with GHB. Once unconscious, the guards would remove the prisoner from the cell under the guise of a medically necessary situation or a suicide. Some woke with abdominal scars and were told they'd had an appendectomy or other operation when in fact they'd had a kidney or lobe of a liver removed, after which they were returned to prison. Those who had hearts and/or lungs removed would be written up as suicide.

As with the rest of the non-surviving donors, most of whom came from the family clinics owned and operated by The Medicus Group, bodies were taken to one of the Golden State Interment facilities where every other marketable part was removed for sale. The scant remains were cremated.

Bryce Weeks told investigators the only person he called by name was Mr. Kaye, and he doubted that was even real. He had no knowledge of Hutch McAfee, Sheldon Birch, or Dr. Brewer.

The surgeons working on Ramon Recendez and the kid were long gone by the time police arrived. The rest of the staff had no useful information. No one could identify anyone else. They explained how anonymity was maintained and said they had been told the hospital was a top-secret government program. They had all signed stacks of official-looking documents, none of which were ever located.

All of the patients at the hospital took the fifth.

Prosecutors took a run at Brewer, McAfee, and Birch under the RICO Act but were unable to put a case together.

As for the death of Ramon Recendez, since Mr. Kaye was the only person who knew the identity of the surgeon who had stopped the heart and removed it, and since no one else would admit being involved, prosecutors had nothing to work with. The lack of cooperating witnesses coupled with the fact that Ramon was an illegal alien, meant no charges were brought against anyone.

***

Mitchell Wick's reality show went through several titles during focus group testing, starting with *Hey, Buddy, Can You Spare a Kidney?* This was rejected on the grounds that the reference was too dated. They tested dozens of others before settling on *Transplant!*

The show started slowly, but increased its audience week after week until it was the number one rated reality show on television.

The donor got the money to open her bakery and, owing to the television exposure, it was an instant success. The network executive's kid got the kidney he needed.

Jake made another fifteen thousand dollars and used it to establish a college fund for Angel.

***

Jake and Detective Densmore met Agent Fuller and Mark Simmons at Taco Bistro. They were on the third round of tequila shots and Mark was trying to explain to Densmore why it was illegal to sell your organs.

"The main argument is that it tends to take advantage of the poor."

"Everything takes advantage of the poor," she said, mystified. "That's no argument."

"I didn't say it was a *good* argument, it's just the one they use most of the time."

"So a wealthy person selling a kidney would be ethically acceptable?"

"Maybe," Fuller said. "But it would still be illegal."

"But why? How come it's not mine to sell? I mean, whose kidney is it?"

"It's your kidney, it's just not yours to sell," Fuller said. "And if you're seriously interested, read *Moore v. Regents of University of California* for the law. My guess is, in our lifetime, it'll change, and our parts will all end up covered under property law. In fact, I heard a story the other day about some women suing fertility clinics for fixing the price of human eggs."

"So you can sell your eggs, your blood, your sperm, your… what else can you sell?"

"Bone marrow," Simmons said. "And you can rent your womb."

Fuller said, "So, Jake, did you find out if Mr. Kaye was an organ donor?"

"He wasn't, unfortunately," Jake said. "I suspect his employer had dibs on his parts."

At the end of the night, the waiter showed up with the bill. It was just under two hundred dollars.

"That include the tip?" Densmore asked.

"Yep."

She pointed at Agent Fuller. "Give it to him."

"What? Why me?"

"We had a bet. Two hundred bucks said you were wrong about Jake."

"Technically, it was two hundred that I was full of shit."

"Either way, I win," Densmore said.

"Fine." Fuller pulled a credit card and handed it over. "But I was right about the transplant hospital. And now they're out of business."

Jake smirked at that. "You still taking bets?"

Agent Fuller was signing the credit card receipt when he received a text. He picked up his phone and stared at the message.

Jake said, "What is it?"

"A courier in San Francisco just got hijacked," Densmore said. "They got another heart."

***

A few days later, Jake was getting ready to return to work. He was looking for something on his desk when he came across the envelope Angel had given him before her surgery.

Inside he found a standard advance directive form filled out and signed by Angel. There was a sticky note attached to it that read, "I'm serious! Pull the damn plug!"

The other document wasn't a final will and testament so much as it was a simple note. It was written in Angel's best cursive:

"Dear Jake, Please don't tell Mom what happened. She'll figure I just ran away and I'm out there somewhere and that's better than knowing I died.

I know this is supposed to be a will but I don't have anything to give you except my thanks. So that's what I'm leaving you. You didn't have to help me but you did. I just wanted you to know I appreciate that.

Love, Angel."

Preview

cover coming soon!

The Organ Grinders
(The Transplant Tetralogy, Book 3)

Paul Symon is an environmentalist who's out to make the world a better place, but he faces too much disjointed information, public apathy, and self-serving talk. Not to mention greedy despoiler Jerry Landis, a venture capitalist dying of a rare disease that accelerates the aging process.

Landis cares only about making more money and finding a way to arrest his medical condition. That brings him and his fortune to the wild frontier of biotechnology, where his people are illegally experimenting with cross-species organ transplantation in California while breeding genetically altered primates at a secret site in the piney woods of south-central Mississippi.

There's also an eco-terrorist on the loose, bent on teaching hard lessons to people who think the Earth and its creatures are theirs to destroy. These forces, together with fifty thousand extra-large chacma baboons, collide in an explosion of laughter and wonder that Bill Fitzhugh's growing league of admirers is coming to recognize as his very own.

COMING SOON

Also Available

Pest Control
(Assassin Bugs, Book 1)

Bob Dillon can't get a break. A down-on-his-luck exterminator, all he wants is his own truck with a big fiberglass bug on top – and success with his radical new, environmentally friendly pest-killing technique. So Bob decides to advertise.

Unfortunately, one of his flyers falls into the wrong hands. Marcel, a shady Frenchman, needs an assassin to handle a million-dollar hit, and he figures that Bob Dillon is his man. Through no fault – or participation – of his own, this unwitting pest controller from Queens has become a major player in the dangerous world of contract murder.

And now Bob's running for his life through the wormiest sections of the Big Apple – one step ahead of a Bolivian executioner, a homicidal transvestite dwarf, meatheaded CIA agents, cabbies packing serious heat… and the world's number-one hit man, who might just turn out to be the best friend Bob's got.

OUT NOW

About the Transplant Tetralogy

Four different tales that consider the possibilities, bizarre inevitabilities, and unintended consequences of one of the greatest achievements of medical science. Each instalment of the Transplant Tetralogy takes you on a darkly comic exploration of the world of organ transplants. This is what happens when demand exceeds supply…

Further titles in the Transplant Tetralogy:

Heart Seizure
Human Resources
The Organ Grinders
A Perfect Harvest

Other series by Bill Fitzhugh:

ASSASSIN BUGS
Pest Control
The Exterminators

DJ RICK SHANNON
Radio Activity
Highway 61 Resurfaced

OTHER
Cross Dressing
Fender Benders

About the Author

Bill Fitzhugh is the author of eleven novels. He still has all of his original organs and plans to keep it that way until the very end, at which point he is willing to let the doctors divvy them up among anyone (with the exception of politicians) who might need them. However, he makes no promises about the quality of his liver. He lives in Los Angeles with his wife and all of her organs.

Note from the Publisher

If you enjoyed this book, we are delighted to share also *The Bug Job*, a new short story by Bill Fitzhugh.
To get your **free copy of *The Bug Job***, as well as receive news of further releases by Bill Fitzhugh, sign up at http://farragobooks.com/billfitzhugh-signup